# THE BODY IN THE KITCHEN

"Can you see anything?" I asked.

Lucy stepped back from the window and shook her head.

I pointed to the driveway. "Let's keep going."

We hurried around to the side of the house and peered through a dining room window. Nothing. Further down the wall we spied a kitchen window, too high for Birdie and me. But Jazz and Lucy could peek inside if they stood on their toes.

"Oh my God!" said Lucy. "She's on the floor. This is like *déjà vu* all over again." Lucy referred to the time two years ago when we discovered the body of a quilter friend the same way—by looking through her window when she failed to answer her door.

We ran around the corner to the back of the house, looking for a way into the kitchen. Jazz didn't need to break down the back door. When he tried the handle, it easily swung open. Forgetting about our promise to call the police first, we rushed inside behind him and stopped when we saw the blood. . .

**Books by Mary Marks**

FORGET ME KNOT

KNOT IN MY BACKYARD

GONE BUT KNOT FORGOTTEN

SOMETHING'S KNOT KOSHER

KNOT WHAT YOU THINK

Published by Kensington Publishing Corporation

...AT
# YOU THINK

## MARY MARKS

**KENSINGTON PUBLISHING CORP.**
http://www.kensingtonbooks.com

KENSINGTON BOOKS are published by

Kensington Publishing Corp.
119 West 40th Street
New York, NY 10018

All Kensington Titles, Imprints, and Distributed Lines
are available at special quantity discounts for bulk pur-
chases for sales promotions, premiums, fund-raising,
and educational or institutional use. Special book ex-
cerpts or customized printings can also be created to fit
specific needs. For details, write or phone the office of
the Kensington special sales manager: Kensington Publishing Corp., 119 West 40th Street, New York, NY 10018,
attn: Special Sales Department, Phone: 1-800-221-2647.

Kensington and the K logo Reg. U.S. Pat & TM Off.

ISBN-13: 978-1-4967-0182-4
ISBN-10: 1-4967-0182-8
First Kensington Mass Market Edition: August 2017

eISBN-13: 978-1-4967-0183-1
eISBN-10: 1-4967-0183-6
First Kensington Electronic Edition: August 2017

10 9 8 7 6 5 4 3 2 1

Printed in the United States of America

*For all my lovely readers.*
*Without you, there would be no Martha Rose.*
*Thank you for your support.*

# ACKNOWLEDGMENTS

Thanks so much to all the usual suspects: Jerrilyn Farmer, Lori Dillman, Cyndra Gernet, and Nancy Jane Isenhart Holmes. You all make me a much better writer than I would be on my own.

Thanks as always to the skillful efforts of my agent, Dawn Dowdle. And thanks to my editor, John Scognamiglio and all the folks at Kensington.

# CHAPTER 1

I hefted the red tote bag stuffed with sewing supplies out of the trunk of my Civic, locked my car, and made my way across my best friend Lucy's newly landscaped front yard. Today was Tuesday, the day we always got together, no matter what.

Peeking through a thick layer of redwood mulch were clumps of blues: pungent rosemary, English lavender, and cobalt salvia. Rows of giant white African Lilies on long stalks flanked the wide, brick walkway. Dots of yellow kangaroo paws and red flax added more color, while pepper trees provided lacy shade. Because of the critical water shortage in California, homeowners in Los Angeles County were being encouraged to replace their thirsty lawns with drought-tolerant plants. Lucy opted for Mediterranean rather than Mojave Desert as a theme for her new garden.

My name is Martha Rose, and in the last seventeen years I'd never missed a week with my quilting friends. I pushed my way through the front door into the colorful interior of Lucy's living room.

"Hey, Martha." My orange-haired friend Lucy waved me over to an easy chair. She wore pink linen trousers, a white cotton blouse, and blue espadrilles with three-inch wedge heels, boosting her height to over six feet. Even though she was in her sixties, Lucy carried herself like a runway model. This morning she held a pencil and notepad instead of a needle and thread. "It's time to plan Birdie's wedding."

Our seventy-seven-year-old friend Birdie Watson wore her signature denim overalls, white T-shirt, and Birkenstock sandals—a style acquired during her hippie days living in a commune. She looked up from her appliqué project and blushed. "At least I won't have to change my last name."

Birdie's long-time husband, Russell, was killed during a bank robbery last year. After his death, she reunited with Russell's younger brother, Denver, the man she always secretly loved. Lately, the couple divided their time between Birdie's house in Encino and the Watson ancestral homestead in McMinnville, Oregon. Very soon she would become Mrs. Watson for the second time.

"Have the two of you picked a date yet?" I asked as I unloaded scraps of fabric from my red tote bag onto a coffee table made of burled tree roots. The blue, overstuffed easy chairs and cowhide rug screamed Wyoming, where Lucy and her husband, Ray, grew up.

Birdie twisted the end of her long, white braid. "Denny and I don't want a big fuss, Martha dear. We prefer a simple ceremony with all our family and friends. The sooner, the better."

The front door opened, and the newest member of our regular Tuesday-morning quilting group breezed into the room. "*Bonjour,*" Jazz Fletcher sang in an exaggerated French accent. The six-foot-tall men's fashion designer crossed the room and claimed an empty space on the brown leather sofa beside Birdie, carefully placing his tote bag on the floor next to his feet.

As usual, his chestnut brown hair was perfectly coiffed. My gray curls, on the other hand, were always a little chaotic. Even though we shared the same age, fifty-seven, I'd never detected a single silver strand on his head. Apparently, Jazz enjoyed a close relationship with L'Oreal or Clairol.

He wore a yellow silk shirt with a banded collar. Small diamond studs sparkled in his ears and on a gold wedding band encrusted with baguettes. The ring came from his longtime lover, Russell Watson, Birdie's dead husband.

When Russell died, Birdie felt free to finally reveal her husband's deepest secret. He'd always been gay, and for the past twenty-five years led a double life. He posed as a straight banker, with Birdie as his wife, while also living with his much younger lover, Jazz Fletcher. When the distraught Jazz turned up after the murder, tenderhearted Birdie befriended him and invited him to join our group.

"Sorry we're late." He reached inside the yellow canvas bag and removed his little, white Maltese dog, Zsa Zsa Galore. She wore a pinafore sewn with the same yellow silk as his shirt and a rhinestone clip in her topknot. "I tried to make a delivery this morning, but it turns out my client wasn't home." Zsa Zsa jumped off his lap and made the rounds, greeting each of us with an enthusiastic tail.

"You left a message about bringing a surprise?" prompted Lucy.

Jazz bent down and extracted a sketchpad from a pocket in the dog carrier and grinned at Birdie. "I've designed the perfect wedding dress for you. *Et voila!*" He flourished a drawing of a white-lace shift with flared, bell-shaped sleeves and a skirt ending mid-thigh. "I remembered seeing an old photo of you in a dress like this in the 1960s." He passed the image to Birdie. "Your legs looked fabulous, so I thought why not show them off again? It's very Mary Quant meets Laura Ashley." A satisfied smile split his face. "What do you think?"

Birdie's mouth fell open, and she seemed to struggle to find the right words. "You've, um, done a beautiful job, Jazz." Long pause. "But it's a little too, ah, youthful for me. My legs don't look like that anymore. I have terrible arthritis in my knees. I'm sorry, dear, but there's just no way I'd ever wear a minidress again. I prefer to cover my legs now."

The more she spoke, the more Jazz's face fell. He slumped his broad shoulders and shrank back into the cushion of the caramel leather sofa, arms crossed and knees pressed together.

Birdie hastily added, "But you're such a talented designer, I'm sure this dress would be perfect for a younger person."

We worked on our individual quilts, enjoying thick slices of zucchini bread with walnuts and cinnamon, courtesy of Birdie's excellent baking. Today,

I sorted through the pile of random cotton prints I intended to cut into rectangles for my newest quilt. I chose a design called Prairie Braid, which consisted of pieces sewn together in a herringbone pattern. This would become a true "charm quilt."

Charm quilts are a special kind of scrap quilt—where no fabric is repeated. They soared to popularity during the nineteenth century, when printed cotton fabrics became affordable and abundant. According to quilting lore, unmarried girls traded scraps of material in order to collect 999 different pieces. The thousandth scrap was supposed to come from the shirt of the young woman's future husband.

"Who are you making that for?" I pointed to the green-and-white quilt cascading over Jazz's long legs. "Isn't it a little big for a dog's bed?" Shortly after he joined our group, the fashion designer opened a second business selling custom-made clothing and quilted bedding for dogs. Now his expert fingers busily sewed the finishing touches on an Irish Chain quilt that seemed much larger than usual.

Jazz ended off his thread and cut a new length from a spool of green. "One of my customers owns an Irish Wolfhound. When the dog stands on his hind legs, he's nearly as tall as me."

"So, business must be good," Birdie said.

Jazz threw his hands in the air and arched his eyebrows. "It's improving. I just finished an order for my manscaper, Dolleen Doyle."

"Man what?" Birdie's eyes widened.

Jazz cleared his throat. "A manscaper is someone who specializes in male waxing."

Birdie seemed mesmerized. "You get waxed?"

Jazz's cheeks colored. "After Rusty died, I sort of let myself go. But I started working out again and regularly visited Dolly's salon. Two weeks ago, I went in for a Brazilian."

*Dear God, please remove that image from my head.*

"While I was there, she ordered an extensive wardrobe for her Chihuahua, Patti, and commissioned three coordinating dog carriers. Dolly's just like me. She takes her dog everywhere. Even to work."

I looked up from my cutting. "What, no quilts?"

Jazz wagged a forefinger. "*Au contraire.* Not only did she order quilts, she wanted four whole bedding ensembles including fitted sheets for her doggie's bed! I agreed to deliver everything last night, but that didn't work out." He closed his eyes halfway and sniffed. "Actually, I'm a little annoyed. I drove all the way to the Valley from my boutique in West Hollywood to deliver everything at the time we agreed. But when I got there, she didn't answer the door, and the house was dark. I heard Patti barking inside, which frankly surprised me. I've never known Dolly to be flaky, let alone leave her dog behind. Anyway, I ended up taking the entire delivery back home with me."

"Why didn't you just leave the package on her doorstep?" asked Lucy.

"Oh no!" Jazz gasped. "You can't leave stuff on the porch anymore. Package pirates come by and steal everything. Don't you watch the news? Anyway,

I thought I'd try again this morning because she lives in Tarzana, not far from here. But when I got there, she still didn't answer the door. I hung around for several minutes and tried calling and texting, but I got no response. That's why I was late."

The hairs on the back of my neck tingled. "You said she never goes anywhere without her dog?"

Jazz nodded.

"Yet she left the Chihuahua alone in the house last night? Even though she knew you were on your way over? And then again this morning?"

Jazz nodded again, this time more slowly.

I immediately thought of the time Lucy, Birdie, and I discovered the body of another quilter in her house and—more than a year ago—how the body of yet another friend lay undiscovered in her bedroom closet for ten months. I didn't want to alarm him, but an unmistakable dread gathered in the pit of my stomach. "Jazz, maybe you should try calling her again. Just to make sure she's not sick or something." My anxiety grew at the possibility of the woman lying helpless on the floor after a stroke, or worse.

His face turned pale and he stared at me. "Now you're beginning to scare me."

Lucy's head snapped up sharply and said just one word. "Martha!" But the tone of her voice spoke volumes.

I clearly heard the caution and the *Oh no, not again.*

Birdie spoke quietly and tugged at her braid. "Well, you have to admit, it does sound suspicious."

Jazz punched his cell phone and waited. After

a minute, he ended the call and looked at me. "Nothing."

I couldn't shake the nagging feeling of dread. "Since she's close by, maybe we should go over to her house and peek in the windows or something. If she's incapacitated, she'll need help."

Lucy scowled. "Or maybe we ought to call the police instead and have *them* check on her. After all, it's their job."

I understood what she left unsaid. If we happened to stumble on yet another suspicious death, her husband, Ray, would *plotz*. The way he saw it, I'd put Lucy's life in jeopardy before, and I doubted he'd have any room left to forgive me if it happened again.

Jazz put down the quilt and jumped off the sofa. "You're right. I'm going over there right now! I'll break down the door if I have to."

At the sound of his outburst, Zsa Zsa trotted over to him and barked once. Jazz picked her up.

Birdie gathered her sewing things and tucked them in a zippered denim tote bag Jazz sewed for her. "I think we should all go. We'd never forgive ourselves if we suspected this woman needed help and did nothing."

Lucy sighed and slowly pushed up from her chair. "Okay, okay. But only to investigate from *outside* the house. If we discover something bad, we're calling the police. Agreed?"

"Agreed," Birdie and I responded together.

Jazz merely pursed his lips.

* * *

The four of us piled into Lucy's vintage black Cadillac with the shark fins in back. Jazz leaned forward in the backseat and tapped Lucy's shoulder. "Take Ventura to Reseda and turn south."

We wound our way through an upscale neighborhood on the flat land at the foot of the Santa Monica Mountains. The original homes, built in the single-story California ranch style, featured rose-colored stucco, English ivy, and palm trees. The neighborhood was changing, however. Some of the nearby homes had been lavishly remodeled or replaced by Mediterranean-style McMansions, so popular among wealthy young families.

"This is it!" Jazz unbuckled his seatbelt even before Lucy parked in the driveway of Dolleen Doyle's home, still preserved in its original mid-century state. We followed him as he marched rapidly to the woman's front porch, hugging Zsa Zsa to his chest. He pounded on the door and rang the bell. All we heard were the frantic yelps of one very small, very agitated dog. He turned to us with deep concern etched between his eyebrows.

We stepped sideways to a large picture window on the front of the house. A petite, buff-colored Chihuahua stood on the back of a red sofa pushed against the glass and yipped at us. Then she raised her head, curled her lips and began to howl. Zsa Zsa tensed, barked in response, and looked at Jazz as if to say, *What are you going to do about this?*

Jazz at six feet and Lucy even taller, with those wedge heels, commanded the best view of the home's interior.

"Can you see anything?" I asked.

Lucy stepped back from the window and shook her head.

I pointed to the driveway. "Let's keep going."

We hurried around to the side of the house and peered through a dining room window. Nothing. Further down the wall we spied a kitchen window, too high for Birdie and me, but Jazz and Lucy could peek inside if they stood on their toes.

"Oh my God!" said Lucy. "She's on the floor. This is like déjà vu all over again." Lucy referred to the time two years ago when we discovered the body of a quilter friend the same way—by looking through her window when she failed to answer her door.

We ran around the corner to the back of the house, looking for a way into the kitchen. Jazz didn't need to break down the back door: when he tried the handle, it easily swung open. Forgetting about our promise to call the police first, we rushed inside behind him and stopped when we saw the blood.

Jazz rocked back on his heels and grabbed the granite counter for support. Zsa Zsa shook violently and whined so pitifully, he carried her outside, using the walls to steady himself. Birdie turned green and followed him into the fresh air. Lucy and I grasped each other for support. Patti looked at us from ten feet away and howled again.

Dolleen Doyle's arms stretched away from her body, and her legs twisted to the side where she'd fallen. Strands of blond hair lay across her face as if blown there by a hostile breeze. The top of her Hawaiian-print halter top slipped open to reveal abnormally large breasts barely contained in an expensive black-lace bra. I estimated her age to be in her thirties, judging by the fine wrinkles just beginning to show at the corners of her unseeing eyes. Who did she remind me of?

Frantic Chihuahua tracks dotted the floor in all directions, from the puddle under her head into the living room and back again. The blood had turned dark brown where it had dried, indicating she'd been lying there since the day before. Clearly, Dolleen Doyle would never get up again.

Lucy closed her eyes and shook her head. "Dang it. I can't believe we found another dead body. Don't say anything to Ray." My Catholic friend made the sign of the cross and looked at the ceiling. "Please God, make this an accident, a simple slip and fall."

I scanned the room to see if I could determine what she could've fallen against. A thready trail of blood on the floor led away from her body to an aluminum trash can. I followed the trail, careful not to step on it. Even though we didn't yet know how Dolleen died, I knew enough not to contaminate the scene. I used my foot to push against the trash can and slide it away from the wall in an effort to preserve any potential fingerprints.

A two-pound metal hand weight had rolled behind the can from where it had been dropped. Blood and strands of blond hair covered one end. The room spun when I stood, so I grabbed Lucy's arm for support.

"This was no accident, Lucy. I'm afraid we've stumbled upon another murder."

# CHAPTER 2

Patti barked at us from the dining area. I moved toward her, careful not to disturb the bloody paw prints on the floor. "Poor little doggie. We can't leave you here." Patti shivered when I picked her up, her little paws stained red.

Lucy blew out a heavy puff of breath. "We have to call Arlo."

I dreaded making the call to Arlo Beavers, a homicide detective with the LAPD and my some-times ex, because our relationship was currently off again. I reached in the pocket of my size 16, stretch denim jeans, pulled out my cell phone, and called his number.

He answered on the second ring. "Beavers."

"Hi, Arlo. It's Martha."

"I know. I have caller ID. What do you want?"

Well, that was a little snarky. To make things worse, I knew from past experience he wouldn't be happy we'd, once again, stumbled across a murder.

"How's Arthur?" I asked in hopes of softening him up before exploding the Dolleen bombshell.

Arthur, a retired police canine Beavers adopted, helped me solve a couple of murders and had saved my life more than once. I loved the German shepherd as much as he did.

"He's fine. Is that why you're calling?" Beavers's tone hadn't changed a bit. So much for avoiding the unpleasant.

I took a deep, calming yoga breath. "As a matter of fact, no. I'm calling to report a murder."

Silence. Then he spoke with a controlled voice. "You're joking, right?"

"I'm afraid not. Lucy and I are standing in the victim's kitchen looking at her body as we speak. Looks like someone whacked her on the back of the head with a dumbbell. It probably happened sometime yesterday."

"Give me the address and get out of the house. You should know by now not to contaminate the crime scene. And don't leave."

"Don't worry, we didn't disturb anything." I ended the call, and Lucy and I joined the others outside. We moved down the driveway to her car and waited.

"I can't believe it." Jazz parked himself in the backseat next to me and stroked the top of Zsa Zsa's head as she tried to wiggle out of his arms.

The Maltese barked a sympathetic greeting to Patti, who trembled and buried her tiny head in the crook of my arm.

"Who would do a thing like this to such a sweet person?" He wiped away tears with the heel of his hand and reached over to stroke Patti's shaking body. "What will happen to this little one?"

Birdie, who sat in the front passenger seat, twisted

around to face Jazz. "I know you must be shocked, dear. We all are. But Arlo Beavers is very good at his job. He'll find out who committed this terrible crime."

Lucy adjusted the rearview mirror so she could lock gazes with me. "And we'll stay out of his investigation. Right?"

I nodded. "Of course! What possible reason would we have to become involved?"

Jazz's phone chirped, and he bent his head to exchange a text with someone. Five minutes later, approaching sirens announced Beavers's arrival. He parked his silver Camry in front of Dolleen's house, while two black and whites parked behind him. The uniforms began stretching yellow tape around the perimeter of the property, and Beavers, dressed in his usual gray suit and tie, marched over to Lucy's Caddy.

Tall and fit, with a shock of gray hair and a white mustache, the sight of him always made my toes tingle. He stuck his head through the open window, and I got a faint whiff of his woodsy cologne. He glared at me, dark eyes glittering, and barked one word. "Where?"

I pointed to the back of the driveway. "Through the kitchen door."

"Don't leave." He disappeared toward the back of the house. Five minutes later he emerged, talking on his cell phone, and headed our way. We heard him say, "Yeah. What's the ETA for SID?"

Jazz mouthed "What's S-I-D?"

Birdie, an avid fan of every crime drama on TV, could easily interpret cop-speak. "*Scientific Investigation Division*," she whispered. "It's what the LAPD calls its forensic team. He wants to know when they'll get here to process the scene."

Beavers put his phone in his pocket and poked his head in the window again. "I want you all to wait for me at the West Valley Station. I'll need statements from each of you." He scowled at me. "You should know the drill by now."

"Really, Arlo? Like you think I go trolling for murder victims on purpose?"

"No comment." He made his way toward the back of the house once more.

Lucy backed out of the driveway and aimed the Caddy toward Vanowen Street in Reseda.

I sank into the cream-colored leather backseat. "I don't know why he has to be so darn rude."

Lucy looked at me again in the rearview mirror. "Yes you do. He's not happy you dumped him for Yossi last year."

Yossi Levy, aka Crusher, was my current boyfriend. After Beavers and I broke up two years ago, Crusher swooped in and tried to stake a permanent claim on me. He wanted to get married. When I refused to make a commitment, he disappeared for five months.

"Arlo invited you to meet his cousins on the Siletz Indian Reservation, remember?" Lucy turned in her seat to look at me. "Doesn't that suggest he was serious about you?"

During Crusher's absence, Beavers said he wanted to try again. One thing led to another, and I kind of accidentally slept with him. I knew I'd made the wrong choice, but when he wasn't grumpy, Arlo Beavers was hard to resist. Even though I'd been incredibly attracted to him, I stopped the affair after one encounter.

Birdie nodded. "And then Yossi came back. No wonder Arlo seems peeved."

When Crusher returned to LA, we sort of resumed our relationship. Like immediately. But I still wrestled with making a permanent commitment. My track record in the romance department scored a great, big goose egg. Zero, zip, zilch. *Efes.*

I shifted in my seat. "My last encounter with Beavers happened eight months ago. He should be over it by now. After all, a handsome guy like him? He's never lacked for female admirers."

Jazz reached over and squeezed my hand. "The heart knows what it wants. I should know."

Did he mean he still grieved over Russell Watson's death, or had he moved on and found a new reason for manscaping and working out again?


Lucy parked in front of the police station and we trooped inside the lobby to wait for Detective Beavers. I dreaded the encounter. Just thinking about his attitude today made me want to throw up.

An hour later my ex arrived. "You first." He pointed at me and began walking toward the hallway holding the interview rooms. I followed obediently, like a bad child in school being led to the principal's office. The blue walls of the eight by ten interview room were covered by those acoustic tiles with the tiny holes in them. I took a seat at a steel table bolted to the floor.

"Are you going to record this?" I asked.

"Always." Beavers slapped a yellow legal pad on the table between us.

"Then as a courtesy to you, I won't comment about your boorish behavior today."

He studied my face for a couple of seconds and his voice softened a bit. "Just tell me what happened."

"Jazz has been very successful over the years designing menswear for the stars. Anyway, he decided to branch into chic canine wear. My uncle Isaac would say he possessed *geldene hendelach*. Golden hands. He's very talented."

Beavers closed his eyes and rolled his hand, urging me forward. "Stick to today. What happened?"

When I spoke again, he began to write. I related what little I knew about Dolleen Doyle's purchase of doggie couture and Jazz's unsuccessful attempt to deliver her order.

"What prompted all of you to troop over to her house? Did you know the woman?"

"Only Jazz knew her. When he told us he could hear her dog barking but she didn't answer her door or her phone, I became suspicious. Apparently, she never went anywhere without Patti."

He sighed. "You could've called the police for a welfare visit, you know."

I looked at the table and shrugged. I didn't want to tell him that Lucy had suggested that very same thing in the first place.

"Jazz insisted on checking it out himself. So, we went along to support him."

"How'd you get inside the house?"

"Lucy looked inside the kitchen window and

spied her body on the floor. Fortunately, we found the back door unlocked, and rushed inside to see if we could help her."

"Did anybody touch anything?"

"Of course not!"

He pointed to the Chihuahua, now curled in my lap, sleeping. "The victim's dog?"

"I couldn't leave the poor thing there."

"Technically, you don't have a right to the dog. I should turn it over to animal services until a relative claims it."

I gazed at the pathetic little creature breathing softly in my lap. She measured only half the size of my cat, Bumper. "Why add one more homeless dog to the shelter? I can do a much better job of taking care of her until her fate is resolved—if that's all right with the LAPD."

Beavers grunted. "Whatever. I've got more important things to worry about right now." He slid the tablet across the table and handed me the pen he was using. "Check this for accuracy. Add anything else you can think of, and sign it."

"And when I'm finished?"

"Sit tight." He scraped his chair back from the table and left the room.

An hour later he collected my statement and released us all with a stern warning for me. "Don't even think about playing detective. Stay out of this investigation."

"What about her poor, little Chihuahua?" Jazz asked. "What will happen to her?"

"I've agreed to let Martha keep it for now. If nobody claims the dog, it goes to the animal shelter."

"You can't do that!" Jazz gasped and covered his mouth with his hand. "If nobody wants Patti, I'll find a home for her. She'll be easy to place, especially with a fabulous new wardrobe and her own cozy little quilts."

By the time we returned to Lucy's house, no one was in the mood to sew. While she prepared an impromptu meal, I took Patti to the bathroom and washed the blood off her paws. Then I put her on the floor, where she and Zsa Zsa did a little polite butt sniffing. The Maltese licked Patti's face, but the little dog just shivered.

Ten minutes later, we sat at the kitchen table devouring turkey sandwiches on sourdough bread with mayonnaise and pickles. I pulled off tiny pieces of meat and fed them to the hungry Chihuahua prancing by my chair.

Lucy fished a barbeque potato chip out of the big bag in the middle of the table. "I hate to say I told you so, but we should've called the police to check up on her instead of going ourselves."

Jazz just frowned and looked at his plate.

"Let's move on and focus on Birdie's wedding," I suggested.

Jazz rose from the table and pointed to Patti. "I can't move on until I know she's going to be safe."

Birdie smiled gently. "I'm sure you can count on Arlo to do the right thing."

"I hope so." Jazz gathered his sewing and placed Zsa Zsa in her carrier. Then he turned toward me. "There's room in here for two, Martha."

"Good idea." I picked up Patti and handed her to Jazz.

He tucked her in the carrier with Zsa Zsa. "Good-bye everyone. Thanks for coming with me today."

I followed him outside and watched as he drove away in his blue Mercedes with the personalized license plate JAZZ FW. The FW stood for Fletcher-Watson, the combined last name he and Birdie's husband Russell secretly shared.

Five minutes later, I also said good-bye, got in my white Civic, and drove home. On the way, I kept going over the crime scene. I couldn't get rid of the feeling Dolleen Doyle looked familiar. How did I know her? We lived in the neighboring communities of Encino and Tarzana. It was quite possible we might have crossed paths at some point. But where? Market? Yoga studio?

My orange cat, Bumper, greeted me as soon as I entered my house. We sat on the sofa together, and I scratched his jaw as he purred in my lap. I certainly understood Jazz's concern for little Patti. I rescued Bumper in much the same way two years ago, when we found his owner lying dead on the floor.

After our five-minute love fest, I pushed a protesting fluff ball off my legs and walked straight to my dining table, where my laptop rested, and Googled the name *Dolleen Doyle*. I got several hits. Then I realized why she seemed so familiar.

# CHAPTER 3

Google is like those old Jewish yentas in bad wigs who trolled the neighborhood sniffing out good gossip. Every scrap of information they collected became their coin, which they used to barter for a position of social importance. When I searched under Dolleen Doyle's name, I found an old newspaper clipping of her engagement to David Shapira and an image of her standing next to him at some big charity event before their marriage.

Only then did I understand why I didn't recognize her right away. After the scandal, she'd gone back to using her maiden name. Probably because she didn't want to carry the stigma of being known as Mrs. David Shapira for the rest of her life.

Of course, everyone in the country knew about her husband—the disgraced owner of the investment firm David Shapira Associates. He was currently serving twenty years in federal prison for securities fraud, grand theft, and a string of other financial crimes. I clicked on dozens of links leading to articles about the man.

According to the stories, he met his young wife while she worked as a male waxer in Beverly Hills. Five months later, he dumped his first wife and college-aged son to marry the young blonde. They lived a very public life until his Ponzi scheme imploded during the Great Recession. He confessed to his crimes and went to prison in 2009.

The Feds were able to locate and seize only some of his assets. Media accounts speculated that most of Shapira's wealth remained hidden in offshore accounts and hinted Dolleen knew where he'd buried the money. Having access to those funds would explain how she could afford to open her own waxing salon on the most expensive street in Beverly Hills. But why bother? Why would she need to earn a living with a pirate's fortune squirreled away?

I was beginning to read another article about Shapira's first marriage when my phone rang.

"Hello *faigela*." My eighty-something uncle, Isaac Harris, the man who raised me, always called me *little bird* in Yiddish. "I haven't heard from you lately, so I thought I'd call. What's new?"

I needed to tell him about discovering another murder before he heard it from someone else. "You know how Tuesday is always our quilty day? Well, we ran an errand this morning and, uh, stumbled across something rather unpleasant."

"Are you all right?" His voice filled with panic.

"Yes, yes, I'm fine."

"So, *nu*?"

"Lucy, Birdie, and I went with Jazz to his client's house. Unfortunately, we found her dead."

"*Oy!* Don't tell me. You didn't find another murder, did you? No, don't tell me."

"Afraid so, Uncle. Of course, we called Arlo right away. Turns out, you might have heard about the victim from the news a few years ago. Does the name Dolleen Doyle ring a bell? She was married to David Shapira. Do you remember the scandal?"

"That *mamser?* Of course I remember." My uncle seldom used such disparaging language, so calling Shapira a *bastard* in Yiddish revealed his deep disgust. "I sometimes played chess with his father at the Jewish Center. Abel Shapira. Anyway, when his *gonif* son went to jail, Abel stopped coming around—too embarrassed to show his face."

Calling David Shapira a thief in Yiddish was like calling Hitler an anti-Semite. The description didn't begin to cover the legacy of devastation he left behind. Especially galling was the shame Shapira brought to the Jewish community. The man ultimately proved to be an embarrassment and a huge liability. His crimes only served to reinforce the worst anti-Semitic stereotypes. Many in the Jewish community also considered him a traitor: counted among his many victims were Jews and Jewish charities.

"The scandal must've been hard for his father," I suggested.

"Worse. Abel persuaded some of our friends to invest with his son. They lost everything. That's when Abel disappeared. Couldn't face the *shande.*" The shame.

My heart skipped a beat. "Did you invest anything?"

"Me? What's to invest?" He laughed. "Besides, I met the son once when he picked up Abel at the center. I'll never forget. David Shapira told his own father, 'Hurry up, I haven't got all day.' Who could trust a *klumnik* like him?" My uncle literally called him an empty person, a person without substance.

*Thank God Uncle Isaac had been so perceptive.* "Well, he got what he deserved. He's in prison for a very long time and won't be able to hurt anyone again. I'm just wondering who killed his wife. Can you still get hold of Abel?"

"Martha . . ." I heard the unmistakable warning in his voice.

"Oh, believe me, I'm just thinking about Dolleen's little Chihuahua. We rescued it before we left her house this morning. I'm hoping to find a relative who'll be willing to adopt her. I thought if Abel had been in touch with his daughter-in-law, he might take the dog himself."

I could almost hear the wheels turning in my uncle's head. "I'll ask Morty if he knows how to get in touch with Abel. Now, enough with the bad news. Let's talk about Pesach."

Pesach, or Passover, was my favorite holiday and arrived in three weeks. We always hosted the Seder at my uncle's home in West LA. With a house full of guests, our celebration and meal involved a lot of planning and cooking. According to Jewish tradition, Uncle Isaac spent the weeks prior to the holiday preparing his house. He conducted a thorough spring cleaning and unpacked special dishes and cookware used exclusively during the eight days of the festival.

Passover celebrated the time when Moses freed the Jewish people from slavery in Egypt and led everyone back to our homeland in Israel, collecting the Ten Commandments along the way. We wandered in the desert for forty years and lived in tents. Back then, all we had to do to clean the house for the holiday was gather the rugs and shake the *shmutz* outside. Now, however, the process had become much more complicated. My *bubbie*, my beloved grandmother, used to be in charge. After her death, may she rest in peace, my uncle and I worked side by side to keep the tradition going.

"Is Quincy coming?" he asked.

"Yes, and she's bringing her fiancé."

He didn't respond.

My thirty-two-year-old daughter, Quincy, would be flying in from Boston with her live-in boyfriend. She said he looked forward to the experience. I wished I could say the same for Uncle Isaac. The issue was the boyfriend. Naveen Sharma was a brilliant nuclear physicist from Mumbai and a perfectly wonderful human being, but not Jewish. Although he was too polite to make a fuss, the prospect of Quincy marrying outside the faith made my very traditional uncle unhappy.

The rest of our conversation addressed the logistics of the upcoming holiday. "Don't worry, Uncle. When the time comes, I'm sure Yossi would love to help us."

"Now you're cookin' with gas." My uncle, a huge fan of Yossi Levy, aka Crusher, said, "You should really go ahead and marry that mensch already."

"Can we not talk about him, Uncle Isaac? We've

been over this a hundred times. I'm just not ready to commit myself again." I wrestled with serious trust issues. My ex-husband, Aaron Rose, and ex-boyfriend Arlo Beavers had both cheated on me.

"Sure, sure, *faigela*. Take all the time you need. Only, hurry up. You're not getting any younger."

By the time our call ended, the clock read four in the afternoon, and the right side of my head throbbed. Between discovering a murder, facing a pissed-off Beavers, and placating my uncle, the stress of the day triggered a fibromyalgia flare-up and a migraine. I swallowed a Soma, my go-to medication for the fibro and another pill for the headache. Then I lay down on my cream-colored sofa, covered myself with my favorite blue-and-white quilt, and closed my eyes. The last thing I remembered before falling asleep was Bumper curling up against my body and purring.

I never heard Crusher ride up on his Harley, nor did I hear him enter the house. Although we hadn't officially moved in together, I'd given him a key to my place. His gentle kiss on my forehead woke me up. "Hey, babe."

I opened my eyes to see all six feet six inches and three-hundred pounds of solid muscle towering above me. On the cusp of turning fifty, Crusher bore the look of a man you didn't want to mess with. His hair, almost invisible under the bandana he always wore on his head, was short, red, and shot through with gray. His neat beard had turned mostly white, except for a red streak down the middle. His blue eyes crinkled at the corners when he smiled at me. Unlike Beavers, who always smelled of patchouli or expensive cologne, Crusher frequently smelled like eau du gasoline.

I stretched and sat up, thankful my headache had dissolved. "What time is it?"

"Time to eat. I brought some Brent's." He referred to one of the last great delis still open in the San Fernando Valley.

Bumper munched on kibble while Crusher and I sat at the kitchen table and unwrapped two mile-high pastramis on rye, plus a pint of deli coleslaw.

"How was your day?" He took a giant bite of sandwich.

"Just the usual. In the morning, I discovered a murder then spent some time at the police station."

Crusher stopped chewing at the mention of murder. With a mouthful of food, he said, "Who was the vic?"

"Dolleen Doyle." As we devoured the salty, moist pastrami, I reported everything I knew about the victim and the events of the day. "Then I took some meds for the migraine and went to sleep on the sofa." I noticed he'd already finished his sandwich, so I pushed the second half of my pastrami across the table. "I'm full. You can have this."

"That must've been quite a shock, babe." He picked up the half sandwich, and the tone of his voice became cautious. "You said you called Beavers?"

*Oh no, here we go.* Crusher believed the reason I wouldn't marry him was because I still had a thing for Arlo Beavers. Maybe I did secretly like him a little, but that wasn't the reason for my reluctance.

How could I be sure Crusher wouldn't cheat on me too?

I took a fortifying breath. "Yes, I called Arlo because he's the best homicide detective in the Valley and because I knew he'd do a good job."

Crusher chewed, grunted, and looked at the table, clearly unhappy about Beavers being back in my life. He'd just have to get over himself.

"Don't worry, Yossi. I doubt I'll be talking to the police again any time soon. Arlo took our statements about discovering the body, and now it's over." I cleared my throat. "I also volunteered you for cleaning out the *chametz* at Uncle Isaac's house."

*Chametz* referred to any leavened food. Torah commanded the Jews to eat only unleavened bread during the eight days of Passover. Therefore, all forbidden foods must be removed and disposed of, including anything made with grains or yeast, such as bread, cereal, cookies, cakes, flour—even beer and grain alcohol. To complicate matters, rabbinic law also banned the use of any dishes or cookware that touched the leavened foods during the rest of the year. So, in addition to the heavy house cleaning, Yossi would help Uncle Isaac pack away his everyday kitchenware and unpack the dishes and cookware used only during Passover.

He nodded. "No problem."

We cleaned up the dishes (that is, we threw away the food wrappings) and settled on the sofa to watch *Jeopardy*. A dapper Alex Trebek read from a card, "The holiest place for Jews."

I immediately said, "The *Kotel*." The Wailing Wall in Jerusalem.

At the same time, Crusher said, "Brent's Deli."

I laughed and playfully punched his arm, then the doorbell rang.

"Ow." Crusher rubbed his massive bicep in mock pain. "Are you expecting anyone?"

"No." I shrugged.

"I'll get it, then." Ever protective of me, my boyfriend got up and opened the door to my unknown caller.

Jazz entered the house, blinking rapidly and biting his lip. A tote bag made of baby blue fabric with a print of fluffy white clouds and little lambs hung from his arm. I grabbed the remote and turned off the TV. "Is something wrong?"

The white-faced Jazz sat across from the sofa in an easy chair and made a table with his lap for the tote. Zsa Zsa and Patti poked their little canine heads out of the bag, wearing matching nightgowns in a petite floral print. Zsa Zsa's topknot was wrapped tightly around a tiny pink roller.

Jazz spoke barely above a whisper. "I think I'm in trouble."

"Talk to me."

"I got a visit tonight from your friend, Arlo Beavers, and his partner."

Crusher glanced at me and frowned.

Jazz didn't seem to notice. "You remember I told you they took my fingerprints today?"

"Yes. They routinely take them if you were present at a crime scene. Right, Yossi?"

Crusher nodded but said nothing.

"Arlo said they found my prints on the metal dumbbell they say killed her."

A picture of the blood and hair I saw on the hand weight flashed through my mind. I leaned forward, not quite believing what Jazz just revealed. "They couldn't be. You didn't go anywhere near the weapon."

"Remember I told you I'd started working out again? Well, last month Dolly said she also wanted to get into shape. Maybe firm up her arms a little. So, I lent her my two-pound weights. My prints were on them because they were *my* weights."

"I didn't know you were so friendly with her," I said.

Jazz twisted the diamond ring on his left hand. "I knew Dolly when she first learned the waxing trade, long before she married David. She came to LA from a small town in Kansas. We were best friends for a while. We stayed in touch during her marriage to David and her move to *Sugar Hill,* as she called her Beverly Hills mansion. I even tailored the occasional suit for him."

"Did Arlo believe you about the weights?"

"I don't think so." Jazz rubbed his forehead.

"I'll get some beer." Crusher headed for the kitchen.

Jazz took a deep breath. "Dolly loaned me fifty thou to start my doggie boutique."

"Really? I thought your menswear business was doing so well."

He bent his head. "I've been too embarrassed to tell everyone the truth. Opening the doggie boutique wasn't just a matter of branching out. My custom menswear business suffered from stiff competition. A couple of hot, new, high-end designers opened their stores on Sunset Boulevard and sucked my business away. You know what they say on *Project Runway,*

'One day you're in, the next day you're out.' I needed the money."

Crusher offered each of us a bottle of Heineken.

Jazz looked up at the big man. "Do you have a glass?"

Crusher glanced at me, raised an eyebrow, and returned to the kitchen.

Something didn't add up. "Didn't Russell leave you anything when he died?"

Jazz's eyes filled with the mention of his dead lover. "When Rusty made out his will, I encouraged him to leave everything to Birdie. Back then, my business was thriving. I was making my own money hand over fist and didn't need any of his. Besides, he'd already given me so much. When he bought our house twenty-five years ago, he put the deed in my name."

"So, when your business suffered, you turned to Dolleen for a loan?"

Jazz sighed. "I agreed to pay her back twenty-five hundred each month, but I fell behind a couple of payments. I texted her and asked for an extension to come up with the money. She texted me back and gave me two weeks to come up with the money or she threatened to put a lien on my house and my business. She was joking, of course. Dolly was the soul of generosity. I joked back and pretended to be this desperate guy when I texted her again."

An alarm clanged in my head. "What exactly did you text in those messages?"

"I called her a heartless bitch who didn't deserve to breathe." Tears spilled down his cheeks. "I swear, we were just being playful. The next day, while she waxed me, she said if I wanted to, I could pay her with a huge order of doggie stuff in lieu of the two payments I'd missed."

"Was her order truly worth five thousand dollars?"

Jazz sat up straight. "There are lots of people who gladly pay premium prices for first-class, one-of-a-kind goods. I charged Dolly exactly what I would've charged anyone else for the same thing. Anyway, I was so grateful. I worked like crazy all week to fill her order. I even threw in a three-hundred-dollar pink, velvet party dress with Swarovski crystals for Patti."

Crusher returned and handed the glass of beer to Jazz, who gratefully accepted the brew.

"And you told Beavers all this?"

Jazz took a hefty swig and burped delicately behind his hand. "Of course. But again, I don't think he believed me. His partner warned me not to leave town." He pleaded with his eyes. "You know Detective Beavers. Can't you talk to him? Can't you tell him I'd never hurt anyone?"

Crusher shifted in his seat, took a long pull from his bottle, and focused on me, his gaze like a laser beam. His face, his posture, even his breathing broadcast his disapproval. But poor Jazz needed my help. That man could no more bash someone over the head than I could roller-skate naked down Ventura Boulevard.

Regardless of how Crusher felt about my talking to Beavers again, I needed to do whatever I could to keep my friend from being arrested for a murder he didn't commit.

# CHAPTER 4

The next morning, I awoke to savory smells coming from the kitchen. Onions simmered in olive oil, hinting that cottage-fried potatoes would be served along with the usual eggs and toast. I hastily pulled on my stretch denim jeans and a pink T-shirt, slipped my feet into a pair of navy blue Crocs, and headed toward the food.

"Morning, babe." Crusher stood over the stove, stirring the diced potatoes in the sizzling oil. He wore a fresh bandana every day in lieu of a more traditional religious head covering.

I added some half-and-half to a fresh cup of dark roast coffee, closed my eyes and took a sip of the life-affirming brew. An egg, spinach, and mushroom mixture steamed in the omelet pan he'd brought over the week before. A stack of already buttered rye toast sat on the table next to a jar of raspberry jam.

My stomach opened in anticipation, like a flower in the morning sun. "Smells great, Yossi."

Crusher didn't behave like any other man I'd

known. Without being asked, he cheerfully stepped up to share in the domestic chores. And since I hated to cook more than I hated the cleanup, this division of labor worked out very well for us. We barely spoke as we made our way through the satisfying meal. Finally, he put down his fork and studied my face. "So, have you decided what to do about your friend Jazz?"

"I'm going to have to talk to Arlo. He's got to know Jazz couldn't hurt anyone." Crusher frowned, and I reached for his hand. "Look. You may not like Arlo, but he's not an idiot. He won't settle for an obvious suspect like Jazz if he thinks there could be others with motives to kill. Think back two years ago when Ed Pappas became the primary suspect in a murder. Arlo didn't stop looking for the real killer just because Ed made a very public threat on the dead man's life."

I guess you could say I could thank my neighbor Ed for meeting the man who had just cooked my breakfast. When someone had beaten to death a baseball coach right behind my house two years ago, my neighbor became the prime suspect. I joined efforts with Ed's biker friends—including Crusher— to prove his innocence. During our investigation, we turned up enough information to point Beavers toward several other suspects. In the end, Ed was exonerated and Crusher proposed marriage.

He ran his fingers through his beard. "My gut tells me Jazz isn't guilty. But I have to admit, you're right. Beavers is a good cop. Unfortunately, he has this thing about both of us right now. Let's just hope he's in a mood to listen to you." Crusher pulled his buzzing phone from his pocket. "Levy. Where? Yeah, I'm on it."

He pushed his chair back from the table and kissed me on the mouth. "Sorry, babe. Gotta go."

He rushed out the front door, stopping briefly to grab his Glock and ATF badge from the hall table. The engine of his Harley growled *brum-rum* and then faded in the distance.

As I cleaned the kitchen, I couldn't decide how to approach Beavers, so I called my best friend, Lucy. "Are you busy? Can I come over?"

"What's up, girlfriend?"

"We've got a serious problem."


Twenty minutes later, I leaned in the doorway of Lucy's kitchen. She stood at the sink, wearing an old-fashioned red-and-white polka dot apron with a bib and rick-rack around the edges. Her husband, Ray Mondello, gulped down the last of his coffee and placed the cup on the counter next to his wife. Thanks to strong Italian genes, despite being in his sixties he still sported a full head of dark hair, with only a few silver threads sprinkled in.

"Okay, sweetheart. Off to the salt mines." He stood two inches shorter than his wife, so when she kissed him good-bye, she bent her head a little. Their embrace was a flawless, graceful dance they'd been practicing since junior high school in their small town of Moorcroft, Wyoming.

Ray walked over to me and gave me a stern look. "Lucy told me about the body yesterday. Can you tell me what I'm thinking?"

I bit my lip and wagged my head slowly, even though I knew perfectly well what he would say next. Ray and Lucy were my staunchest friends over the years. But he was fiercely protective of the mother of his five sons.

"Stay the hell out of it. I don't want either of you playing detective and getting hurt. *Capiche?*"

I widened my eyes, raised my eyebrows, and nodded.

Ray knew me so well. "I know that look, Martha Rose . . ."

"What look?"

Lucy rescued me. "Ray, hon, like I told you yesterday, there's no reason for us to get involved. Right, Martha?"

I smiled and crossed my fingers behind my back. "No reason."

He grunted. "Keep it that way." Then he gave me a peck on the cheek and headed for his car.

Once we were alone, Lucy poured me the last of the coffee, and we sat at the kitchen table. "Okay, what's this serious problem?"

"Jazz got a visit from Arlo last night." I repeated the story about the loan from Dolleen and the playful text messages on her phone.

"How ridiculous. Just because he texted something silly doesn't prove he's a murderer."

"I'm afraid there's more. Jazz's fingerprints were found on the metal hand weight that killed her. The evidence is pretty damning."

Lucy's mouth fell open. "How did his prints get on the weapon? Do you think he's guilty after all?"

"No! I don't believe for a second he killed her.

Jazz lent those weights to Dolleen last month. They were his to begin with, so of course his fingerprints would be on them."

"Well, there you go." Lucy waved her hand dismissively. "Circumstantial evidence. Wasn't Arlo satisfied?"

"Apparently not. He told Jazz not to leave town."

"What can we do? You heard Ray. He'd have a cow if we got involved in another murder investigation."

"You don't have to get involved if you don't want to. But I have to convince the police Jazz is innocent. Since Arlo is still pissed at me, I need you to help me figure out a way to approach him."

Lucy closed her eyes for a second and tapped the table with her fingertips. "*Hmm.*" She opened her eyes and looked at me. "Why not approach this sideways?"

"What do you mean?"

"I mean, don't talk to Arlo. Instead of poking the bear, why don't you talk to his partner?"

"Detective Kaplan? That little weasel?" I'd had a couple of run-ins before with Beavers's much younger partner Noah Kaplan. He bore the looks of a movie star, the swagger of a pimp, and the judgment of a sixteen-year-old. In his zeal to arrest my neighbor Ed for the coach's murder, he unwittingly leaked important information to the real killer. "What makes you think he'll listen to *me*?"

"Easy. He's got a giant ego. Figure out a way to play on that."

Maybe Lucy had a point. While both Beavers and Kaplan might be equally disposed to ignore me, Kaplan might be easier to influence. I decided approaching Kaplan was my only shot at helping Jazz.

"Okay, let's go to West Valley Station and talk to him."

Lucy held up her hand. "Didn't you hear what I just said about Ray? I'm afraid this time you're on your own, girlfriend."

Facing my old nemesis Kaplan without Lucy's support wouldn't be easy. But I respected her position. She needed to consider her husband's feelings. However, as far as I was concerned, that was another argument against marriage. When you were single, like me, you didn't have to ask permission.


The West Valley Station of the LAPD sat near a park on the corner of Vanowen and Wilbur. Tall windows filled the recently remodeled lobby with light. I stood in a short line, waiting to speak to the uniformed officer at the desk. Bruises covered the face and arms of the woman in front of me. More bruising probably hid beneath her clothes. She spoke in a timid whisper so I could barely overhear what she said.

"Boyfriend Randal . . . rent money."

Thank God this poor woman possessed the courage to come forward and name her abuser. How many other bullies like Randal got away with this kind of crime? I appreciated the way the officer's voice turned gentle at her story. He made a call, and a minute later a female dressed in street clothes appeared and escorted the victim through a door. My turn came next.

"I'd like to speak to Detective Noah Kaplan. I have some important information about a homicide he's investigating."

The officer took a fresh form from a pile and poised his pen to write. "What is your name, ma'am?"

"Martha Rose."

He printed my name in block letters. "Address and phone number?"

I gave him the information.

"And which case are you talking about?"

"Dolleen Doyle."

"Please have a seat, and I'll let Detective Kaplan know you're here." He picked up my intake form and disappeared briefly through the same door as the poor, battered woman.

I sat in one of the gray plastic bucket chairs, hoping Beavers wouldn't come walking through the lobby and spot me. Kaplan kept me waiting for fifteen minutes, the petty little ferret.

Finally, a door opened, and he appeared with a smirk I wanted to slap away. Noah Kaplan had the kind of looks that made young women weak: flawless physique; dark, curly hair; and liquid, brown eyes. He sauntered over to me. "Mrs. Rose. I shoulda known you'd be back."

"Hello, Detective. How have you been?"

"You said you have some important information about Dolleen Doyle's murder?"

I cleared my throat and stood. "I do. Can we talk?"

"This oughta be good for a laugh." He crooked

his finger at me in a condescending signal to follow him. I swallowed my anger and trooped behind him to the same blue interview room where I'd given Beavers my statement the day before. Kaplan sat back in his chair, crossed his legs, and smirked at me across the steel table.

I leaned forward in my chair. "I want to get off on the right foot with you this time, Detective, so let's be honest here. We haven't gotten along in the past. As a matter of fact, we probably don't like each other very much."

He drew his head back and raised an eyebrow. "So, why did you ask to speak to *me*?"

"As you know, I've successfully solved a few murders. You could say I've earned some credibility. But when I came to you in the past with important information, you not only ignored me, you arrested me. Turned out I was right and you were wrong. If you'd listened to me over the years, you could've chalked up a couple of big wins. But because of your stubbornness, you lost the chance to be a hero and scored a zero." For emphasis, I touched the tip of my forefinger and thumb together to form an "O."

"You're right. I don't like you."

I shrugged. "I'm offering you a chance to get out in front of this investigation. Arlo Beavers is going down a path that will lead him nowhere. But if you're smart, you'll listen to me this time. You can be the hero and solve this case."

"You know I can't discuss an ongoing investigation with anyone. Least of all you. Why don't you set your boyfriend Beavers on the right path? Oh, wait."

He sat back and turned up the corner of his mouth. "He dumped you a while back, didn't he?"

*No, you little putz. I dumped him the last time.* I forced a smile. "Now you understand why he's not the right person to talk to. I believe you're more capable than he is of setting aside any differences we might have felt in the past."

"Dream on," he grunted.

"Look, Noah. May I call you Noah? You can call me Martha." I didn't wait for an answer. "I have real information about Dolleen's case to share with you."

His eyes narrowed, but he didn't reach for a pen. "Go on."

"Jazz Fletcher came to me last night in a panic. Totally distressed. He explained to me about the text messages on Dolleen's phone and the fingerprints on the murder weapon."

"So?"

"So, despite the fact it looks bad for him, I can tell in my gut he didn't do it. And my gut is never wrong. I'm sure you know by now how his fingerprints got there. I concede Jazz said some suspicious things in those texts, but the two of them were just playing a game. Neither one of them meant those messages. Jazz Fletcher is incapable of killing another human being. It's just not in his nature."

"Let me get this straight. You want us to eliminate him as a suspect because he's your friend?"

I took a deep breath. "No. I want you to eliminate him as a suspect because he didn't do it. Look: Dolleen Doyle married a man responsible for stealing millions from a lot of people. The Feds weren't able to find it all. Some of his victims might think she could still get her hands on those hidden accounts. Surely there are plenty of potential suspects out there who might've tried to get their investments back from her or were angry enough at her husband to seek revenge."

Kaplan seemed unconvinced. "If you know all those details, you must also know a witness puts Fletcher's Mercedes outside the victim's house around the time of her murder."

*Actually, I know nothing about a witness. But thank you, Detective, for the information.*

I threw up my hands. "Yes, but he never went inside. He drove all the way from West Hollywood to make a delivery. But when Dolleen didn't answer the door, he left. She must've already been dead. I'll bet your witness never saw him enter the house."

Kaplan didn't answer. Instead, he rose. "I'm sorry, Mrs. Rose."

"Martha. Please call me Martha."

"I'm sorry, but you haven't really told me anything new about the case. Fletcher's in deep trouble. He needs more than your say-so. He needs a good lawyer."

"Jazz is cash-strapped. Where would he get the money to hire a top-notch attorney? Will you at least consider the possibility there may be other people with a reason to kill Dolleen Doyle?"

"Your objections are duly noted. Now let me give you a word of advice. If you interfere in another investigation, *Mrs. Rose*, I won't hesitate to arrest you, just like I did two years ago. And this time, I doubt your ex-boyfriend would bother to help you get out of jail."


I drove back to Lucy's house and drowned my anger in a slice of zucchini bread with walnuts.

Lucy listened to my story and lowered her chin to her chest. "Well, it was worth a try."

"We can't let them arrest Jazz. You know what happens to gay men in jail."

"I know, I know. But what did Kaplan warn you? If you start *poking* around," she wagged her fingers in air quotes, "you're the one liable to end up in the *pokey*." She ignored my groan. "And Kaplan spoke the truth when he said Jazz needs to get a good lawyer."

"I don't think he can afford one right now. Yet, I'm not willing to leave his fate to an overworked public defender. What can we do?"

Lucy frowned and pursed her lips. "What about Birdie? She's very fond of Jazz. Maybe she'll help him pay for an attorney. She's confided many times that Russell left behind a huge life insurance policy and more money than she could ever spend."

I laughed. "What a scenario. A widow paying for the legal defense of her dead husband's boyfriend. But you have a point. What could it hurt to ask?"

Lucy walked to her front window and looked at Birdie's house across the street. "She's home now. I see someone moving in her living room."

"Let's go."

# CHAPTER 5

Birdie Watson sat across from us at the green farm table in her kitchen, wearing her denim overalls. "How much does it cost to hire a criminal defense attorney?"

"What'd you do this time, Twink?" Birdie's fiancé strolled into the kitchen, wearing jeans and brown cowboy boots with scrollwork tooled into the leather. Denver Watson had combed his white hair back behind his ears, where it curled over the collar of his blue shirt. He nodded a greeting to Lucy and me.

"It's not for me, Denny." She gestured for him to sit next to her. "It's for poor Jazz. The police suspect him of murdering that woman we found yesterday."

"He do it?" The chair scraped across the floor as he drew it next to Birdie.

"Of course not. But apparently he's short on cash right now. So, I told the girls I'd be happy to pay for an attorney."

Denver grabbed her hand. "I'd expect no less

from you." He raised her fingertips to his lips and gently kissed them.

My heart expanded with pleasure as I watched the two of them talk in their own private language of gestures and looks. After decades of separation, they were making up for lost time.

Lucy said, "Shall I call Jazz and tell him about the attorney, hon?"

Birdie absently reached with her free hand for the end of her white braid. "It's probably better if I call him. He won't turn me down." Of course. Jazz and Birdie shared a special connection.

I smiled at the elderly lovebirds. "While Lucy and I have the two of you here together, why don't we talk about your wedding? There's a lot of planning to do."

Denver chuckled once and stood. "I think this is where I suddenly remember I left the engine running in the RV. Or something like that." He gestured toward Birdie with his chin. "I'll let Twink, here, make all the decisions. Whatever she wants is fine with me." A faint smile curved Birdie's lips as she watched him mosey out of the room.

I turned to the older woman. "I've been dying to ask you, Birdie. Why does he call you *Twink*?"

Her cheeks colored. She dipped her chin and lowered her voice. "It stands for *Twinkle*. I told him once, when we were young, that when we made love, I saw stars." She giggled and whispered, "I still do, and I'm in my late seventies."

Lucy laughed. "I used to wonder if the magic would eventually fade from our love life, especially as we got older. But our fiftieth anniversary is coming up, and I stopped worrying a long time ago. I feel the same way about Ray today as I did when we were kids in high school."

"Pleasure doesn't have an expiration date," I said. "Look at the story of Abraham and Sarah in the book of Genesis. She conceived her only son, Isaac, when she was in her nineties. So, we better get you married soon, Birdie, before you become an unwed mother."

I instantly regretted my remark when I saw her reaction. Birdie and Russell never had children. She stared into the distance and squeezed her hands together. "I'm afraid that train left the station a long time ago, dear. But you're right about one thing. Denny and I want to get married soon. We've chosen May tenth. It's an auspicious day, according to Phoebe. And she's going to perform the ceremony for us."

"The Phoebe from your old commune?" I pictured the elderly woman, who officiated at Russell's funeral last year, wearing a white robe and a crown of flowers in her long gray hair.

"Yes. I'm glad you remember."

How could I forget? Phoebe Marple talked to ghosts and summoned forest deities with drums. "We have less than eight weeks to get everything done," I said.

Birdie reached over and patted my hand. "No need to panic. Denny and I don't want anything formal. We're getting married at home on the ranch."

Lucy reached in her purse and produced a pad of paper and a pen. "How many guests are you inviting?"

"Denny's family has lived in McMinnville, Oregon, for generations. There are quite a few of his relatives in the area. Plus, he knows all the old-timers." She paused and chewed the inside of her cheek. "Let me see. Including families with children, a couple hundred could show up."

My mouth fell open. "What about food? How're you going to feed so many people?"

Birdie patted my hand. "Don't worry. We're doing this family-style. My friend, Rainbow, has insisted on coordinating everything. A couple of the Watson cousins will barbeque the meat. The rest of the dishes will be potluck. We're inviting guests to bring a dish to share, instead of a gift."

I tried to picture how we could organize the chaos of a hundred potluck dishes. "But what if everyone brings a green-bean casserole?"

Birdie waved her hand. "These things always work out, dear. We'll let each family decide what they want to contribute. All we have to do is spread everything out on long tables and let people help themselves."

Lucy wrinkled her nose as if she smelled something bad. I knew my super-organized, orange-haired friend was completely out of her comfort zone. "Are you sure you want to leave everything to chance? Wouldn't it be safer to have someone cater your party? You'll need an army of helpers for two hundred people."

"What would be the fun in catering?" Birdie smiled. "The nice thing about potluck is the food expands with the crowd. On the other hand, if you

commit to catering for two hundred people and
only fifty show up, you've wasted a whole lot of
food. As for helpers, Rainbow's got that covered.
You'll see."

"How many toilets do you have at the ranch?" I
had to ask. The mere logistics of accommodating so
many people would've sent my *bubbie* straight to a
big-box store looking for the best bargain on a case
of Quilted Northern. She'd routinely kept a reserve
of forty-eight rolls in the closet. God forbid we
should run out.

Birdie gave me a blank stare, but Lucy nodded
her head vigorously. "Martha's right. How are you
going to accommodate two hundred guests?"

After a short pause, Birdie brightened and said
"Porta Potties."

I shuddered. *Bubbie* would plotz.

We talked about table rentals, flowers, and wedding cakes.

Then I stood and stretched. "Time for me to
go. Whatever you want to do, Birdie, we're here
to help."

"I know, and I'm grateful. Now I'd better help
Jazz hire a good attorney. You don't happen to
know of anyone, do you?"

"As a matter of fact, I do," I said. "Remember the
fancy attorney who helped me handle Harriet
Gordon's estate a couple years ago? Deacon Abernathy? He's in Westwood. If he doesn't do criminal
defense, he'll know someone good who does."

Lucy put her notepad back in her purse. "Be sure
to mention your wedding date when you speak to
Jazz, Birdie. He still needs to make your dress."

We said our good-byes and left. Denver tinkered under the hood of the Winnebago parked a few feet away in Birdie's driveway. Lucy walked me to my Civic sitting across the street in front of her house. She put her fists on her hips. "Can you believe the two of them are actually going to invite a couple hundred people? Do you even know that many? I don't."

I shook my head. "No. But I really like the idea of celebrating the occasion like a block party. Everyone participates, and everyone helps."

As I drove home, I thought about how the custom of potluck dinners reflected the neighbor-helping-neighbor tradition in America, especially in rural communities. Constructing a barn to shelter a farmer's animals and crops was hard work and took time away from other vital chores. So, families gathered together on a neighbor's land to help him erect a building in one day—an event called a *barn raising.*

The men came with their tools, and their women-folk brought enough food to feed everyone. While the men and boys worked together with hammer and nails, the women and girls busied themselves in the kitchen or sat around a large quilting frame and helped the farmer's wife stitch a quilt or two. When it came time for a break, the women fed everyone with food they'd cooked together, along with all the other dishes they'd prepared ahead of time.

This kind of mutual aid became an important part of the social fabric and survival of farming communities. Quilters commemorated this time together—as they did with so many of their experiences—through their handiwork. One special quilt pattern came to be known as *Barn Raising*.

I loved the fact Birdie and Denver's wedding would celebrate this tradition. I'd have to talk to Lucy and Jazz about working together to make a Barn Raising quilt as a surprise wedding gift for the couple.

As soon as I got home, I hurried to the kitchen. The clock read two in the afternoon and my stomach reminded me I hadn't eaten anything since Yossi's excellent breakfast. I slapped some chunky peanut butter on a couple slices of challah and went straight to my sewing room to cut more rectangles for my Prairie Braid quilt.

Working with fabric made me happy in a way nothing else could. I developed a personal attachment to every piece of material I handled. If I ironed it, I made sure not to injure the fibers with too much heat. If I cut it, I lined up the edges with a ruler for accuracy and economy. And finally, I made a *shidduch*, a match, and only joined patterns which complemented each other. I'd be so engrossed, hours could pass in this way and I wouldn't know it.

Because I was in the zone, I jumped when my doorbell rang. I stood on my toes to get to the peephole in the door and my jaw dropped. What the heck? Detective Kaplan stood on my front porch. I opened the door.

"Hello, Detective. I'm surprised to see you."

He didn't pause for niceties. "Where's Fletcher?"

*This can't be good.* "How should I know? Why are you looking for him?"

"Something new has come up, and he's wanted for questioning. If you're hiding him . . ."

I held up my hand like a stop sign. "Whoa. Let's not get ahead of ourselves. You'd better come inside."

He hesitated, looked past me into my living room, then entered my house.

I closed the door behind him and extended my arm. "You're welcome to search my house, but you won't find him here."

Kaplan quickly walked through the house. I heard closet doors open and close. Two minutes later he returned to the living room.

"Why do you think I'm hiding him?" I asked.

His shoulders relaxed a tad and he raked his fingers through his dark curls. "Since you were so . . . interested, I thought he might be here. He's not at his shop, he's not at home, and he's not answering his phone."

My stomach tightened. Where could he be? I hoped he was consulting with a criminal defense lawyer. "He's probably not even aware you're looking for him," I offered.

Kaplan blew out his breath. "We warned Fletcher not to leave town. If you talk to him, tell him he'd better show up at the station if he knows what's good for him." He handed me his business card. "And call me."

*Oh my God.* "Are you going to arrest him?"

The detective didn't answer. He just gave me a hard stare then turned to leave.

"Wait!" I rested my hand on his arm. "Does this have anything to do with the witness you spoke about earlier this morning?" His silence provided me with the answer. "Well, whoever this mysterious witness is, he's lying!"

"How can you say that?" Kaplan seemed genuinely surprised. "You don't even know what she's testifying to."

*The witness is a woman? Thanks for the info, Detective.*

"Because I know Jazz Fletcher. He didn't kill Dolleen Doyle."

"Then he has nothing to be afraid of, does he?" Kaplan strode to his unmarked car and drove away.

Who was this so-called witness? And why would she lie? And where did Jazz disappear to?

I ran to the phone. "Birdie, this is Martha. Have you spoken to Jazz yet?"

"He's here now."

"Let me talk to him."

A moment later he said, "What's up?"

"You're wanted for questioning. Detective Kaplan's looking for you. He just left my house. Have you talked to the attorney yet?"

"Yes. Birdie and I met with Deke Abernathy this afternoon. He's going to take my case."

"You'd better call him back right now and ask him what to do about Kaplan."

I breathed a sigh of relief as I ended the call. Thank God. Deke would take good care of Jazz. Jail was a dangerous place for a gay man.

# CHAPTER 6

Thursday morning, we gathered in Birdie's kitchen, eager to hear about Jazz's interrogation at the police station. A platter of freshly baked sticky buns sat in the middle of the table, cinnamon rolls topped with a gooey syrup of pecans, brown sugar, and melted butter.

Jazz posed an elegant picture in a perfectly tailored gray pinstriped suit with a pink dress shirt and purple tie. "I really felt good about the interview this morning." He stretched out his long legs and took a sip of coffee. "I must say, Abernathy got the best of that young detective. In every way. Deke was much smarter and dressed way better. He obviously wears bespoke suits, because he's not an easy man to fit. He's rather beefy in the arms and around the middle, you know, but he's still quite attractive.

"In lieu of cash, I offered to pay him back by designing a more updated wardrobe. We just received some gorgeous Italian woolens that would really complement his skin tone. Deke turned me down. He said I wouldn't be able to sew anything if I went to jail." Jazz's cell phone twittered. He read a message, typed a hasty reply, and put the phone away without comment.

"So, tell us about the interview," said Lucy.

Jazz crossed his arms. "Some witness identified my car by the personalized license plate and picked me out of a lineup using my DMV photo. But Deke said the statement only proved I'd been telling the truth when I said I went to Dolly's house to deliver packages."

"Did the witness claim she saw you go inside the house?" I asked.

"Deke asked the same question. He also asked for the name of the witness, but we didn't get an answer to either question. So, he said, 'Either arrest my client, or we're done.'" Jazz took another bite of sticky bun. "Divine. Sugar always calms me down."

I could relate. "I wish we could talk to the mysterious witness. I have some questions of my own."

"Wait." Lucy held up her hand. "We could ask a much better witness. One who saw everything." When she noticed the confusion on my face, she continued, "The victim herself! Surely Dolleen can identify her killer. And we know the very person who can talk to her spirit. You know who I mean."

"Oh my God. Are you referring to Paulina?" Paulina Polinskaya, a medium and a fortune teller, had been involved with my late friend Harriet Gordon. "You can't be serious."

"As serious as a one-eyed hog on a truffle farm." Lucy crossed her arms. "Think about it. She could point us to the real killer."

My natural skepticism told me a visit to Paulina

would be a waste of time. Still, she did have an eerie way of predicting the trajectory of my love life the last time I saw her. "No disrespect, Lucy. I know you believe in all that stuff. But even if Paulina could come up with a suspect, do you actually think the police would take us seriously?"

Jazz twisted his wedding ring. "You say this woman can speak to the dead? Could she talk to Rusty?" He used the pet name for his dead lover. "I need to ask him something."

I gave Lucy the stink eye. Why did she have to plant this seed in Jazz's mind?

"That's right, hon." Lucy's voice softened as she answered Jazz's question. "Paulina is a well-known medium and psychic. It's possible she could help us solve this case and also talk to Russell."

"Then we have to go see her!" Jazz squared his shoulders and stood. "This is an emergency." He bent to pick up Zsa Zsa and Patti and placed them in a denim carrier matching their tiny rhinestone-studded jackets. "Who will come with me?"

"I'm so sorry, dear, but I can't leave right now," said Birdie.

"Neither can I, although I'd love to." Lucy smoothed the wrinkles on her sleeve. "I can't risk Ray thinking I'm snooping around again."

All eyes turned to me. I stood reluctantly. "Okay, okay, I'll go with you. But I don't want you to get your hopes up."

Two minutes later we climbed in his Mercedes, and I gave him directions to Venice Boulevard in West LA.

* * *

Paulina's house stood as the last vestige of a bygone neighborhood that commerce transformed long ago. Her pre-World War II bungalow sat squeezed between a strip mall and an auto body shop. A large wooden sign stood in the cracked concrete of what used to be a front yard.

### PSYCHIC
TAROT READINGS
PAST LIVES
### SPIRITUALIST

Since I'd last been there, Paulina had painted the house lavender with white trim. The dying hibiscus in the Mexican pot on her front porch had been replaced by a morning glory vine with purple flowers climbing up a fan-shaped trellis. The paint flakes had been scraped off her front door, which now stood smooth and white. The fortune-telling business must be good.

I knocked shave-and-a-haircut on her front door and almost immediately it swung open. A messy bun captured Paulina's long black hair at the nape of her neck. A purple caftan in an extravagant floral print swathed her short, plump body. Fuchsia lipstick and thick, black eye-liner completed the exotic look. I guessed her age to be somewhere in the range of late twenties to early forties; I could never be sure.

She grinned at me and said in her hard, East

Coast accent, "Long time no see, Martha. I knew you'd show up today."

Jazz's mouth fell open.

I rolled my eyes. "Hello, Paulina. This is my friend Jazz Fletcher."

She craned her neck and measured the tall man with her eyes. "Your aura tells me you suffered a recent loss. I also detect fear. Enter."

Jazz looked at me with wide eyes and whispered, "She's really good!"

"She's a good guesser," I whispered back.

The terra cotta walls of her living room seemed to suck up the light from twelve white candles. Paulina gestured for us to sit at a round table covered by a purple velvet cloth and stuck out her hand. "I charge $150 per session, payable in advance."

"Your prices have gone up," I said. "Last time I visited, you were only charging a hundred."

She shrugged. "I'm more in demand than ever, thanks to good reviews on Yelp. Maybe you've seen my tweets at hashtag PaulinaPredicts?"

"Afraid not," I said.

Jazz opened his wallet. "Do you take credit cards?"

Paulina reached behind her and produced an electronic reader. "Visa, Discover, and Master Card but not American Express. They take 3 percent. Go ahead and swipe your card." She completed the transaction and handed Jazz a receipt. Then she poured tea from a porcelain pot and passed each of us a cup. I added sugar and stirred, watching the brown leaves settle to the bottom.

She adjusted the cushion on her chair. "You still quilting, Martha?"

I nodded. "Yes, and Jazz has joined our little group."

"Did I ever tell you my *bunica*, my grandma, sewed quilts? I'd like to make one someday. Purple."

I loved the idea of helping another new quilter get started. "Just tell me when you're ready. I'd be happy to get you started."

"Thanks. I'll take you up on that." She shifted her focus to Jazz. "Tell Paulina why you're here today."

"I'm in trouble." He spread his hands on top of the purple tablecloth. "The police think I murdered someone, but I didn't."

"*Um hmm*. As I suspected. You got a brownish tinge on the edges of your aura. Go on."

"You can speak to the dead, right? The woman the police think I killed is Dolleen Doyle. Can you ask her who the real killer is?"

"I can try." Paulina nodded gravely. "But you gotta be prepared. When someone passes over to the other side, especially after a sudden or violent death, they can be confused. Frightened. If this Dolleen is still trying to get her bearings in the spirit world, she might not hear me calling. It could take several sessions to break through to her."

Several sessions? Paulina wasn't the only so-called psychic in the room. I heard the distinct *cha-ching* of her internal cash register.

"Fine." He leaned forward. "I'm desperate. When can we start?"

"Slow down." Paulina motioned with her hands.

"I'll need an item that belonged to her. Something she touched, or wore. Do you have an object like that?"

"Kind of. I have her Chihuahua, Patti." He reached into the denim tote and lifted out the small, sleepy dog and passed her across the table. A curious Zsa Zsa poked her head out of the same bag but didn't attempt to follow.

"Even better," Paulina said. "A beloved pet is just the thing to draw her spirit back to our world." She cuddled the dog and, after a moment, spoke to the quivering, miniature canine. "I don't blame you. Size can make a difference." She paused and stared in the dog's brown eyes. "I know this adjustment must be difficult for you. You've been through a lot. But these people really seem to care. You'll be okay from here on out." The Chihuahua visibly calmed down.

Jazz nudged me with his elbow.

I cleared my throat. "You're a dog psychic too?"

Paulina's bracelets clattered as she turned her palm up. "You still doubt me? I have many gifts, including the ability to speak to animals. I've just learned that in her previous life, Patti was a bilingual Rottweiler from my old neighborhood in New Jersey. She could bark in Romanian. The problem is, she's having trouble adjusting to her new, diminutive stature. In her other life, she wouldn't have just quivered helplessly while someone attacked her poor mistress. She would've jumped the guy and torn him to pieces."

The Chihuahua wagged her tail and barked twice.

The rational part of me didn't want to believe a word she said. But what if she really could communicate with animals? Against my better judgment I asked, "Can Patti identify the killer?"

Paulina looked into Patti's eyes again for a moment then shook her head slowly. "Unfortunately, witnessing the event traumatized her, and she doesn't remember much. All she remembers is the attacker wore white sneakers."

I rolled my eyes. "That only describes everyone in LA."

"Give the poor thing a break." Paulina stroked the Chihuahua's head. "She's got PTSD and traumatic amnesia. With time, she may remember more."

Jazz's mouth slackened. "This is amazing. Can you contact Dolly now? Ask her about her killer?"

"Turns out Patti's still too fragile emotionally to participate in a séance. I'm afraid we'll need to use something else to summon the dead woman's spirit. Can you bring a possession she might've really valued? Like a good piece of jewelry?"

Jazz frowned. "Not without breaking into her house."

I didn't like the direction of this conversation. "Oh my God. No offense, but can't you do your medium thing without a prop?"

She pursed her lips. "Sometimes. But it takes longer. I'm under the impression your mission to contact her is urgent."

"Very," said Jazz.

Paulina raised one shoulder. "Well then, I could speed up the process by holding one of her most cherished items."

She reached for Jazz's cup of tea and briefly turned it upside down to drain the leftover liquid in the saucer. "I'm gonna read your leaves." She peered inside. "*Mmm-hmmm.* Just as I thought. Something big is about to change your life. Also, your freedom is in peril." She put down the cup. "I will give you careful guidance through these treacherous times. Unfortunately, our time is up for today."

"But I need to talk to Rusty," said Jazz.

"Who?" Paulina frowned.

"My fiancé. He died last year. I need to ask him something."

Paulina reached up and rearranged her hair bun, lifting it to the top of her head. "Come back tomorrow."

"Really?" I said. "Does this mean he's going to have to fork over $150 every time he comes here? Because I don't think he can afford you right now."

"Luckily, I have a special going this week. Pay for three visits and get the fourth one free."

Jazz nodded vigorously and reached for his wallet again. But I stopped him with a hand on his arm. "We'll have to think about it, Paulina. Come on, Jazz, let's go."

She held up her left hand. Silver rings sat on each finger, and bangle bracelets tinkled once more on her wrist. "Wait. Before you get up, I'll read your leaves too. Consider it a finder's fee for bringing me new business."

Again, despite my misgivings, I handed over my cup. She studied the pattern made by the brown leaves. "I see struggles ahead. *Hmm.* I also see a wedding."

Jazz piped up, "You're really good at this. Our friend Birdie is getting married in a few weeks."

"I don't think that's the wedding I'm seeing. This one will come at the end of the summer." Paulina put down the cup and winked at me.

"You can't be talking about me." I shook off her prediction as nonsense. In spite of Crusher's regular proposals, I didn't plan to ever remarry. Then again, could she be talking about my daughter, Quincy, and her fiancé? "We've gotta go."

Jazz said, "Yes, thanks for fitting us in your busy schedule. I'll be back tomorrow with something of Dolly's and something of Rusty's."

"Only one séance at a time," Paulina said.

An alarm clanged in my brain.

Jazz sighed. "Okay. I guess we should contact Dolly first." He reached across the table for Patti, but she bared her tiny fangs and growled. Jazz furrowed his forehead. "What's wrong, sweetheart? Come to Daddy. I have a teeny little biscuit in the car for you," he sang.

Patti barked once and refused to move.

"She doesn't want to go with you," Paulina said.

Jazz stared at the psychic. "Why not?"

"For one thing, she hates the dresses."

Jazz's hand flew to his chest. "Oh no, Patti! Is it the lavender print? Just tell Daddy what colors you like best."

Paulina shook her head. "It's all part of her conflict over being so small."

"But what about Zsa Zsa?" He pointed to the Maltese still sitting in the tote bag on his lap.

"Doesn't Patti want to go home with her? The two of them are BFFs."

She shrugged. "Let me keep Patti overnight. Maybe I can help her work through her issues." The little dog jumped up and down and licked Paulina's face.

Jazz got up from the table. "Okay, but I'm taking her home tomorrow."

As soon as we were in the car, I turned to Jazz. "You told Paulina you'd be back with an object belonging to Dolleen. Just what did you have in mind?"

He turned on the engine. "I'm going to her house tonight to find something."

"You can't do that! You'll be arrested for burglary."

"Only if someone catches me, and I don't intend to be caught. I can't go to jail, Martha. Making me wear one of those neon orange jumpsuits would be cruel and unusual punishment."

He pulled into traffic on Venice Boulevard and glanced my way. "The only thing is, I kind of need a lookout."

My stomach turned queasy. "Are you crazy? Not only would we be committing burglary, we'd be messing with a crime scene."

"I don't have anyone else." He reached over and squeezed my hand. "Please, Martha, you've just got to help me."

# CHAPTER 7

Later that night, I lay in bed listening to Crusher snore softly beside me. The digital clock on the night stand told me I had fifteen minutes to get dressed and meet Jazz in front of my house. I crept through the darkened bedroom into my sewing room where, earlier in the evening, I'd stashed black yoga pants, a T-shirt, a black sweatshirt, and sneakers. I dressed hurriedly, stuffed my flashlight, cell phone, and keys into a fanny pack, and pulled back the curtain to peek outside. Jazz's Mercedes idled in front of the house. I silently sneaked out the front door.

"How long have you been here?" I slipped into the passenger seat and clicked on my seatbelt. The digital clock on the dashboard read 12:55.

Jazz also wore all black, from the stocking cap on his head to his Nikes. "Five minutes. I forgot the freeway would be so open this time of night. The ride from West Hollywood only took me twenty-five minutes. Did you remember to bring gloves?"

I pulled a pair of bright red leather gloves out of

the front pouch in my hoodie and waved them in the air. "Yes, although I don't know why I'll need them since I'll be sitting in the car the whole time." I studied his profile as he drove.

He pressed his lips together all the way to Dolleen's house.

As we turned south on Reseda Boulevard, I asked, "What's your plan?"

"I figured we could get the job done faster if there were two of us looking through her things."

My stomach tightened. "Wait. I'm supposed to go inside with you? No way. I thought we agreed I'd be the lookout. Lookouts stay outside."

He glanced at me. "These expensive neighborhoods were developed with a network of alleys behind the houses for more discreet garbage collection. It's one in the morning. Nobody's going to notice my car parked in the alley."

I reluctantly agreed. At this time of night, we could enter the rear of the property without being seen. Dolleen's house was the fourth from the corner on her street. Yellow police tape still decorated the front door. Jazz circled the block and turned off his headlights as we entered the alley. We rolled to a quiet stop behind house number four.

A six-foot-tall cinder block wall stretched from the garage clear across the back. Without a garage-door opener, we were going to have to scale the wall. We got out of the Mercedes, put on our gloves, and approached the barrier. "You can probably climb over this, but in the absence of a ladder, I'm way too short. Maybe I should just stay in the car like we planned."

He stepped up to the wall, interlaced his fingers, and bent slightly at the knees. "No problem. I'll give you a boost." He gestured with his head. Clearly, he wasn't about to let me stay behind. "All aboard."

Despite the warning bells in my head, I raised my right foot, stepped into the sling made by his hands, and held on to his shoulders. He propelled me vertically until I could grab the top of the wall and throw my left leg over. I stayed on my stomach and peered down into Dolleen's backyard. A vine of creeping fig covered the inside of the cinder blocks with a carpet of tiny leaves. I slithered over and dropped to the soft lawn below. Jazz soon followed and flicked on his flashlight.

A light burned in the back of the house next door. "Turn off your flashlight," I whispered. "Her neighbor's awake. If they see us back here, they'll call the police."

Jazz snicked off the beam. "I didn't even think of that. See? It's a good thing you came with me."

*Right. So, we can keep each other company in matching orange jumpsuits during our criminal trial.*

"Kitchen door?" I grabbed his hand.

He squeezed it in response.

Bent over at the waist, we sprinted through the darkness across the backyard. Halfway there, my foot hit something and I fell hard on my left knee and elbow. *What the heck?* My body exploded in pain. I curled in the fetal position and cradled my knee, fighting not to make a sound.

Jazz dropped beside me and whispered. "Oh my God. Are you okay?"

"Just ducky," I hissed through the fire in my leg.

"Help me stand." With his hands under my arms, he pulled me upright. I carefully shifted my weight to the injured side. When my leg didn't buckle, I took a small step forward. Aside from the intense throbbing in my left knee, I could manage on my own. From decades of experience with fibromyalgia, however, I knew I'd be aching for days from the jarring my body just took. "I'll be okay. Let's just hurry inside before we're seen."

Hanging on to his arm for support, I limped the rest of the way to the kitchen door, where two days earlier we'd entered the house and found Dolleen's body.

Jazz rattled the knob. "Closed tight."

"Do you know how to pick a lock?"

"*Mais non*! I'm a fashion designer, not a thief. But everyone knows you can open a lock by sliding a credit card in the crack of the door." He removed a Mobil Oil card from his pants pocket. "Like this one."

He poked the plastic in the crack and rattled the knob, but the door stayed stubbornly shut. After a couple of minutes, he wiped his forehead with the back of his hand. "Well, it always works on TV."

I turned on my flashlight and briefly swept the back of the house before turning it off again. "There's a set of French doors farther down. Let's try those."

We crept along the back of the house until we came to the old-fashioned doors. I turned the knobs, but they held firm. Jazz tried the credit card trick again, but the door remained locked.

"Fortunately, these are not double-paned," I said.

"We should have no problem breaking the glass next to the lock."

"How will we do that without making any noise?" He looked nervously at the light in the neighbor's window.

I pulled my black hoodie over my head and handed it to Jazz. "I watch TV too. Wrap your flashlight in this, and hit the glass. The cloth should muffle the sound."

After a couple of whacks, the glass shattered and fell inside the house. He swept the shards of glass away from the mullion until he could safely reach through the hole and click open the lock. We were in.

A blue LED bulb plugged into a wall socket near the floor provided enough illumination to navigate the dark room.

I drew the heavy drapes across the windows. "We should close these first."

Jazz waited until all the windows were covered before clicking on his flashlight. A giant four poster king-sized bed with two nightstands dominated the wall to the right of the French doors. To our left, a long wooden dresser stood next to the bathroom door. An entry to the hallway and mirrored closet doors lined the far wall.

"Paulina said to bring something Dolly valued, like a piece of good jewelry," he said.

Dolleen must've owned some really nice bling in the heyday of David Shapira Associates. But even if the government didn't confiscate it, I seriously doubted she'd be careless enough to leave the valuable stuff lying around. Still, we had to start somewhere. "Let's begin with the obvious. First the drawers, then the closet."

We stood side-by-side and rummaged through the dresser drawers. Lacy panties and bras with giant cups were neatly arranged in the top drawers. Camisoles, stockings, T-shirts, and sweaters filled the rest. A search of the closets yielded nothing interesting. "Obviously, Dolleen didn't keep her jewelry with her undies or her shoes," I said. "Let's try the nightstands."

We each took a side of the bed and rifled through the small cabinets. "Oh, Lord." Jazz curled his mouth with distaste and took one step backward. "You better come over here."

*What in the world?* I hurried to the other side of the bed and looked in the drawer where Jazz trained his light. Under some papers and a curling iron with a pink handle, I could just make out a black leather box with gold curlicues embossed along the edges. "Looks like a jewelry box."

"That's what I think," said Jazz. "You pick it up."

Why did he act so deferential? "We don't have to stand on ceremony. Go ahead and grab it."

"*Ew.*" He turned the corners of his mouth down and took another step backward. "I'm not touching that thing."

"What are you talking about?" I asked, confused by his reluctance.

Jazz waved a beam of light at the drawer. "Look again."

I got closer and peered inside. All became clear.

The pink object wasn't a curling iron. A very personal massager sat within easy reach of the bed.

"Oh."

I used my gloved fingers to push Dolleen's love wand aside and lifted out a black leather box measuring six inches by four inches. A small brass key nestled in the black velvet interior. I picked it up and turned it over in my hand. The words *Master Lock* were stamped into the top. "This opens a padlock, not a jewelry safe."

Jazz bobbed his head rapidly then stopped abruptly. "Listen!" he hissed.

We froze. Hinges squeaked as someone entered the house. The door closed with a bump.

"Someone's here." My heart sped as I replaced the empty box and closed the drawer. "We've got to hide." I pointed to the large four poster bed. "Under there."

We switched off our flashlights and dove to the floor. Scooting underneath the bed, we lay side by side on our backs. Dolleen hadn't been the best housekeeper.

My nose began to itch from the accumulated dust. "I have to sneeze," I whispered.

Jazz reached over and pinched my nostrils shut. "*Shhh.*"

Footsteps shuffled on the hardwood floor in the hallway, heading our way. I pushed Jazz's hand off my face and watched a narrow beam shine on the floor inches away. A chill shook my body. The cops would have switched on the overhead lights, but the mysterious intruder only used a flashlight. Just like us.

The feet shuffled over to the nightstand and yanked open the drawer. I rolled my head to the side and stared at a pair of small ladies' white sneakers. My heart hammered in my throat when I remembered what Paulina said. *Get a grip, Martha. Just because Paulina made some vague comment doesn't mean you're looking at Dolleen's killer. Everyone wears white sneakers in LA.*

A woman's voice muttered, "What the . . . ?" I heard her throw something across the room. "Crap! The cops took it."

She must've been looking for the key I still clutched tightly in my hand. The intruder stepped away from the bed and shuffled back down the hallway. We listened to the door squeaking open and shut again. Unable to hold back any longer, I exploded in a sneezing fit.

We scooted out from under the bed. Jazz grabbed my hands and helped me stand. My knee still throbbed a little, but the adrenaline now coursing through my body helped mitigate the pain.

"Let's keep looking," I said. "Maybe we'll find the padlock this key opens." As we left the room, I spied the leather box open on the floor, where the mysterious intruder threw it. She definitely knew right where to find the key. Did she kill Dolleen? If so, why didn't she take it the night of the murder?

In the second bedroom, we found a four-foot-tall wooden jewelry armoire with seven drawers. "*Voila!*" Jazz reached it in two strides. "We should be able to find something here to satisfy Paulina."

The top of the armoire lifted to reveal over fifty pairs of earrings arranged in rows by color: lapis and turquoise, peridot and jade, citrine and amber, amethyst and garnets, pearls and opals. Yellow gold hoops in several sizes sat next to a similar selection in sterling silver.

He picked up a pair of cloudy emerald studs. "These are okay for every day, but I don't see anything so far screaming *valuable.*"

Each of the seven drawers contained a different category of adornment: necklaces in one, bracelets in the next, watches, rings, pearls and beads. Not one item in the entire collection seemed to be worth more than two or three hundred dollars. For someone like Dolleen, who probably owned high-end jewels, this assortment seemed like chump change.

Jazz sighed. "None of this stuff is going to lure Dolly back from the spirit world."

"Why don't we take one of these items anyway? After all, they did belong to Dolleen."

He closed his eyes and set his jaw. "No. *Uh-uh.* No way. Paulina said only something significant will work."

By two in the morning, we'd gone through every room in the house without finding the padlock the little brass key would open.

Jazz crossed his arms and pushed on his lips with a thoughtful fist. "I honestly don't know what to do. I hate to leave empty-handed."

"But we do have something." I reached in my fanny pack and held out the brass key. "The woman who broke in tonight obviously wanted this. So, maybe the key itself is powerful enough to summon

Dolleen's spirit. Not that I believe in such stuff, because I don't."

Jazz brightened. "Of course! Forgive me, Martha, but for someone who has such uninspired taste in clothes, you're really sharp."

"Seriously? You want to talk about my wardrobe right now?"

"I'm just saying." He turned toward the hallway leading back to the bedroom.

Apparently the crime scene tape on the outside hadn't deterred Dolleen's mail carrier. I bent down to pick up some letters on the floor right under the mail slot on the front door. One window envelope caught my attention. The return address indicated a self-storage facility on Burbank Boulevard in Tarzana. "Jazz. Wait up. This mail must've been delivered in the last day or so." Tampering with someone else's mail constituted a federal crime; another count to add to the list of offenses we'd be facing if Jazz and I were ever caught. Oh well, in for a penny . . . I slid my finger under the flap and tore the envelope open.

Inside was a statement for a monthly rental unit at Tarzana Relocation and Storage Services. I handed the bill to Jazz. "Dolleen maintains a storage unit on Burbank Boulevard nearby. What do you want to bet there's a padlock on the door matching this key?"

"I say we go over there right now." He glanced at the paper. "Unit 309."

"*Mmm.*" I gnawed on my lip. "Even if it's open twenty-four hours, going there now isn't a good idea. We'd be noticed at this time of night. Best to wait until business hours tomorrow, when we'll blend in with all the other customers coming and going."

We slipped out the French doors and looked around. The neighbor's house was dark. Jazz gave me a boost to the top of the wall and helped me down the other side so I wouldn't have to drop on my injured knee. We drove down the alley with the headlights off, only turning them on when we got to Reseda Boulevard.

We turned east on Ventura Boulevard, a busy thoroughfare when the rest of the world was awake, but empty at this time of the night. "I'm exhausted." He rubbed his eyes. "Who do you suppose the burglar was? You were closest to her. What did you see?"

"I only glimpsed small feet with white sneakers."

Jazz gasped. "Oh my God. That's what Patti remembered about Dolly's killer."

"No, that's what Paulina *claims* the dog said."

Jazz sniffed. "Patti would never lie."

# CHAPTER 8

As soon as I got home, I took some pain meds and a cold gel pack from the freezer to put on my swollen knee. Rather than wake Crusher, I nestled on the sofa under my favorite blue-and-white quilt and drifted to sleep. I don't know what woke me up first, the smell of fresh Italian roast coffee or the pain and stiffness in my body.

I gingerly pushed myself up to sitting and yawned. "Good morning," I called from the living room.

Crusher clumped across the floor in heavy boots and brought me a steaming cup of coffee with cream, just the way I liked it. He wore his black leathers and a fresh red bandana. "Morning, babe. Where'd you disappear to last night?"

"What makes you think I went anywhere?"

He chuckled and pointed to the black T-shirt and yoga pants I still wore. "As I recall, that's not what you wore to bed last night."

One of the things I really liked about Crusher was the way he didn't try to "manage" me. Arlo Beavers would've delivered a stern lecture about sneaking around and getting into trouble. Could Uncle Isaac be right about Crusher? I wasn't getting any younger. Maybe I should think about marrying such a mensch.

My head cleared with each sip of the milky coffee. "I didn't want to wake you up. Jazz and I went to Dolleen's house last night."

"The dead woman?"

"Yeah." I told him about our visit to Paulina and the prop she needed for a séance. "We searched the bedroom but only found a padlock key."

"How did you get inside the house?"

"We broke a pane of glass in the French door leading to the bedroom."

"Did you wear gloves?"

See what I mean about Crusher? Did he scold me about breaking and entering? No. Did he point out I could go to jail? No. His first concern was whether I'd been smart enough not to leave behind finger-prints. Working undercover for both the *Shin Bet*, the Israeli Secret Service, and the ATF, Crusher wasn't fastidious about breaking rules.

"While we were there, we hid from another in-truder who entered the house through the locked kitchen door. She used a key, because we didn't hear any sound of forceful entry."

"Did you get a good look at her?"

"No. From my vantage point under the bed, all I could see were her feet and ankles. There's more. She knew where to look because she came directly to the bedroom looking for the padlock key. She was pissed when she didn't find it, and left. I suspect she was Dolleen's neighbor."

"Why do you think so?"

"First of all, neighbors exchange keys all the time to help each other out in case of an emergency. It's not a stretch to think Dolleen trusted one of her neighbors with a key. Second of all, Jazz and I didn't arrive at Dolleen's house last night until one in the morning. Yet, her next door neighbor must've still been awake because we saw a light burning in the house. All the other houses were dark."

"You seem pretty sure."

"I am. And I intend to go back to make certain I'm right. If the neighbor is the intruder from last night, she could also be the mysterious witness who told the police she saw Jazz the night of Dolleen's murder. Detective Kaplan let it slip the witness is a woman."

"Slow down, babe. If you're right about both things, confronting this woman could be dangerous. How do you know she's not the killer?"

"According to Dolleen's Chihuahua, she could be." I told him about Paulina claiming to talk to Patti. "Supposedly, the dog said the killer wore white sneakers. The woman last night wore white sneakers—like everyone else in LA. Except, maybe, for Jazz and Elizabeth Taylor, and she's dead."

He gathered me in his arms. "Be careful, babe. Let me know if you need backup. You know I'll always have your six."

I loved his use of military slang to assure me he had my back.

Later in the morning, I sorted fabric alone in my sewing room, thinking about the sweet way Crusher said good-bye in the bedroom. Before he left, he twisted one of my long gray curls around his finger and said, "Your hair is so beautiful. It reminds me of a flock of goats moving up Gilead."

The phone jolted me out of my cloud. "Hey, girlfriend. What happened with Paulina yesterday?"

I knew Lucy would want to hear every detail, so I gave her the long version, including our trip to Dolleen's house. "Jazz and I are going to check out the storage space today. I'm just waiting for him to pick me up." I didn't ask if she wanted to come with us, because I didn't want to cause a conflict with her husband, Ray.

She hesitated at first and then said, "I'll be over in five minutes. Don't leave without me. What Ray doesn't know won't hurt him."

When Jazz and Lucy arrived, I said, "If we're going to break into Dolleen's storage unit, we have to take my car."

"Why?" They both spoke at the same time.

I looked up at the tall man. "Because your license plate says *Jazz FW*. It's too easy to remember. And, Lucy, your vintage Cadillac with the shark fins is a standout wherever you go. We need to blend in, not be conspicuous. There are a gazillion white Civics on the road, just like mine. Nobody will remember my car."

Tarzana Relocation and Storage Services occupied a beige, concrete building resembling a fortress the size of Costco. I parked in the back of the lot, away from the entrance to the building.

"What're we looking for?" asked Lucy as we got out of the Civic. A silk scarf tied around her head babushka-style hid her orange hair, and a large pair of dark sunglasses hid her face.

Jazz and I spoke at the same time: "Dolly's spirit." "Clues to the killer."

"Like what?" she insisted.

"We'll know it when we see it." I pressed the lock button on the Civic's fob.

Two entrances stood in front of the building. A glass door with TARZANA RELOCATION AND STORAGE in gold lettering led to a small reception area. The sign on another steel door said simply, UNITS. A keypad next to the door stopped us.

"Uh-oh," said Lucy. "We need a code to get in."

"Hold on." I reached in my purse and pulled out the monthly statement we'd stolen from Dolleen's house the night before. Printed under the item-ized charge for storage unit 309 was *Code for April: 0412309.*

"Dang!" said Lucy. "It's still March. Is there any way you can get the current code?"

I shook my head. "Not without going back to the house and looking for last month's bill. We got lucky once. I don't want to chance getting caught in there again. Let me see if I can charm the recep-tionist into giving me the code. Wait for me here."

I pushed through the glass doors and approached a bored-looking teenager sitting behind a Spartan counter. She sported long, navy blue hair and a silver ball pushed through her nostril. She looked up from her cell phone. "Can I help you?"

I slid the monthly statement across the tan-colored Formica. "I'm Dolleen Doyle. I want to get into my unit, but I forgot the code for March. Can you please give it to me one more time?"

Sharper than she looked, the girl said, "Why don't you look on your bill for March?"

"I threw that away weeks ago."

"Let me see your ID."

*Crap.* This wasn't going to be as easy as I thought. I rummaged through my large, brown leather shoulder bag, pretending to look for my wallet. After a minute, I looked up. "Darn it. I must've left my wallet in my other purse." I smiled my most endearing, motherly smile. "Can't you save me a trip home and give me the code just this once?"

The girl shook her dark blue hair back from her face. "Sorry. We have a strict security policy here. I need to see an ID."

I joined my friends standing next to the Civic in the parking lot. "No dice. They take security seriously here."

Lucy reached under her chin and tightened the knot on her scarf. "Maybe we can figure out the code. Let's see the bill again." We scooted closer to each other and studied the code for April.

"Do you think this is a coincidence?" Jazz pointed to the bill. "Her unit number is 309 and the last three numbers on the code are also 309."

Suddenly it all became clear. "Of course! And the first four numbers, 0-4-1-2, stand for the month the code is good for, the fourth month of 2012." I tapped the bill with my fingertips. "So, the code for March must be 0312309."

"Let's go for it." Lucy grabbed my arm and tugged me toward the steel door.

When we got to the keypad I punched in 0312309. The electronic release on the door clicked.

I grinned. "We're in."

Two elevators waited on our right. We pushed a lighted button in the wall and almost immediately a bell dinged and the doors opened. Gray furniture pads covered the interior walls of the lift. We hurried inside and Jazz pressed the button for the third floor.

The cables creaked as we slowly ascended. None of us spoke a word. The car jerked to a stop, and the doors opened to a hallway identical to the one we'd just left. The corridor appeared to be deserted. Black arrows were painted on the pink concrete wall in front of us. The one leading to the right pointed the way to units 301–310.

Odd numbered units were on the right side, even numbers on the left. Unit 309 sat clear at the end of the hallway. All along the way, automatic sprinklers, recessed lights, and the half-dome lenses of security cameras dotted the ceiling. An identical roll-up steel door closed off every unit.

When we reached the end, I took Dolleen's brass key out of my pocket. "Here goes nothing." Almost immediately the padlock sprung open. I looked up and grinned a second time.

Jazz rolled the steel door high enough for us to

enter comfortably and found a wall switch to an overhead light.

Lucy spoke in hushed tones. "Quick, close the door again before anyone sees us." I didn't enlighten her about the overhead cameras.

The room measured twenty feet deep and ten feet wide. Boxes and cartons were neatly stacked on the back wall. Dolleen had arranged the rest of the space like an office, with a walnut-colored desk, gray steel filing cabinet, computer, and printer. She'd even placed a red Persian carpet on the concrete floor and plugged in a space heater.

Jazz whistled. "This is a set-up for some serious business."

"Yeah," I said. "*Clandestine* serious business."

"I think we may be in way over our heads." Lucy bit her bottom lip. "We should let the police handle this."

"And tell them what? That Jazz and I broke into Dolleen's house, opened her mail, stole the key, and broke into this place as well?"

Lucy raised her eyebrows and shrugged. "Can't we call in an anonymous tip on the crime hotline?"

"I hate to break it to you, Lucy, but we wouldn't remain anonymous for long. This facility is loaded with security cameras. They already have us on tape entering this unit. Besides, it's just a matter of time before the police go through her financials and discover she's been paying rent here."

She nodded slowly. "You're right. And when they do, they'll swarm all over this place like black ants on a picnic blanket." She looked at her watch. "We'd better get to work."

I agreed. Not only were we trespassing, we were messing with the evidence in a murder investigation. The longer we stayed, the greater our chance of being caught.

# CHAPTER 9

I quickly assessed the contents of the storage locker. "Let's divide up the work. Lucy, you're the best with computers. See what you can find. Jazz, you're the strongest, why don't you start going through those boxes? I'll tackle the filing cabinet. Use your cell phones and take pictures of anything significant you come across."

Jazz removed his cell phone and answered a text. When he noticed me looking at him, he looked away and quickly put the phone back in his pocket, almost as if he were hiding something.

I opened the top drawer of the filing cabinet. Inside sat a presentation box from Harry Winston, jeweler to the rich and famous. Wouldn't Paulina just love to get her hands on this! I opened the large leather box, expecting to find a gem-encrusted necklace. It was empty. The Feds seized all of the Shapira's assets they could locate. They probably took all of Dolleen's good jewelry as well. Maybe she kept the box as a memento.

Jazz ripped tape from the first carton. "Doesn't look like much. A piece of Lladro and some rather gauche art even the Feds weren't interested in." He continued to open cartons and occasionally called out the contents. "Men's clothes. Photos. Books. Nothing earth shattering."

I turned to Lucy. "Have you found anything on the computer yet?"

She nodded. "There's an Excel document with names, dates, and dollar amounts. The last entry was made seven days ago."

"Can you tell where the money came from?"

"No. It's just a list."

"We need a copy. Can you print one?"

'I'll do better than that." Lucy removed a cord around her neck with a thumb drive on the end. "I came prepared. I'm going to copy all these files. We can sort through them later."

I opened the second drawer of the filing cabinet. Inside were dozens of file folders. Five of them were labeled with different banks: Royal Cayman, Sheffield's, Cayman National, First Cayman, and Caribbean Savings. The statements inside revealed balances of seven to eight digits each. "I think I've found David Shapira's hidden offshore accounts. There are millions here." I took photos of the latest statement from each bank.

Lucy leaned back and looked at Jazz. "You knew her best. If she could access so much money, why did she live in Tarzana?"

He shrugged. "I knew her before she ever met David Shapira. Dolly was a girl from Kansas with simple tastes. The smallest things made her laugh. Her smile was like sunshine in a cornfield. I don't think she ever really knew how gorgeous she was, but David sure did. And he wanted her. He was a charmer who always got what he wanted. Neither of us had any idea about his true nature. We just thought he was a successful businessman. Nevertheless, I tried to warn her against getting involved with a married man, but she was stupid with love."

I remembered an old Yiddish proverb. "You know what they say: 'With money in your pocket, you are wise, and you are handsome, and you sing well too.'"

Jazz grunted. "Rusty and I went to their wedding, and then David whisked her off to the world of the ultrarich. Completely not our social scene. Poor Dolly. When he went to prison, the Feds took everything they owned and all her rich friends abandoned her. I reached out, and we carried on our friendship, almost as if the whole David thing never happened."

"How did she wind up owning a salon in Beverly Hills?"

"Dolly was determined to survive. When she told me about opening her own business, I asked where she got the money. She just said, 'David didn't leave me without resources.'"

"Do you know what she meant?"

"Not really."

"Well, the money came in from somewhere," said Lucy.

I shook my head. "I have to confess; I'm having a hard time figuring out who would want to kill such a nice person. Did she ever talk about any enemies who might want her dead?"

Jazz shrugged. "That's the thing. She was always nice to everyone, not just me. Whoever killed her probably just wanted to get back at David. That's the only explanation I can think of."

If Jazz was right, we were no closer to finding her killer. David Shapira had left behind scores of enemies. I turned back to the filing cabinet and opened the third drawer. I found a stack of dozens of letters still in their envelopes and printouts of e-mails. After I opened the first few, I realized they were all hate mail. Maybe this was where we'd find the killer. I knew I didn't have time to take a picture of each one, so I grabbed the lot and shoved it into my large bag. Eventually, I'd have to figure out a way to hand them over to the police anonymously. I'd think of something later.

Lucy looked at the steel door and rubbed her arms. "I'm getting one of my bad feelings." She stood abruptly, removed the flash drive and turned off the computer. "We need to leave." I used to think her "bad feelings" were mere intuition sharpened by raising five boys. Lately, however, I learned not to ignore her premonitions. I shut the filing cabinet.

"The things in this office hold the answers to a lot of questions." I held up the padlock key. "This is valuable because it unlocks the information preserved in this room. Let's just give this key to Paulina to use as a prop in the next séance."

Jazz picked up the tote bag with Zsa Zsa inside.

"Okay, maybe you're right." He rolled up the steel door and turned off the light.

Lucy walked swiftly toward the elevators. "Hurry up."

Jazz closed the door and replaced the padlock and the two of us rushed to catch up with her.

She kept jabbing at the elevator button until the bell dinged. As soon as the car door opened, she darted inside and repeatedly pressed the button for the first floor. "Come on," she muttered.

Another bell dinged announcing the arrival of the second elevator. We heard the doors open and a familiar voice said, "It's to the right."

*Crap!*

The doors of our car slid toward each other. Just before they shut tight, I glimpsed two men walking past. The taller one with white hair held a bolt cutter.

As the elevator descended, Lucy blew out her breath and gave me an *I told you so!* look.

Who could argue? We'd barely missed being discovered by Detectives Noah Kaplan and Arlo Beavers, my ex. Once outside, we hurried toward my anonymous white Civic.

When we were safely back on Burbank Boulevard, Lucy said, "That was too close! I don't know what Ray would have done if I'd ended up in a police station again."

Zsa Zsa poked her face out of the tote bag, and Jazz kissed the top of her head. "Thank God you have ESP, Lucy. Speaking of which, I'm going to call Paulina and see if we can have our séance now."

"I'm in!" Lucy rubbed her palms together. "I've always wanted to go to one. What about you, Martha?"

Jazz was in a very vulnerable place, which made him an easy target. And Lucy's beliefs in the metaphysical predisposed her to believe whatever Paulina said. Someone needed to protect both of them. "Yes, I'm in."

# CHAPTER 10

We parked on Paulina's cracked driveway. A pneumatic tool burped loudly in the auto body shop on one side of her lavender-and-white house. The smell of cilantro and onions escaped from the taqueria in the strip mall on the other side. My stomach rumbled in response. I didn't need to consult my watch to know it was time for lunch. Jazz took Zsa Zsa out of her tote bag and walked her over to the curb to let her pee before we entered the house.

Paulina, wearing thick makeup, greeted us at the door and put a sign on the doorknob that read

DO NOT DISTURB, SÉANCE IN SESSION

Today she hid her plump figure in a long-sleeved beach caftan made of lavender crinkle cotton. A gold lamé turban sat atop her long, black hair. She smiled up at Jazz from her diminutive stature of around five feet. "Enter. Today's a favorable day for contacting the spirit world."

I suspected any day with a paying customer was favorable.

The smell of frankincense hung heavily on the air inside, giving the room an ambience of the inside of a church. Plum-colored drapes darkened all the windows. One purple candle flickered in the center of the round table surrounded by four chairs placed at precise intervals. Paulina sat in the chair with a red velvet cushion, which boosted her height, and gestured for us to join her. I took the chair directly opposite, where I could better observe her. Zsa Zsa sat in the tote on Jazz's lap, happily crunching on a tiny bone-shaped biscuit.

After she swiped Jazz's credit card, Paulina squinted at Lucy. "I recognize you from Harriet Gordon's funeral a couple a years ago. You've got an interesting aura."

Lucy's eyes widened. "I do?"

"Yeah. Green and purple. I can do a reading for you. Only twenty bucks since you're a friend of Martha's."

Lucy opened her purse.

I grabbed her wrist. "Let's just get on with the séance."

The psychic rolled her eyes. "Alright, geez. What'd you bring to summon Dolleen's spirit?"

I handed over the padlock key. "This opens up a room in a storage facility where she hid all her valuable secrets."

Paulina wrapped her hand around the key and closed her eyes, exposing extravagant lines of liquid black lid liner painted after the fashion of Egyptian hieroglyphs. "Excellent." She opened her eyes. "This is vibrating with energy."

She placed the key right next to the flickering candle in the middle of the table. "Okay, here's how this works. We'll all hold hands to form a circle. You will send the departed gentle thoughts of love. I'm going to go into a trance, and if she feels safe, Dolleen's spirit will speak through me. However, there's one rule you must follow. Under no circumstances are you to let go of the circle or the connection will be broken. Understand?"

Jazz said, "Can we ask Dolly questions?"

"Of course." Paulina swiped her hand in the air. "I've got five-star reviews on Yelp and a following on Twitter, remember? I've ridden this subway before. As long as you don't break the circle, you won't be disappointed."

We joined hands. Paulina closed her eyes, made a low, droning sound, and raised her face to the ceiling. "I call on the spirit of Dolleen Doyle to join our circle. Your friend Jazz wants to talk to you."

Suddenly, she flopped forward until her forehead touched the table. When she sat up again, her gold lamè had shifted slightly down her forehead.

Lucy stared with rapt attention. Jazz's eyes were huge and his mouth hung slightly open and he licked his lips.

*Give me a break!*

Paulina opened her eyes and gazed at a distant point over my shoulder. In a reedy voice she said, "Jazz?"

He squeezed my hand hard and leaned forward in his chair. "Dolly? Is it really you?"

Paulina's eyes shifted toward him. "Yes, it's me, Jazz."

"Oh, Dolly, I'm so sorry about what happened to you." His eyes filled with tears. "You would've been so pleased with the things I made for Patti. I even threw in a pink party dress with Swarovski crystals."

Paulina hummed in response. "*Mmm. Hmm.*"

"I need your help. I'm in deep trouble because the police think I killed you. Can you tell me who did it?"

The spirit of the dead woman from Kansas said in a New Jersey accent, "It's all still foggy. I only re-member a little bit. It was a woman. We were close." Paulina closed her eyes, dropped her head and then looked up again. "An argument. A hit on the head. Pain. Blackness."

Lucy strained sideways toward Paulina and spoke slowly, over-enunciating each word as if speaking to a deaf person from Mongolia. "Hi, hon. I'm Lucy. Friend of Jazz's. Can you describe the woman?"

Tiny beads of sweat appeared on Paulina's upper lip. "White sneakers. All I remember."

"Amazing," Jazz whispered. "Patti said the same thing."

I couldn't restrain myself any longer. "What did you argue about?" I was certain Paulina couldn't sustain this ridiculous farce.

The medium swayed slightly and transferred her glassy-eyed gaze toward me. "Money. Lots of money."

It didn't take a psychic or a genius to come up with that one. Dolleen had access to her husband's millions.

Paulina suddenly slumped forward and gripped

the edge of the table, breaking the circle of hands. Then she slowly sat up and blinked. "She's gone." Clear-eyed but sweating, she straightened out her turban. Then she retrieved a box of tissues from someplace behind her chair and dabbed at the tiny beads of moisture on her lip and forehead. Was the sweat the result of being in a trance or did her heavy turban cause her to perspire?

Jazz also helped himself to a tissue and wiped his eyes. "That was amazing. But I'm disappointed she left before I could ask her about Rusty."

Paulina's whole body sagged like a rag doll with fatigue. "We'll contact your other friend next time."

"Fiancé," Jazz gently corrected her. "Russell Watson was my fiancé."

The Maltese poked her head out of the tote bag and barked once.

Jazz said, "Zsa Zsa's ready to take Patti home now."

Paulina held up a forefinger encircled by a wide, silver band. "Not so fast. Patti has improved over the last twenty-four hours. Fortunately, we both speak Romanian. She now accepts the fact there's no shame in being small. I'm slowly getting her to stop thinking like a Rottweiler. But she's not ready to go home with you."

Jazz put his hand to his throat. "Why not, for heaven's sake?"

"She doesn't trust men."

*I can relate.*

"Well, she seems to trust me. After all, we're not strangers."

Paulina nodded. "Maybe. But leave her with me a while longer. We're making such good progress. It would be a shame to interrupt her therapy now. She's slowly overcoming her traumatic amnesia. As a matter of fact, a new memory broke through. She said a woman killed her mistress."

"Amazing!" Jazz gaped. "That's exactly what Dolly just told us." He paused. "Can I at least see Patti once before we leave?"

Paulina stood. "Sure. She's in the other room. I'll take you to her, but you have to leave your dog out here with Martha."

Jazz's face fell. "Why?"

"The Chihuahua's in a bitchy mood."

Jazz stiffened and handed me the tote with Zsa Zsa inside. "Daddy will only be gone a minute," he cooed. Then he followed Paulina out of the room to the back of the house.

As soon as they disappeared, Lucy snorted and pointed to the tote. "You've got to admit, he is a little over the top with this dog."

"And you don't think Paulina is a little over the top, period?"

Lucy's eyes widened. "I think she's brilliant. I can't wait to come back and have her read my aura."

"Well, I can't wait to take a closer look at the stuff we found on Dolleen's computer and in her filing cabinet today."

Lucy reached into her purse and gave me the flash drive with Paulina's computer files. "Be my guest. If Ray caught me looking at this, he'd have a cow."

I tucked the small device into my bag, alongside the stack of hate mail I'd taken from the filing cabinet earlier in the morning. I hoped Jazz could help me comb through everything—if I didn't perish from hunger first.

We left Paulina's house and walked to the strip mall next door for a quick lunch of spicy grilled carne asada and salsa verde wrapped in steamed corn tortillas and icy glasses of a sweet rice drink called *horchata*. Then we drove back over the Sepulveda Pass to Encino with enough material to keep us busy for hours.

With any luck, we just might uncover a clue to the identity of the real killer this afternoon.

# CHAPTER 11

Jazz and I sat at my dining room table. He took Zsa Zsa out of the tote and she promptly chased my cat, Bumper, down the hallway to the bedroom. A minute later they came running back, this time Zsa Zsa in the lead. Eventually, they headed for my cream-colored sofa and settled down together.

We began to sort through the stack of hate mail I swiped from Dolleen's storage unit. "Listen to this." Jazz read out loud from a letter written with a shaky hand on blue stationery.

*The money you stole from me was all I had in the world. How am I going to keep my sister in assisted living now that our money is gone? I'm 75. I can't go back to work. You're a despicable thief. I hope they lock you up for the rest of your life!*

*Very truly yours,*
*Emma Fishblatt*
*Los Angeles*

We put Emma's letter into an "angry-but-harmless" pile along with similar letters and e-mails Dolleen printed out. We were more interested in the letters containing actual threats. Would we find a clue to the killer in one of those?

"Thanks to what Dolly told us, we only have to look at the letters written by women." Jazz began sorting the threatening letters into two piles.

I grabbed his arm. "Listen, Jazz. We can't rule out the men because of what happened in the séance."

"But you heard Dolly yourself. She told us her killer was a woman. So did Patti."

"No, what I heard was Paulina the psychic *claiming* to be Dolleen. The police would never accept that as proof. Until we have some real evidence, you need to keep an open mind."

We sifted through the dozens of printouts of threatening e-mails. "Oh my God," said Jazz. "Here's one from someone called Kurt Nixon. He's the devil himself. Listen."

> I know where you live, Jew. If I don't get my money, I'll make you watch as I pour acid on your pretty wife's face until she dies screaming. Then I'll do the same thing to you.

I shuddered. "How gruesome!"

"Right?" His eyes widened. "Here's another from C. Evelyn."

> You betraying S.O.B. No one in your family will be safe.

Jazz waved the printouts in the air. "These could exonerate me. Both of them threatened to hurt Dolly. We need to show these to the police right now."

"Slow down. I agree those messages are compelling. They should force Beavers and Kaplan to take a closer look at those two people. But we have to figure out how to hand over the files without admitting how we got them in the first place."

"They probably took her computer from the storage unit this morning. Maybe the messages are in a file." Jazz frowned and tapped his lips with his fingers. "*Hmm.* I know! We could phone in an anonymous tip."

"Let's check it out to be sure." Thanks to Lucy's flash drive, we could examine all the files from Dolleen's computer. I began a search. The threatening messages were nowhere to be found. Where had Dolleen gotten them? "Sorry, but it looks like we have the only copies, Jazz."

He threw his hands in the air. "If we keep these messages, the police will never know about the threats. If we turn them in, they'll arrest us for stealing evidence. Either way, you might as well shoot me now because my life is over."

"Maybe there's still a way." I looked at his honest face and wondered if he could pull off the lie I was about to propose. "Since you were a friend of Dolleen's, you could tell them she gave you the letters to keep, with instructions to take them to the police if anything happened to her."

"But how do I explain why I didn't hand them over right away? That'll be the first thing they ask."

"You can say you were so rattled, you forgot and only now remembered the letters existed. But whatever you do, don't talk without your attorney present."

Jazz nodded. "I'll do anything to avoid those garish orange jumpsuits."

"Good. Let's make copies of these before we give them away." We gathered the stack of papers and envelopes and fed them to my copy machine for the next hour. By the time he left, I had half an hour to get ready for Friday night Shabbat dinner. Studying more of Dolleen's computer files would have to wait until tomorrow.

This week, Crusher and I would drive over the hill to Uncle Isaac's house in West LA. I jumped in the shower, washed and dried my hair, and sprayed on a liberal mist of Marc Jacobs before dressing in a long, black skirt and pink blouse. I stood in front of the bedroom mirror, fastening my grandmother's pearls when I heard Crusher come through the front door. "Be there in a sec," I yelled.

A minute later he appeared in the bedroom doorway with a lusty grin on his face. He'd showered and dressed at his own place. My heart melted—as it always did—when I saw him in his Sabbath clothes: dark slacks and a white shirt. A white crocheted yarmulke replaced the do-rag normally covering his head.

He came up behind me, wrapped his arms around me, and nuzzled the back of my neck. "Babe. You smell so good."

I briefly closed my eyes and sank back into his embrace, enjoying the electricity coursing through my body. "Later, Yossi. You know Uncle Isaac wants us there before sundown."

"Promise?"

Oh yeah. I had big plans for later. A tub of Cool Whip sat waiting in the refrigerator.

On the drive over the hill to West LA, I told him about Dolleen's secret office, the séance, and our scheme to turn over the hate mail to the police without incriminating ourselves.

He chuckled. "You've been busy, babe. I'll help you look through her files tomorrow if you want."

I saw it again—the stark difference between Crusher and Beavers. Did Crusher have a hissy fit the way Beavers would have when he learned we'd broken into the storage facility and stolen evidence? No. He was more interested in what the evidence revealed.

"You can't. You're supposed to help Uncle Isaac start to clean his house for Passover. Remember?"

He pulled up to the curb in front of my uncle's house and shut off the engine. He glanced at me with a lopsided smile. "The things I do for you."

Yeah. Big plans.

The succulent smell of baked chicken and rosemary potatoes embraced us as soon as we walked inside. A faint hint of cinnamon told me we were having Uncle Isaac's fabulous babka for dessert. My stomach rumbled in anticipation.

He greeted me with a kiss on the cheek. Not very tall to begin with, the years shrunk him down until he stood only a couple of inches taller than my five feet two. He wore slacks, a white shirt, and brown leather slippers. An embroidered Bukharian skull cap covered his white, curly head. "Good Shabbos, *faigela*. I saved the candles for you."

"Shabbat Shalom, Uncle." I walked over to the dining room table set for five. I assumed Uncle Isaac's friend, Morty, no stranger to this table, would bring his girlfriend, Marilyn. Candles in silver holders stood in the middle of the table. Twin loaves of homemade, braided challah sat on a plate covered with a cloth my *bubbie*, may she rest in peace, had embroidered. A silver kiddush cup filled with sweet red wine sat next to the plate—all the elements necessary to bless the beginning of the Sabbath.

Next to the candles, my uncle had placed a neatly folded silk scarf for me. I covered my head with the scarf and picked up a box of matches. The front door opened behind me. Morty must have arrived. After lighting the pure white candles, I circled my hands three times over the flames then covered my eyes and recited in Hebrew the blessing ushering in the Sabbath. *Blessed art Thou, oh Lord our God, King of the universe, who has sanctified us by Thy commandments, and commanded us to kindle the Sabbath lights.*

Four male voices standing next to me echoed, "*Omein.*"

I opened my eyes to find my uncle's long-time friend Morty standing next to me. He'd slicked his sparse white hair straight back and wore a diamond stickpin in his tie. To my surprise, he didn't bring his girlfriend. An older man I didn't recognize stood next to him. His shoulders sagged, and the corners of his mouth turned down like an old dog's. An expensive Rolex watch peeked out from under the cuffs of a green dress shirt. Uncle Isaac opened a drawer in the sideboard and handed both Morty and his friend black silk yarmulkes.

Morty introduced his friend as Abel Shapira. Bless Morty and Uncle Isaac! They knew I wanted the contact information for David Shapira's father, so they went one better. They produced the man himself.

We took our places around the table. Crusher sat next to me and gently held my hand while my uncle recited the prayers and blessings over the wine and bread.

Afterward, I went with my uncle to the kitchen to help bring the food to the table. When we were out of earshot, I said, "Why didn't you tell me you invited Abel Shapira here tonight?"

"I only found out an hour ago, myself. Morty got the bright idea. He did some fast talking to get him here, especially when Abel learned you were the one who found his daughter-in-law's body." He put his hand on my arm. "Go easy on him, Martha. He's been deeply shamed by his son. Besides, it's Shabbos. We shouldn't talk about unpleasant things at the table."

"I'll be as gentle as I can, Uncle."

Shapira helped himself to large portions of food and acted as if he hadn't eaten a decent meal in days. Poor guy was probably sick over Dolleen's death. Losing a child, even an in-law, could be especially traumatic for the elderly. Crusher helped my uncle clear the dinner dishes.

When Morty excused himself to use the bathroom, I took the opportunity to speak to the old man. "I'm so sorry for your recent loss, Mr. Shapira."

"Thanks," he mumbled. "Dolly was a wonderful girl. She stuck by my son, David. She wasn't Jewish, you know. But she stayed very active in the Reconstruction *shul* they belonged to." Abel referred to a liberal branch of Judaism that welcomed couples in interfaith marriages. In those situations, it was possible the Gentile spouse might embrace the Jewish Sabbath and holidays while still adhering to their Christian faith.

"They never divorced, then?"

He looked up sharply. "No! They were in love. My son gave Dolly everything and she supported him even after he . . . went away. When David found out she'd been killed, he cried. If a man can do that, do you think he could cheat people the way they said he did? *Feh!*" His face reddened and he squeezed his fists. "My son was railroaded."

I felt sorry for Abel. The evidence against David was overwhelming. Besides, he freely confessed to swindling hundreds of millions. But I refrained from reminding poor Abel of that painful fact.

"Do you have any idea who might've killed Dolleen?"

"Nah." He looked down and wagged his head. "No one I know could do such a thing."

"Does David know who could've killed her?"

"Nah. He's got no idea, either."

Why did I get the impression the old man's answers came just a little too fast?

"My friends and I found her," I said softly.

"So I heard."

"We rescued her Chihuahua, but the dog needs a new home. Would you be interested in taking her?"

He looked up sharply and waved his hand rapidly in the air. "No. No dogs."

"Well, does Dolleen have other family who might be interested?"

"No. David was her only relative."

"Besides you," I corrected him.

"Yeah, yeah. Besides me. And Johnny."

"Johnny?"

"My grandson, Jonathan. David's son from his first wife."

Ah, yes. I remembered researching old newspaper articles online and reading about their ugly divorce in 2005. David left his wife, Shelley, and their college-aged son for a beautiful young woman he found in a waxing salon. He married Dolleen the day his divorce became final. Shelley accused David of trying to screw her out of community property. They didn't reach a settlement until years later. When the great recession hit and the assets dwindled, Shelley finally settled for considerably less than she'd asked for.

Shelley must've found it galling to see David's new wife with money that might have been hers. Was this a motive to kill Dolleen? What about the son? Would he want to kill the woman who broke up his home?

"Do you think Jonathan might want the dog?"

Abel sat up a little straighter and pushed his shoulders back. "Johnny's a big-shot lawyer now. Beverly Hills. He's got no time for Dolly's dog."

"So, you won't mind if we find a home for Patti?"

"Do what you want . . ." His voice trailed off.

I tried not to upset the man with my next question. "I just need to ask one more thing. Do you know when her funeral is? My friends and I would like to pay our respects."

"Johnny's handling those details. You could ask him."

Morty joined us once again at the table, and Crusher and Uncle Isaac returned with piping hot glasses of mint tea on a tray and a round, cinnamon babka—a Russian pastry from my *bubbie*'s dairy-free recipe.

As the three old friends slurped their tea from Moroccan glasses, they debated whether one could properly sit *shiva* for a non-Jew. *Shiva* means *seven* and refers to the seven days of formal mourning observed by close relatives beginning on the day of a Jewish person's burial. Various traditions are observed, like covering all the mirrors in the house, sitting on the floor, not wearing leather, and reciting certain prayers daily.

Uncle Isaac looked across the table. "What do you think, Yossi?"

Crusher put down his fork. "I think if you loved the person who died, it doesn't matter how you mourn. You should do what brings you comfort and meaning. Your intention is what matters to God."

Uncle Isaac smiled. "Spoken like a true mensch."

The three old men bent their heads together again and returned to their discussion.

Crusher leaned over to me and whispered in my ear, "I love you, Martha Rose." He raised my hand to his lips and kissed it. "Marry me, already. Don't wait too long. Isaac isn't getting any younger, and neither am I."

I sighed. He was right about my uncle. While I was content with the life I'd made for myself, my being alone in the world caused my uncle a lot of anxiety. Not to mention I grew fonder of Crusher every day and couldn't imagine my life without him. The thought of marriage didn't scare me as much as it used to because deep down I was pretty sure he'd never cheat on me. Didn't he always have my back?

I squeezed his hand. "I'm thinking about it. Okay?"

A wide grin split his face. He whispered, "This is the first time you haven't said *no*. Are we engaged? I'll buy a ring. You can choose whatever you want. I know a guy downtown." He was referring to the thriving diamond district in downtown LA.

"Wait. I only said I'd *think* about it."

"Coming from you, that's as good as a *yes*." Crusher raised his glass of tea and declared in a loud voice, "I have an announcement to make. Martha has finally decided to marry me."

I'd decided no such thing.

But before I could say anything, the old men exclaimed together, "Mazel tov!"

My uncle beamed with tears in his eyes. "*Oy*! You have made this old man very happy, *faigela*."

Morty raised his glass and grinned at Crusher. "It's about time. *Yasher koach*." Good job.

Even Abel smiled. "*L'chaim*." To life.

I started to open my mouth to protest, but Crusher covered it with a deep kiss. Right in front of God and everybody.

# CHAPTER 12

Saturday morning the phone woke us up. Crusher reached toward the nightstand. "I'll get it." He pushed aside the empty tub of Cool Whip, handed me the receiver, and rolled out of bed.

"Hey, girlfriend," Lucy greeted me. "What did you and Jazz find out yesterday?"

I told her about the hate mail and our scheme to hand it over to the police. I also described my conversation with Abel Shapira. "Apparently Dolleen didn't have other family, so her stepson, Jonathan, is handling the funeral."

"Did he say he'd take Patti?"

"He said we could do what we wanted with the dog. I'm planning to examine Dolleen's secret financial records today. I hesitate to even mention this because I don't want to cause any trouble with Ray. But I'd welcome a second pair of eyes."

"How about four more eyes? I'll bring Birdie with me. You know how good she is with puzzles and codes and stuff. I'll call Jazz too."

Crusher emerged showered and dressed with a

fresh blue bandana on his head. He sat on the edge of the bed to pull on athletic socks and his brown motorcycle boots. "Is that Lucy?" When I nodded, he flashed a wide grin and gently took the phone from my hand. "Hey, Lucy. Did Martha tell you? We're engaged."

He pulled the phone away from his ear as Lucy screeched loud enough for me to hear.

"Get out! Really? So now we have two weddings to plan?"

He laughed and handed the phone back to me. I put my hand over the mouthpiece and squeaked, "I never said yes. You can't go around telling people we're getting married."

"Lucy isn't people. She's your best friend." He bent down and kissed my forehead. "Later, Mrs. Levy." He clomped out of the bedroom, heavy boots echoing down the hallway.

The sound of Lucy's voice brought me back. ". . . happy for you. This is the smartest thing you've done in a long time. I'll round up Birdie. We can be at your place in less than an hour."

I barely had time to shower, dress in stretch pants, and pick up the trail of clothes leading from the living room to the bedroom when my doorbell rang. Lucy and Birdie burst into the house and hugged me in a three-way embrace.

Birdie wore her usual light blue denim overalls and smelled like vanilla. She handed me an almond coffee cake in a green jadeite baking dish still slightly warm from the oven. "Congratulations, Martha dear. Lucy told me the good news."

"Crusher is jumping the gun, as usual. I didn't actually say *yes*."

Lucy's hands landed abruptly on her hips. "So, where did he get the idea you were engaged?"

"I didn't actually say *no.*"

She gave me a knowing look. "Paulina was right. You'll be married by the end of the summer."

I rolled my eyes and retreated to the kitchen, not willing to argue with another one of Lucy's "strong feelings." Ten minutes later, the three of us sat in front of my computer with fresh coffee and warm cake, the best breakfast ever. We stared expectantly at the blue screen and a number of items popped up.

Lucy pointed to a folder labeled *Ledger.* "This is where you'll find the Excel document I mentioned yesterday morning. It's got names, dates, and dollar amounts."

After I sent the file to the printer, I downloaded the photos of the bank statements from my cell phone and printed them as well. Five minutes later we pored over the documents.

Birdie adjusted her glasses and peered at the ledger. "I wonder why she collected $9,000 each from all these people. Were they rent checks? Even for LA, the amounts were a bit steep unless she rented out commercial space."

"I don't think so," I said. "The Feds would've confiscated any obvious assets, like real estate, back in 2009, when David Shapira confessed and went to prison. Dolleen would now be reporting any legitimate income, like rent checks, to the IRS on a completely different set of books."

Birdie twirled her hair around her fingers, which she did whenever she tried to figure something out. "Martha's right. Dolleen hid these transactions for a reason. Her ledger shows she received nearly $90,000 this month. Let's follow the money trail back to the bank accounts."

Lucy spread the bank statements side by side on the table. "I don't see any corresponding deposits in any of these offshore accounts, but I do see regular withdrawals of around $200,000 a month."

I gasped when I realized what we were looking at. "Oh my God, we're going at this the wrong way."

Lucy tilted her head and frowned. "What are you saying?"

"I'm saying the $90,000 weren't payments made *to* Dolleen. This is money she paid *out*." I picked up the ledger and ran my fingers down the list of nine names. Just as I suspected, one immediately jumped out. "Here she is. Emma Fishblatt."

"Who's she?" asked Lucy.

"She's an old lady swindled out of her life savings by David Shapira. Don't you get it? Those are restitution payments!" I stretched to reach the copies of hate mail sitting at the end of the table since yesterday. "I'll bet we'll find more names from that list in here."

We cross-referenced the list of names on the ledger with the letters and e-mails and found three more matches. A common thread seemed to unite them: according to the letters, all the recipients were elderly investors who complained David Shapira's Ponzi scheme wiped out their savings. Missing from the list of recipients were wealthy individuals or organizations better able to sustain a big loss.

I was getting the pot of coffee for refills when the doorbell rang. Jazz stood on the porch wearing a black pin-striped suit, lavender shirt, and sky-blue tie. He breezed past me and headed for the dining room table and plopped in a chair. He placed the black tote bag on the floor and liberated the Maltese. Zsa Zsa wore a jumper made of the same fine wool pinstripe and a sky-blue bow in her topknot. Bumper approached her slowly, delicately sniffing her face. Zsa Zsa shook her head rapidly and headed for the water bowl on the kitchen floor.

"I just came from the police station," he said. "Deke met me there. Remember Agent Kay B. Lancet?"

How could I forget? Kay investigated Russell Watson's murder last summer. Not just a special agent for the FBI, she also happened to be Arlo Beavers's ex-wife.

Jazz accepted a cup of coffee and a slice of cake. "Well. As Deke and I walked into the station, she was leaving. I said 'Hello. Remember me?' She nodded but just kept going. Detective Beavers and Kaplan took us to an interrogation room. Kaplan said he already knew about the e-mails. He said the FBI downloaded those same messages years ago from David Shapira's computer."

I nodded. "Kay probably showed up to deliver copies of David's case files. What did Arlo have to say?"

"Nothing. He let Kaplan do all the talking."

"Did they ask how you came to be in possession of the messages?" I held my breath.

"They totally bought the story about Dolleen giving them to me for safekeeping." He smoothed his hair. "I channeled Rock Hudson for my role."

I exhaled, relieved the police didn't suspect we'd actually stolen the letters from Dolleen's storage space.

Jazz paused to take a sip of coffee. "Anyway, Deke said, 'In view of this new evidence, you can no longer consider my client a viable suspect.' Kaplan got all pissy again. He said, 'Fletcher's not off our list yet.' Deke stood up and said, 'We're done here. My client came forward in good faith. We have nothing more to contribute.' We moved toward the door and Kaplan snarled at me as if I were some sort of serial killer. He warned me again not to leave town."

"What about Arlo?" I asked.

"I don't even think he was listening. He was too busy separating out the written letters from the e-mail messages."

"He would," I said. "Obviously, the snail mail was new evidence for them."

Jazz looked around the table. "Have you found anything on Dolly's computer yet?"

We told him about the victim-paying restitution to nine of David's investors, including Emma Fishblatt. "According to what you and I read in her letter yesterday, she'd be nearly eighty by now. I'm hoping she can tell us about these disbursements from Dolleen."

"Do you know how to contact her?" asked Birdie.

"The return address on the envelope indicated she lives on Detroit Street in LA."

"And if she's moved?"

"Dolleen sent out regular monthly payments to these people. She must've kept their addresses somewhere on her computer." I clicked a few keys and hit pay dirt—a spreadsheet with nine addresses. "Emma Fishblatt still lives on Detroit, near Park La Brea. There's also a phone number. Let's hope she can tell us more." I printed out the contact information.

Jazz's voice broke. "You know, I'm not at all surprised Dolly paid those people back. She had a soft spot for animals, children, and older people. Who would want to hurt such a sweet person?"

I grabbed a stack of e-mails. "Maybe someone knew about those restitution payments she made to a handful of David's investors and became furious when she refused to cut him in. Like someone who sent one of the scary messages."

"Don't worry," said Lucy. "Arlo is thorough. He'll question every one of those clowns."

I began to form a new idea. "Wait. What if the killer is someone closer to home? Like the ex-wife, Shelley, or the son, Jonathan? They could've blamed Dolleen for breaking up their happy home."

My list of people to interview kept expanding. It started with Dolleen's sneaky neighbor, who claimed to have seen Jazz in the victim's house the night of the murder. And now the list had grown to include Emma Fishblatt, Shelley Shapira, and Jonathan Shapira. Interviewing all those people was a huge responsibility, and the sudden weight of it translated into physical pain and the beginnings of a headache.

So, I did what always made me feel better: I cut another slice of cake. I firmly believed in sugar's effectiveness as an analgesic and antidepressant. However, the unfortunate side effect of my self-medicating in this way could be observed in my size 16 jeans.

Jazz removed a sketchpad from an outside pocket of the black tote. "To change the subject a little, I've come up with another design for your wedding dress, Birdie. It covers your legs like you asked for. You'll look very regal on your special day." He handed her the drawing. "What do you think? Can't you just see yourself gliding down the aisle with that picture hat instead of a veil?"

We stared at a colorful satin dress with a high neck, mutton chop sleeves, and an impossibly tiny waist. A bustle ballooned over an exaggerated derrière and cascaded into a ten-foot train. Perched on the head sat a hat the size of an umbrella, with huge bows, flowers, and ribbons streaming off the side.

Birdie swallowed. "It's very grand, Jazz dear. Very turn of the century."

"Yeah, two centuries ago," Lucy muttered out of the corner of her mouth.

Jazz seemed to ignore her. He sat back in his seat and beamed. "Do you remember I once told you I worked in San Francisco in the eighties? I made all the costumes for Finocchio's nightclub. Well, I designed an outfit similar to this for the headliner, a female impersonator named Kevin. I may still have a bolt somewhere of the same green and black striped satin we used back then."

Birdie managed a weak smile. "She—or he—must've looked lovely in this. But it's a little too, ah, dramatic for me." She handed the drawing back to Jazz. "Denny and I will be married on the ranch. Such a lot of fabric in the train would be hard to maneuver in the great outdoors. And it would get soiled from the dust and dirt."

Jazz closed his eyes and pouted. "First you reject the Mary Quant mini dress, now this. I never thought you'd be so finicky."

Lucy pointed toward the sketchpad. "Think flower child, hon. Peasant skirts. Gauzy fabric. You can't go wrong with something simple and comfortable for Birdie. And while you're at it, why don't you design a wedding dress for Martha? She and Yossi just got engaged last night."

Jazz whipped his head toward me. "Really? I've been dying to get my hands on your wardrobe. I'll redo everything in a combination of both Rizzoli and Isles."

*Oh brother.*

"I'm so jealous." His whole body slowly sagged. "Everybody has someone except me."

"Don't worry." Lucy winked. "If Martha can get married again, there's hope for anyone."

I dismissed the conversation with a wave of my hand and turned my attention to the Internet. A second later, Jonathan Shapira's contact information filled the screen. I sent it to the printer. I figured he'd be out of the office today, but I'd call him first thing on Monday morning.

I phoned Emma Fishblatt next.

"Hello?" She spoke cautiously.

"Mrs. Fishblatt?" I put her on speaker. "My name is Martha Rose. May I come to visit you today? I'd like to talk to you about Dolleen Doyle."

"It's *Miss* Fishblatt. Are you with the police?"

"No. I'm her friend."

Jazz whispered. "She's an old lady. It's not nice to lie."

I shrugged. "I know she helped you financially, and I was hoping we could speak about that."

"If you're a friend of Dolly's, maybe you can help me. Two police detectives just left, and I think I'm in big trouble."

Where had I heard that before?

# CHAPTER 13

Emma Fishblatt lived on the first floor of a large two-story duplex in a mid-Wilshire neighborhood in which, decades ago, middle-class Jewish families thrived. Over the years, the duplexes and small apartment buildings fell one by one into the hands of developers. The lovely old interiors—with plaster medallions on the ceilings, real hardwood floors, and art deco tiles in the bathrooms—were obliterated by multi-story condos covering entire blocks and finished inside with drywall and pressed wood flooring.

Underground parking replaced narrow driveways once leading to wooden garages. Long gone were the orange trees and jasmine that had perfumed the spring and summer air of an entire city. Now the neighborhood smelled like the exhaust from hundreds of cars trolling the streets for the rare parking space.

We pulled into Emma's driveway behind a light blue Oldsmobile.

"Oh my God," said Jazz. "This is a 1999 Cutlass,

the last year the car was ever made. It's like we stepped back in time."

"In more ways than one." I shut off the engine of my Honda and we all got out.

Lucy stood next to the car and looked up and down Detroit Street. "I wonder why she held on to her home in the midst of all this tumult and change."

"She's probably lived here forever," Birdie said. "Change is always a bit overwhelming for a senior." This, coming from a woman in her late seventies about to marry her former sweetheart and move a thousand miles away. "Let's hope she's not also over-whelmed with the four of us descending on her."

I marched toward the porch and rang the bell.

A tiny window opened in the solid oak door at face level. Cautious blue eyes peeked through the little, iron grate covering the opening. "Yes?"

"Miss Fishblatt? I called you earlier. I'm Martha Rose, and I've brought some other friends of Dolleen's." I made quick introductions.

The window closed, a dead bolt clicked, and the door swung open. "Come in," said an elderly woman with short white hair in a tight perm. "I didn't expect so many people, but never mind."

Emma wore a hand-knitted pink cardigan. The thermostat must've been set at seventy-nine degrees. The unmistakable aroma of boiled chicken and onions lingered in the air. She gestured toward the living room with a spidery hand. "Please sit down and I'll just go get some *mandle broit*." *Mandle broit* was Yiddish for *almond bread*, those crispy biscotti you always see in the bakery case of a delicatessen.

She reminded me so much of my *bubbie*. God forbid you didn't have a few cookies to serve guests.

I settled on the sofa and waited while she shuffled on fuzzy pink slippers into the kitchen. Emma returned moments later with a plate of Jewish biscotti, placed it on the coffee table, and sat in an oversized recliner with her feet dangling.

I cleared my throat. "Miss Fishblatt, when we spoke earlier, you mentioned you might be in trouble with the police?"

She wrung her hands. "They said I'd been helping Dolleen with money laundering, hiding income, tax evasion—I don't remember what all. Here's the card." She handed me an LAPD business card with the name *Noah Kaplan*.

I could just picture the arrogant Detective Kaplan scaring an old woman with threats, probably the only way he could impress a female over the age of twelve. "I'm sorry to hear that."

Emma briefly closed her eyes and sighed. "My memory isn't the best these days. Dementia runs in my family, you know. My sister, God love her, ended up in assisted living because of the Fishblatt curse. I've been taking care of her expenses for years. I tried telling that to the young detective, but he didn't care. I'm pretty sure he's Jewish, but he has no manners. Have you noticed the lack of respect in younger people these days?"

I waited for her to finish then gently brought her back to the reason for our visit. "What did you tell Detective Kaplan?"

"Dolly said if anyone ever found out about our, um, arrangement, I should say she was paying me back a loan. And that's what I did. I told him, 'The only dirty laundry I know about is in my washing machine. And I don't have to report the money to the IRS because I already paid taxes on it before I lent it out.'" She chuckled. "I played dumb, and he bought it because young people expect the elderly to be stupid."

Emma Fishblatt might be approaching her eighties and her memory might not be what it used to be, but she certainly wasn't a fool.

"Did you talk about anything else?" I picked up a piece of *mandle broit.*

"He asked if I knew of anyone who might've wanted her dead." The old woman took a tissue out from under the cuff of her sleeve and wiped her eyes. "I told them *no.* Dolly, may she rest in peace, was a good person. Whoever killed her took an angel from the face of this earth."

Birdie nodded sympathetically. "I'm so sorry, dear."

"Did you know she often took me to the Farmers Market for dinner?" Emma sighed. "She once said 'Emma, you're the closest thing I have to a mother.' I never had children of my own, you see. My sister, Sarah, and I never married. We grew up in this house and always lived together. At least until she came down with the Fishblatt curse."

I bit into a very cold biscotti. Apparently, Emma stored them in the freezer. I pointed to the only man in the room. "The police think her friend Jazz, here, could've killed her. He's innocent, of course, but they don't agree. We're hoping to uncover the true identity of the murderer. It would really help us to understand your arrangement with Dolleen and how it came about."

Emma settled back in the chair. "It all began years ago when I wrote an angry letter to David Shapira. After he went to prison, Dolly found it among his things and contacted me. I told her I didn't know how I could pay for Sarah's care. Assisted living had gone up to $7000 dollars a month."

"Yes," I said. "I saw your letter."

"Well, Dolly said she'd found a way to pay me back but let me know she couldn't do it in one lump sum. She'd found others just like me and wanted to help us all. I had to swear never to tell anyone about our agreement, and I never did."

"Tell me about your agreement."

"Dolly gave me monthly checks in amounts that wouldn't alert the IRS. So far, she's paid me back over $250,000, half of what I lost in the first place." She wiped her eyes again. "She was the soul of kindness. Not like the rest of them."

My ears perked up. "The rest of them?"

"Her family. I trusted her scoundrel of a husband, David Shapira, with all of my savings. I never knew what Dolly saw in him. In my day, if a man like that came courting, my father would've thrown him out of the house." Emma patted her hair. "Plenty of boys were interested in me, but Papa was very traditional. He insisted my older sister, Sarah, must be the first to marry. He said it was only proper."

"But Sarah never did," Lucy said.

Emma shook her head. "No. She was too picky. By the time my parents died and I could finally choose for myself, it was too late. All the good ones were gone."

Once again, I had to reel Emma in. "What can you tell me about Dolleen's relationship with her husband? I understand she never divorced him."

Emma's mouth turned down at the corners. "She stayed loyal to him, even after he went to prison."

"She must've loved him a lot," said Lucy.

Emma sighed and gave a quick shake of her head. One curl flew free and settled on her cheek. "You could call her 'one of a kind.'"

"What about his son, Jonathan, and David's ex-wife, Shelley?" I asked. "Can you tell me about Dolleen's connection to them?"

"Dolly spoke very fondly of Jonathan. But the ex-wife, Shelley, really hated her. Apparently, she blew her top when she found out Jonathan and Dolly traveled together to Leavenworth to visit David."

Often a divorced spouse resented any relationship a child might have with the new partner of their ex. Yet Emma described Shelley as still being jealous years after the divorce. Jealous enough to kill?

"I met Abel Shapira last night," I said, "and he seemed to think the world of Dolleen."

Emma sat up straighter. "I would take whatever he says with a huge sack of salt."

"You know Abel Shapira?"

"Unfortunately, yes." She pushed the stray curl back off her face. "We dated years ago. We both belonged to the senior center on Pico Boulevard. He persuaded me and several others at the center to invest. When it all went bad, he disappeared. Too ashamed to show his face." She tugged on the end of her sleeve. "I would have broken it off anyway. He was a sloppy kisser. False teeth."

"Do you know Isaac Harris?" I asked. "He practically lives at the center. He's my uncle."

Emma beamed. "Of course I know him. You're *that* niece? Why didn't he ever get married? He's such a sweet man, and very smart, *keinehore*." She used an expression that came from the phrase *kein ayin ha ra,* meaning *no evil eye.* God forbid a compliment should attract envy and malice.

"I guess you'd have to ask him." I steered the conversation back to the murder. "Emma, did anyone else from the center receive payments from Dolleen?"

She played with a button on her cardigan. "Dolly asked me to confirm the identity of other seniors at the center like me. Investors who lost everything because of her husband. She made payments to a group of us."

I asked her to create two lists of names: those seniors receiving reimbursement payments, and other investors from the center who were not being compensated. Emma retrieved a notepad from the kitchen.

While she wrote down names, I asked, "Did Dolleen ever mention having a conflict with anyone over her scheme to reimburse some of you? Maybe from one of her family members or from one of her husband's victims?"

She furrowed her forehead. "If she had trouble with anyone, she never shared it with me. All I know is she promised to return every penny her husband stole from us." Emma's eyes welled with tears and her lips trembled. "Now it's too late."

A car drove by, blaring rap music that penetrated the stucco walls and made the bay window vibrate.

Birdie looked out. "This area seems to have turned into a nightmare of condos and traffic. Wouldn't you be more comfortable living someplace more quiet?"

"When I lost my savings, I needed a new source of income to support Sarah. So, I took out a reverse mortgage." Emma's jaw tightened. "Now I'm stuck here."

I hated the reverse mortgage business. Financial predators took advantage of vulnerable seniors who owned their homes. If Emma ever wanted to sell her duplex, the bank would first recover all the past payments, plus interest, plus an administrative fee. The poor woman would be lucky to get a fraction of her equity back. But if she stayed in her home, the monthly checks from the bank were guaranteed for life—even if she used up all the equity.

Zsa Zsa poked her tiny face out of the black tote bag.

Emma noticed her for the first time. "What a nice little dog. Dolly carried around a tiny Chihuahua with her. What happened to it?"

"Patti's fine," Jazz said. "But she needs a new home. Would you be interested? She comes with a fabulous wardrobe, matching tote bags, and several sets of custom-made bedding, including adorable quilts." He winked. "And such a stylish little dog would be a stud magnet at the senior center."

Emma's stomach moved up and down when she laughed. "I'm not very good with pets."

"Just think about it," he said. "Maybe a little companion is what you need."

I thanked Emma for her time and stood to leave.

She fluffed her tight curls. "Come back any time, Martha. And bring that nice uncle of yours with you."

# CHAPTER 14

On the way back to the Valley, I reviewed the conversation with my three friends. "We should double-check the list of names Emma gave me against the list in the ledger. I'm guessing we'll find matches for all those names."

"What about the other names she gave us?" Jazz asked. "Could one of the seniors not being reimbursed have been angry enough to kill Dolly?"

Birdie reached for the grab bar as I accelerated onto the freeway. "This reminds me of a similar case I saw on an episode of *Forensic Files*. My money's on the ex-wife, Shelley."

"Yeah!" Lucy nodded vigorously. "Emma said Shelley went ballistic when she learned Jonathan and Dolleen visited Leavenworth together. She probably felt her son was being disloyal by even associating with Dolleen. Some women can't stand that."

"Maybe her anger went much deeper," I said. "Leavenworth's in Kansas. A trip would involve an airline flight and maybe even an overnight stay. What if Shelley believed the young and pretty Dolleen, who had an affair with her husband and broke up their marriage, went on to have an affair with her son?"

"If you're right," said Lucy, "how far would she go to stop them? Remember, both Dolleen's spirit and Patti the Chihuahua identified the killer as a woman."

I shrugged off the paranormal claims of the so-called medium, Paulina. I was far more interested in pursuing the information we'd just gotten from Emma.

Back at my house, we compared the eight other names on Emma's "reimbursement" list to the names in the ledger. As I suspected, they all matched.

Jazz rubbed his eyes. "Okay. We can assume none of these seniors wanted to hurt Dolly. They all stood to lose with her death. But are we any closer to identifying the real killer?"

Birdie gestured toward Jazz. "You have a point. There are maybe hundreds of individuals and organizations all over the country who never got their money back. Any one of them could be the perp."

I smiled at my seventy-seven-year-old friend's use of cop speak.

When Birdie excused herself to go to the bathroom, Lucy reached in her purse and handed me a pile of Log Cabin quilt blocks, each nine and a half inches square, in a Ziploc bag. "I made forty of them for Birdie's surprise wedding quilt, just like you asked. Tell me if you need more."

Jazz passed me a similar package from his tote bag and whispered, "Does Birdie suspect anything?"

"Not that I'm aware of. With the forty blocks I just made, we now have a total of 120. I'll sew them together in rows of ten across and twelve down. The quilt top will measure 90 inches by 108 inches—plenty big enough for a queen-sized bed."

I found endless fascination in the geometry of traditional quilts. Depending on how you placed quilt blocks next to each other in the top, secondary overall patterns could emerge. Blocks with strong contrast between light and dark fabrics were especially amenable to creating such designs. Our Log Cabin quilt blocks would be joined together in a unique configuration called Barn Raising; a perfect theme to commemorate Birdie and Denver's country wedding.

I quickly hid the plastic bags behind a sofa cushion when I heard Birdie emerging from the other room.

She looked at her watch. "It's almost four, Martha dear. I need to get home."

Jazz waited until Birdie and Lucy were out the front door. "I can come over tomorrow and help you assemble the top. Do you have what we need for basting the quilt?"

*Basting* is shorthand for structuring the three-layered quilt "sandwich" with fabric backing on the bottom, a sheet of batting in the middle, and the pieced design on top. The three elements are temporarily joined with either large stitches, safety pins, or plastic tacks. This prevents the layers from shifting during the quilting process.

"Yes. I have nine yards of a brown-and-red plaid flannel for the backing. And I bought a package of wool batting for extra warmth during those cold Oregon winters."

Jazz scooped up Zsa Zsa and put her in the tote. "Sounds very rural and log cabiny. I'll be here by ten with bagels and cream cheese." Before he walked out the door, he sent me an air kiss via his fingertips. "*Mwa!*"

I picked up my phone and called Crusher. "Yossi, can you use your law enforcement connections to get a phone number for me?"

"Sure, babe. Who do you want to talk to?"

"Shelley Shapira."

Ten minutes later he called me back with the information.

Shelley Shapira's phone went straight to voice mail, so I left a message. "Mrs. Shapira, my name is Martha Rose. I'm a friend of your former father-in-law, Abel Shapira. If you can spare a moment, I'd really like to talk to you about a personal matter." I left my contact information and hung up.

True to his word, Jazz arrived Sunday morning with bagels and helped me assemble the Barn Raising quilt top. The overall pattern featured diamond-shaped ripples emanating bigger and bigger from the center of the quilt. The ripples alternated between dark and light.

First we taped the red plaid backing to the hardwood floor with masking tape around the edges, pulling it taut and wrinkle free. Next we arranged the wool batting over the backing, smoothing it with our hands, starting from the middle of the quilt and working toward the edges. Finally, we stretched the Barn Raising quilt top over the first two layers and pinned around the edges to hold it in place.

The following two hours were spent on our hands and knees basting the quilt sandwich together with long, temporary stitches. I dreaded this step, because my fibromyalgia invariably flared up from the bending and squatting. And my left knee still felt tender from falling on it Thursday night. But I endured the temporary discomfort for the sake of Birdie's quilt. Using the masking-tape-on-the-floor method for basting large projects was still the best way I knew of ensuring a large quilt would be perfectly square and wrinkle-free when the layers were stitched together.

"Is it just me, or is my needle really gliding through this batting?" asked Jazz.

"No, it's not just you. I find that wool is way easier to needle than cotton batting, especially if the cotton has a scrim." *Scrim* referred to the thin adhesive film applied to the cotton fibers to hold them in place so they wouldn't bunch. "You'll see when you begin to quilt this. Your stitching will go much faster. Especially if you keep the point of your needle sharp."

When the three layers were basted together, we pulled off the tape, took out the pins, and liberated the quilt from the floor.

Jazz glanced at his watch. "I've got to get back home for some face time with a friend on the Internet." He threw me another kiss and disappeared out the front door.

I folded Birdie's quilt and put it in my sewing room. Then I took a Soma for the aching in my body and stretched out on the sofa for an afternoon nap. Tomorrow promised to be a big day, and I needed to recover. I needed to be strong and clear-headed when I spoke to both Shelley and Jonathan Shapira.

# CHAPTER 15

Monday morning, I entered the law firm of Edelman/Schwartz in Beverly Hills. The receptionist showed me to an office with a removable name plate on the door reading *Jonathan Shapira*. Abel claimed his grandson was a Beverly Hills big shot. But the temporary sign on the office door told a humbler story.

I took a seat inside a modest office, while a young man in his late twenties spoke into a cell phone and paced behind a slightly battered wooden desk. He wore jeans and white sneakers. The sleeves of his navy-blue cashmere sweater were pushed up, revealing tan, muscular forearms. Behind him, a narrow bank of windows overlooked the street six stories below.

He smiled briefly in my direction with an apologetic look on his handsome face. "I've got a new client sitting in my office. We'll have to talk later."

He stopped moving. "I'm sorry for the interruption, Mrs. Rose." He pushed his sleeve farther up his arm and briefly came around the desk to shake my hand. Then he slid his elegant body into the black leather desk chair. "You said over the phone a friend of yours needs help with an urgent legal problem?"

"It's *Ms.* Rose, actually." I returned the smile. "My friend's name is Jazz Fletcher. He's innocent, of course, but the police think he killed your stepmother, and they don't seem willing to look at anyone else for the crime."

Jonathan's face remained fixed in a pleasant expression, but his pupils contracted and his jaw tightened. "If your friend is seeking representation, I'm hardly the one to ask. First of all, we practice entertainment law here. Second, I should think the conflict of interest would be obvious." He pushed his chair back from the desk and stood. "I'm sorry, but I'm afraid I can't help you."

I ignored his signal to leave. "That's not why I came. Jazz already has excellent representation."

"Then why are you here?"

"I found a witness who says your stepmother's killer may have been a woman." I wasn't going to tell him my information came from a so-called ghost and a reincarnated Rottweiler who spoke Romanian.

"What does that have to do with me?"

"Maybe nothing. But I didn't want to go to the authorities with my information until we had a chance to talk first. I mean, it's no secret your mother, Shelley, had every reason to hate Dolleen. With this new evidence, she might be the first person the police will suspect."

A storm gathered in his eyes. He swiftly walked to his door and closed it. Then he sat back down and leaned across the desk. "Are you accusing my mother of killing Dolly? Is this some kind of a shakedown?"

I held up my hand. "God forbid. I'm trying to learn more about Dolleen Doyle in hopes of uncovering any suspects with a motive to kill her. Your mother may be an obvious person of interest, but that doesn't have to mean she's the killer. So, I'm postponing handing the information over to the police."

He sat back. "What exactly do you want?"

"Information. Did you know Dolleen had been withdrawing money from hidden offshore accounts on a regular basis? She used some of it to pay restitution to a small group of seniors who lost everything in your father's swindle."

He frowned. "How do you know all this?"

"You'd be surprised what you can find out if you just ask the right people."

"That's the job of the police."

"I agree. But so far, they're fixated on an innocent man. At the moment, it appears I'm the only one who's interested in finding out the truth. Can you please answer my question? Did you know about Dolleen's scheme to reimburse those elderly investors?"

He raked his fingers through an abundant head of dark hair. "Dolly had a very generous side."

He still evaded the question, but I pressed on. "Apparently, she reciprocated your admiration. Someone close to Dolleen said she was quite fond of you."

"Your point?" His nostrils flared.

"Last Friday night my uncle invited a friend to join us for Shabbat dinner. He turned out to be your grandfather, Abel. We chatted a little and he told me he really liked Dolleen because she stuck by your father."

Jonathan drummed his fingers on the desktop. "Is this going anywhere?"

"Abel couldn't think of anyone who'd want to kill Dolleen, yet someone did. Can you?"

Jonathan glanced at his watch. "I thought you said you have a witness who says the killer was a woman. So far I've heard nothing implicating my mother. And I'm getting a little tired of this fishing expedition."

"*Could* have been a woman. But I'm exploring every possibility. Didn't you and Dolleen travel to Kansas together to visit your father in prison? Maybe she confided her troubles to you during such a long trip."

"No. Now I really . . ."

My voice softened. "A beautiful woman, almost the same age as you. . . . Maybe you turned to each other for comfort? Those things happen."

He looked up sharply. "What you're suggesting is disgusting. Dolly loved my father. End of story."

"Forgive me for that, but I had to ask. So what, exactly, was your relationship with Dolleen?"

He blew out his breath. "I didn't blame her for my parents' divorce. Their marriage was already over long before my father met Dolly. She never treated me badly. She made sure my father did right by me."

"How so?"

"After my father went to prison, Dolly gave me a living allowance and money to pay for law school. She checked in with me from time to time to see how I was getting along."

"Then you were on good terms with her?"

"Yes."

"How did your mother feel about that?"

"You're back to my mother? Leave her out of this!" He stood and walked toward his office door. "I think we're done here."

I stood and followed him. "I'm sorry to upset you. But ask yourself this one thing. Don't you want to know who's responsible for Dolleen's death?"

He glared at me and yanked open the door. "Of course I do. But it wasn't me or any member of my family."

I left the building convinced Jonathan Shapira hadn't been totally forthcoming. Only when I got to my car did I realize I failed to ask him about the funeral.

# CHAPTER 16

My watch indicated I had an hour to get to Paulina's. Jazz made me promise I wouldn't tell Birdie about the séance today. He wanted to contact Russell on a very personal matter.

Paulina's house on Venice Boulevard was only fifteen minutes away from Beverly Hills. The mid-morning traffic was light, and even with a stop at Starbucks for two mocha lattes, I arrived a half hour early. I parked in the short driveway next to her black BMW.

Paulina answered the door with a welcoming smile on her fuchsia lips. Her gold lamé turban teetered loosely on top of her black hair. "Hi, Martha. Jazz said you'd be coming, but you're early. Do you want a reading before he gets here?"

I thrust one of the mocha lattes toward her and stepped inside the dim living room. "No thanks. I just thought we could hang out while we wait. It's been a long time."

"Thanks." She took the cup and gestured for me to sit at the round table with the purple cloth. "I'll be right back." She headed for the kitchen and returned with an open bag of Oreos. She pulled out the half-empty plastic tray and set it in the middle of the table.

The first time I met Paulina, I'd been trying to solve the mystery of my friend Harriet Gordon's murder. In the beginning, I suspected the psychic might've been involved, since Harriet was one of her most lucrative clients—that was, until the day she suddenly cut Paulina off. But it turned out Paulina's only vice was using her sharp instincts to hustle customers. She knew how to make them happy because she told them what they wanted to hear; just like every politician and every miracle-diet guru.

"Thanks for introducing me to your friend Jazz." She took a sip of Starbucks and left fuchsia lip marks on the white plastic top. "He's a sweet guy, but he needs a lot of help. And I don't mean with the cops. His problem goes much deeper."

I reached for an Oreo stuffed with chocolate frosting. "Like what?"

"He's lonely."

*Duh.* It didn't take a sixth sense to notice the wistful expressions and sadness in his eyes. Jazz Fletcher had been genuinely in love with Russell Watson, whose death left a huge hole in his life. I washed down the Double stuffed chocolate Oreo with some mocha latte. I sighed as the sudden infusion of sugar activated the pleasure center in my brain.

The Chihuahua trotted into the room and begged to sit in Paulina's lap. "Tell me honestly, Paulina, what's the deal with Dolleen's dog?"

She smirked and shook her head slowly. "It's a shame you're such a skeptic, Martha." She picked up the dog, who furiously licked her face. "She felt very loved by Dolleen, but she doesn't want to be called Patti anymore. That was her slave name. From now on, she wishes to be known as Hathor."

"Who?"

"The Egyptian goddess of love." She stroked the dog's tiny head. "This one is an old soul."

"What a relief. It should be much easier to place an old soul with a new owner."

Paulina bristled against my sarcasm. "Hathor cannot be owned. She's made that very clear. She chooses to stay with me."

I shrugged. "Fine by me. Nobody else seems to want her. And it's your lucky day. She comes with couture clothes, tote bags, and quilts."

"Wearing human clothing is beneath Hathor's dignity." Paulina sniffed. "But she'll accept the tote bags and quilts."

Jazz arrived just as we finished our coffee. Paulina removed the cups and cookies from the middle of the table. In their place, she lit a purple candle and three joss sticks in a brass holder. The flame on the candle swayed slightly and the jasmine-scented smoke curled upward in a lazy spiral.

She looked at Jazz. "Go ahead and take a seat."

He placed a yellow tote bag on the floor and put his finger to his lips. "Zsa Zsa's asleep."

Hathor's nose twitched, and her little body shivered slightly.

Paulina looked toward the door. "Is anyone else coming, or is this it?"

He scratched the back of his neck. "No one else. I didn't think Birdie would be comfortable listening to Rusty and me, and Lucy wasn't available." He reached over and briefly squeezed my shoulder. "Martha knows me best. We've been through a lot together."

"No problem. Did you bring something belonging to the deceased?"

Jazz removed the diamond-encrusted gold wedding band from his left hand and gave it to Paulina. "If Rusty had lived, we would've been married. This is the ring he intended to surprise me with. But he died before that happened."

"How did you end up with it?" Paulina asked.

"Birdie found it and gave it to me. She's such a sweet person. She knew Rusty was gay when she married him. She covered for him all those years. And she would've been okay with a friendly divorce so Rusty and I could be married. There's nothing but good emotion attached to this ring."

Paulina hefted the heavy band in her hand and eyed it like a jewelry appraiser. "Yes, I feel a strong, positive energy." She placed it next to the purple candle. "Tell me the full name of the deceased."

"Russell Watson," said Jazz.

Paulina nodded. "Are you ready?"

The three of us joined hands. Nervous sweat moistened Jazz's palm.

He swallowed. "Go ahead."

Paulina closed her eyes and hummed. Hathor sat

at attention in her lap and stared at Jazz with dark, liquid eyes too big for her tiny face. Even when Paulina slumped forward onto the table, the Chihuahua never moved.

Paulina sat up again, eyes still closed. She chanted three times, "*Amor junxit, mors non separabit.*" I didn't understand a lot of Latin, but I pieced together *love, death, not separate.* Or something like that. "Russell Watson. Please join our circle." After five seconds, she made a noise in the back of her throat like a duck choking. "*Ack, ack ack.*"

Paulina's voice dropped an octave from her normal mezzo-soprano to baritone. "I am here, Jazzy Joe."

"Oh my God. *Jazzy Joe* was his pet name for me! Rusty, are you really here, honey?" He squeezed my hand so hard my fingers went numb. "I've missed you so much." He paused. "Are you okay? What happened to your voice? Do you have a cold?"

Paulina cleared her throat and spoke in a slightly higher register. "Yes, it's really me. I'm very happy where I am. It's peaceful and green."

By now tears streamed down Jazz's face. "First of all, I'm sorry about what happened to you. Did you hear Martha caught your killer? And Birdie's finally going to marry your brother, Denver. I know the two of you didn't get along in the last years of your life, but I hope you don't plan to haunt them. Anyway, I want to thank you for the wedding ring. It means the world to me you were finally ready to get married."

"Yeah, we woulda been happy." Paulina speaking.

Jazz leaned toward the medium. "Rusty, honey, your happiness is still important to me. Otherwise I wouldn't ask what I'm about to ask." He paused. "I'd like to get your permission to start dating again."

*I was right about the reason for manscaping and working out.*

"Do you have someone in mind?" Paulina.

*Just what I'd like to know.*

Jazz blushed and looked at the table. "Kind of. We met last year. We've been texting and e-mailing for the past few months, and he wants to come to LA for a visit. He's interested in taking our relationship to the next level. But I've been putting him off. I didn't want to be disloyal to you."

*Oh my God. I think I know who he's talking about.*

Paulina opened her left lid just a slit and watched me as her voice slid into the lower register again. "Let me think about it."

I gave her the stink eye. "Hi, Russell. It's me, Martha. Jazz has really suffered since your death. I think it would be cruel to force him to come back for another séance in order to get your answer." I nudged her leg with my foot under the table.

"Okay. Okay. I want you to be happy, Jazzy. You should go for it. I give you my bless . . ."

She stopped speaking and shivered. When she spoke next, her voice became raspy, almost a whisper. "You and Martha must be very careful. The murderer you seek will kill again in order to hide their secret."

"Who is it?" Jazz asked.

*Thunk* went Paulina's head on the table again. The gold lamé rolled off her skull and travelled toward the lit candle. She slowly sat up, let go of our hands, and blinked her eyes open. Suddenly the turban burst into flames.

# CHAPTER 17

Jazz deftly smothered the fire with the purple tablecloth and doused the smoldering turban with water in the kitchen sink. Satisfied Paulina's place was in no danger of burning down, I drove back to the Valley, leaving the two of them to hash out custodial arrangements for Hathor.

Time to talk to Dolleen's neighbor. I was pretty sure she was the person who sneaked into the victim's house the night Jazz and I broke in. She knew what to look for and where to find it. How much more did she know about the secrets inside Tarzana Relocation and Storage?

I also suspected her to be the mysterious witness who reported seeing Jazz at the victim's house the night of the murder. If so, what exactly did she tell the police?

I got back to Encino before three, a little light-headed from skipping lunch. Rafi's Falafel beckoned me and I stopped for a half hour to fortify myself with a shawarma plate and a side of baba ganouj with pita bread. Hunger satisfied, I headed toward

Tarzana and parked on Dolleen's street in front of the neighbor's house. For the first time, I noticed the similarity between her and Dolleen's California ranch-style houses.

A gray Toyota pickup and a red Corvette sat next to each other in the driveway. The raised garage door revealed two bicycles and two sets of golf clubs hanging neatly on one wall. Two mopeds were parked in tandem next to a golf cart. A workbench took up the back wall with tools hanging in an orderly array on a pegboard above it. The owners of this organized space would probably be horrified at the random and dusty contents of my cluttered garage.

The grass had that newly mown smell; yet not one stray blade lingered on the cement walkway leading to the front entrance. Flanking the front door were two pots of freshly watered pink azaleas with white granules of fertilizer sitting on top of the soil. I took a calming yoga breath and pressed the doorbell.

A petite woman around forty pulled open the door a crack. She brushed back a long strand of dull blond-turning-gray hair from her face. "Oh. I thought you were the FedEx guy."

Bingo! I recognized the voice as the same one from the other night inside Dolleen's house. I spread my sweetest smile across my face. "Hello. My name is Martha Rose. I was a friend of your neighbor, Dolleen Doyle. I'm hoping you can help me. You are Mrs. . . . ?"

"Hawkins. Kiki Hawkins." She didn't open the door any farther. "What do you want?"

"Oh, you're *that* Kiki. Dolleen spoke so highly of you." I was amazed at how easily the lies flowed from my lips. "I just need a moment of your time. Her family asked me to tie up some loose ends. Understandably, they're extremely upset over her awful death, so I volunteered to step in and help. I understand you were close to Dolleen . . . Dolly?"

"A little." The door remained in a defensive position.

Since I was right about the neighbor being the intruder, I decided to test my other theory. "The police told us you came forward as a witness and identified someone as a possible killer. Can you tell me more? The family would be greatly comforted knowing there's an actual suspect."

She glanced over her shoulder and lowered her voice to a whisper. "The police promised they wouldn't identify me!"

*Bingo again!*

I also lowered my voice and spoke behind my hand. "Did you talk to Detective Kaplan?"

She nodded.

"Figures. I hate to say this, because you and I are stuck with him. He's not the sharpest crayon in the box. We could do a much better job of finding the killer than him!"

One corner of her mouth turned up. She opened the door two inches wider and whispered, "Some men think women are stupid, but we have our ways. Right?"

"Absolutely." I could now see past her all the way through to the backyard. I caught a glimpse of a shirtless young hunk in a baseball cap skimming leaves from a swimming pool. He could've been a cover model for a paperback romance. His well-oiled biceps and smooth chest glistened in the sun. *Must be the pool guy.* My feet and legs began to ache from standing in one position; one of the miseries of fibromyalgia. "Uh, do you think I could come in and sit down?"

She glanced over her shoulder again and shook her head rapidly. "No."

*What is she hiding? Does she have a thing going with the pool guy?*

"No problem." I shifted my weight, hoping to find a more comfortable position. "What can I go back and tell the family about the person you saw the night of the murder?"

Kiki licked her lips. "My husband likes to have his dinner every night at six sharp. I was standing at the kitchen sink cleaning up, so it must've been around seven. I looked outside and saw a tall man with brown hair. He seemed really upset." There was something automatic in her response, as if she'd rehearsed this speech beforehand.

"In what way?"

She shrugged and looked down. "He had an angry look on his face."

"What exactly was he doing when you noticed him?"

"Walking toward his car. The license plate said *Jazz* something."

"Did you see him actually going into or coming out of the house, or did you just see him walking toward his car?"

She licked her lips again. "Uh, coming out of the house, I think."

*Something's not right.* "Are you sure? Did you see

him exit the doorway and shut the door behind himself?"

"I'm pretty sure that's what he did." Kiki took one step backward and began to close her door.

I put my hand up to stop her. "Thank you so much, Kiki. What you've just told me is really helpful." *Just not in the way you think.* If, God forbid, the police did arrest Jazz, his attorney would demolish her I'm-pretty-sure testimony under cross-examination.

I plunged ahead to test another theory. "Dolleen told me she gave you a key to her house in case of an emergency."

Kiki blinked several times.

I continued, "I do the same thing with my neighbor. Dolleen also said you knew about her secret office in Tarzana. You know the one I'm talking about, right?"

"Well, I guess if she already told you . . ."

*I love it when I'm right.*

"Dolly did mention it a couple of times, but she never went into detail." Kiki swallowed. "She just said she kept some memorabilia there she didn't want the FBI to know about because they'd take it from her. Did she tell you where she kept the key?"

Kiki looked away. "*Nuh-uh!*"

*Another lie.* Jazz and I were hiding under the bed when she came looking for it. "Dolleen must've trusted you. It sounds like you were more than just 'a little' close."

Kiki's voice trembled. "If you must know, we were like sisters. We confided in each other. Along with the key to her house, she gave me a phone number to call in case of emergency."

"Whose number was it?"

"Her stepson, Jonathan. She said he'd know what to do."

"Did you call him when they discovered her body?"

"Right away."

"How did he take the news?"

Kiki frowned and took a half-step backward. "I thought you said the family sent you. If that's true, you should know how Jonathan felt."

*Darn! Please God help me here.* "I'm here on behalf of her Kansas family."

"Dolly said she grew up in an orphanage."

"She did, but she had an aunt. Emily Doyle. Auntie Em."

She looked at me skeptically. "Dolly never mentioned her."

*Oh dear God, please let this woman believe me.* "They didn't really keep in touch." I cleared my throat. "Anyway, when you called Jonathan, how did he react to Dolleen's death?"

She chewed her lip. "He seemed really upset. And worried."

"Worried? Did he say why?"

Kiki lifted one shoulder. "No."

Why was she being so guarded? "Can you think of anyone who might've wanted to kill Dolleen?"

"You mean, besides the ex-wife?"

"Why do you say that?"

"Kiki?" A voice called from inside the house.

She began to close the door. "That's my husband. I have to go now."

Before the door clicked shut, I caught a glimpse of the pool guy with the six-pack abs. Through the door I heard him ask, "Who've you been talking to, precious?"

*Six pack is her husband? He's got to be fifteen years younger.*

I walked over to Dolleen's front porch and turned to look at the Hawkins' house. Only the living room windows were visible. As in Dolleen's house, their kitchen windows were toward the back. If Kiki washed the dishes the night of the murder, she couldn't possibly have seen what she claimed. I aimed my cell phone toward their house and snapped a photo.

Back at home, I cracked open a chilly can of Coke Zero and opened my computer. I combed through Dolleen's files, beginning with her e-mails. A folder labeled *J* contained a number of brief messages from Igo4you. The most recent one, sent two weeks ago, read **Harlequin at 3. She's suspicious.** Another message dated a month before read **Harlequin, Tuesday at 2.** Over the past three years, there must have been dozens of similar messages.

A brief online search showed a boutique hotel in West Hollywood called the Harlequin. Why would Dolleen arrange frequent meetings at a hotel? Did she indulge in some afternoon delight with someone named Igo4you? Did the *J* stand for *Jonathan?* Did he lie to me about being involved romantically with Dolleen in order to shield his mother from suspicion?

I fished around inside my purse and found

Jonathan Shapira's phone number and called him again. "This is Martha Rose."

"I told you we have nothing more to discuss."

"Don't hang up. I've acquired files from Dolleen's computer which seem to suggest you and your step-mother were closer than you would admit."

"That's a lie! I didn't . . ."

"The thing is, this evidence could've given your mother an even stronger motive to go after Dolleen. We need to talk, but not on the phone."

"I don't want you in my office. I'll meet you at Bergin's." Tom Bergin's Irish Pub on Fairfax Boule-vard had been an LA landmark ever since it opened in the 1930s, right after Prohibition.

Crusher would be home by six, so I felt perfectly safe in what I was about to propose. "It's been a long day for me, Jonathan, and I'm through run-ning around. You'll have to come to my house in Encino. Eight this evening."

"And if I refuse?"

"Would you and your mother rather be talking to the police about what I found?"

I called Crusher next to make sure he'd be home.

"I'll make a point of it, babe. What're you hoping to get from this dude?"

"The truth." I told him about my earlier conver-sations with Jonathan and with Kiki. "My gut tells me they're both hiding something."

"Your gut is usually right." He chuckled. "By the way, have I told you how delicious your gut is? Next time we should try some Nutella."

After I ended the call, I thought about the bland little Kiki Hawkins and her younger, good-looking husband. The Corvette and expensive sports toys suggested at least one of the Hawkinses had money. I took a wild guess and decided it wasn't Mr. Hawkins. A hunk like him—who could choose from dozens of beautiful, young women—would only marry a mousy older woman for one reason. Money.

I didn't have the same problem with Crusher. We were equals in every respect. He'd always been gentle and supportive of me. He never tried to dominate, except sometimes late at night when he pretended to be Ogg the Caveman. *Don't ask.*

I loved Yossi Levy's intellect and his commitment to those Jewish traditions that were also important to me. Yet The ATF and Israeli Secret Service knew him as a tough agent, and bikers knew him as Crusher. This complicated man would never bore me.

Instead of my usual panic, my chest filled with a warm glow at the thought of spending my life with such a man. I carried around serious trust issues because of bad experiences in the past with my ex-husband and ex-boyfriend. But, deep in my heart, I sensed Crusher would never betray me. Was I ready to confess the L-word? Was I finally ready for the M-word?

# CHAPTER 18

What other secrets lurked in the victim's computer? The more I learned about the dead woman, the more questions popped up. But before I could do any more digging, Crusher came home.

He sniffed the air like a dog. "I smell something delicious."

"Huh?"

"What're we having for dinner?"

*Oh, crap!* Tonight was my night to cook. But because of my late lunch, I'd completely forgotten about food. "I've been looking through Dolleen's digital files and must've lost track of time."

He strode over to the dining room table and bent to kiss me. "That's what I love about you, babe. You're not only tenacious, you're unapologetic."

I regarded the big man towering over me with a soft smile. He wasn't the least bit annoyed at my failure to uphold my end of our domestic deal. "Sorry, Yossi."

"You can make it up to me later." He looked at his

watch. "It's six thirty. I'll go to Mick's and bring back a couple of foot-longs. The usual?"

Mick owned a sandwich shop on the corner of Lindley and Ventura and made the best egg salad this side of heaven. I always ordered a crispy baguette with extra fresh onion sliced paper thin and pickled jalapeños. So what if I'd eaten a large lunch a mere four hours before? By the time Crusher returned, it would be four and a half hours. I could eat again.

While I waited for him to bring the food, Jazz called. "I just heard from Deke. He got a copy of the autopsy report. He said if the coroner has released the results, he's also released her body. How can we find out about the funeral?"

"I'm going to see Jonathan tonight. I'll ask him about Dolly's funeral and fill you in tomorrow morning when we meet at Lucy's for quilting."

Crusher came back with our sandwiches, and I updated him on the e-mail messages from Igo4you. "Dolly carried on a long-term affair with some guy. It's got to be Jonathan."

"You said he already denied everything this morning. What makes you think he'll admit to anything tonight?"

"Because this new information makes things look worse for his mother, Shelley. She'd already lost one man to Dolleen. Maybe she didn't want to lose a second one."

At ten past eight, Yossi answered the door still wearing his ATF badge.

Jonathan Shapira stepped inside, wearing an expensively tailored black leather jacket and Aviators, completely unnecessary at night. He peeled off his glasses and scowled at me. "I thought you said you weren't going to the cops."

"Relax. He lives here." I gestured toward the living room, hoping the soothing neutrals and light blues would calm him down. "Please have a seat."

Jonathan chose the easy chair with the slipcover and perched on the front edge of the seat cushion. He leaned forward, resting his forearms on his legs and looked from Crusher to me. "What do you want?"

"The whole truth this time." Out of the corner of my eye, I saw Crusher take a surreptitious picture of Jonathan with his cell phone. "Dolleen kept copies of e-mail messages in a folder labeled *J*. I think that's shorthand for *Jonathan*." I pointed my finger at him. "I know all about the Harlequin Hotel, Mr. Igo4you!"

He looked up sharply. "Who?"

"Don't pretend you don't know what I'm talking about. I'm good at uncovering secrets. Do you deny you used a secret e-mail account to arrange afternoon trysts at the Harlequin Hotel? Do you deny your mother found out and killed Dolleen?"

"That's exactly what I'm saying. My phone app keeps excellent records of my appointments and my whereabouts. All the data is retrievable." His body relaxed, and his face held a slightly triumphant expression. "You've got the wrong guy."

I sat back. I hated to admit it, but he could be telling the truth.

He narrowed his eyes and leaned in my direction. "Stay away from my mother. If you harass her in any

way, I'll get a restraining order. If you smear her
reputation, I'll ruin you."

Crusher had remained silent until that moment.
He stirred beside me, like a huge bear coming out
of his winter cave. "Dude."

One look at Crusher's intimidating face made
Jonathan sit back again, but he didn't remain silent.
"My mother has suffered enough."

"Not as much as Dolleen," I said. "She had friends
who loved her. They want to pay their respects and
say good-bye. I understand you're handling her
funeral."

He stood. "Forest Lawn Glendale. Wednesday
morning at eleven. Now go to hell."

Crusher walked beside him. Before opening the
front door, he wrapped his hand around Jonathan's
shoulder in a vise-like grip and murmured something I couldn't hear. Jonathan took one last look at
me and left.

I went into the kitchen and opened a bottle of my
favorite Ruffino Chianti Classico, filled two red
Moroccan tea glasses with gold curlicues, and handed
one to Crusher. "I saw you taking his picture earlier.
Why?"

He shrugged. "I figured we could set up our own
murder board in your sewing room."

"You mean like the ones on *Castle* and *Major
Crimes*?"

He laughed at the references to my favorite TV
cop shows. "More like the ones we use in real life."

Quilters often used a design board when planning a new quilt. Mine consisted of a white flannel
sheet tacked to one wall of my sewing room. Small

pieces of cloth easily stuck to the fuzzy nap of the
flannel. At the moment, swatches of various green
cotton prints were pinned next to each other, waiting to be selected for my next project. I removed
the little bits of fabric to make room for a new kind
of display.

Crusher printed out the photo of Jonathan from
his cell phone. He also printed separate images of
Dolleen, David, and Shelley he found on the Internet. I added the photo of the Hawkins' house I'd
taken from Dolleen's front porch.

I used straight pins with spherical glass heads to
stitch each photo to the flannel sheet and fetched a
pen and some note cards. I wrote whatever information I'd gathered and pinned the comments below
each photo.

DOLLEEN—VICTIM
hidden millions
still married
paid restitution
affair, Harlequin Hotel, (Igo4you?)

DAVID—HUSBAND
prison 2009
hidden millions
threatening e-mails

JONATHAN—STEPSON
received allowance
friendly with Dolleen
lover (?)

SHELLEY—EX-WIFE
angry divorce
unhappy $ settlement
jealousy (?)
suspicious of affair (?)

ABEL—FATHER-IN-LAW
believes David framed
fond of Dolleen
proud of grandson
dated Emma

Although I didn't have photos, I pinned up notes on two more people.

KIKI HAWKINS—NEIGHBOR
lied to police about Jazz
has key to house
knew about key to storage space
older than husband (she has the money?)

EMMA FISHBLATT—MOTHER FIGURE
small investor, lost everything
reimbursed by Dolleen
mother figure
once dated Abel

"You've talked to all these people?" Crusher asked.
"Yes." I studied the board for a moment. "This would be so much easier if we were the LAPD. We could grill some of them and demand an alibi for the time of the murder."

"Babe." Crusher chuckled. "Don't forget to look for a motive. Motive, means, and opportunity."

A wave of fatigue washed over me after the wine and the long day. I rubbed my eyes. "You're right. But right now, my brain is cooked."

Crusher kissed my forehead. "Go to sleep. I'll clean up."

"Thanks." I stumbled toward the bedroom with barely enough energy to get into my pajamas and collapse into bed. Just before falling asleep, I pictured the murder board and a vague feeling nagged at me. *I'm missing something important.* Whatever it was would have to wait.

# CHAPTER 19

I woke up late on Quilty Tuesday morning, aching from sleeping in the same position all night. A note from Crusher waited for me in the kitchen next to a pot of coffee.

*Dear Mrs. Levy, Had to leave early. Fed the cat.*
*Love, Mr. Levy.*

I wasn't Mrs. Levy yet, but the idea was slowly growing on me, and he knew it. I poured a cup of Italian Roast and called my best friend. "Hey, Lucy. Do you think you could bring Birdie to my house this time for quilting? I want to show you something in my sewing room."

"Have you assembled the top of Birdie's Barn Raising quilt already?"

"Jazz and I did that on Sunday, but I'm talking about something different. Yossi helped me turn my design wall into a murder board."

"You mean like they do on *Castle* and *Major Crimes*?"

See? No wonder we were best friends.

I called Jazz next. "We're meeting at my house instead of Lucy's today. There's something I want you to see."

I dressed quickly and dashed over to Bea's Bakery in Tarzana for a pink box full of chocolate lace cookies and almond bear claws to serve with coffee. I also bought a loaf of deli rye.

The familiar aroma of garlic, savory cold cuts, and chicken soup embraced me the minute I walked into Mort's Deli next door. I bought sliced beef pastrami and chopped chicken liver for sandwiches and a pint each of fresh coleslaw and potato salad. The white butcher paper crinkled as the counterman wrapped my food and winked. "I threw in some kosher pickles and green tomatoes."

I rushed home, set out the pastries, and started a fresh pot of coffee. The clock read fifteen minutes before ten, so I walked to my sewing room to look at the murder board before everyone arrived. Bless him. While I slept last night, Crusher added more items: the list from Dolleen's computer of seniors who were receiving reimbursements; the list Emma gave me of the seniors who were not receiving reimbursements; and copies of the messages from Kurt Nixon and C. Evelyn specifically threatening Dolleen's life.

As I stared at the board, an elusive thought darted around in my head, daring to be captured. Something was still missing. What was it?

Everyone arrived at the same time and headed for the living room, carrying tote bags full of their current quilting projects. Jazz put Zsa Zsa's carrier on the floor and the little Maltese jumped out wearing a red gingham sundress with toenails painted scarlet. She greeted each of us and then trotted down the hall, probably looking for my cat Bumper.

"Okay, girlfriend, let's see this murder board." Lucy rubbed her hands together.

I led the troop to my sewing room and stepped aside so they could approach the white flannel sheet that once served as my design wall. "What do you think?"

Birdie's eyes sparkled. "Oh, Martha dear, it looks just like the ones on TV. Very professional."

Jazz raised his eyebrows and pouted. "Where's *my* picture?"

"You're not a suspect."

"You may not consider me a suspect, but the police still do." He pushed his shoulders back. "I think I deserve a space up there." He removed his cell phone from the pocket of his red gingham shirt and took a selfie. "Here. I'm sending this to your e-mail right now."

I rolled my eyes, printed out his picture, and pinned it on the murder board. "There. Satisfied?"

He studied the photo. "I think I can do better. There's a shadow under my nose. Where is some paper?"

I handed him the note cards and a pen. He wrote

JAZZ FLETCHER—FALSELY ACCUSED
 SUSPECT
loyal friend of victim
incredibly talented fashion designer and quilter
Wouldn't hurt a fly

"Okay. Put this up." He handed me the note with a flourish.

I noticed he omitted the hyphenated WATSON at the end of his name. I wondered if it was an indication he was already moving on. At the séance yesterday, Russell's spirit had supposedly given him permission to date again.

"Do you see any pattern emerging?" Birdie gestured toward my design wall.

I shook my head. "Not yet."

I told them about my meeting yesterday morning with Jonathan Shapira. "He denied knowing anyone with a motive to kill Dolleen and defended his mother. I basically came away with nothing from our first conversation. But later in the day, I combed through Dolleen's e-mails and found a bombshell."

I told them about her trysts in the Harlequin Hotel. "I confronted Jonathan with this new information in our second conversation, last night, but he still denied being Mr. Igo4you."

"Do you believe him?" asked Birdie.

"I found him very convincing." I sighed. "He could be telling the truth."

"Or he's a good liar," said Lucy. "Like father, like son."

"You're right." I pointed to his photo. "To find out for sure, I'm going to take this picture to the hotel and see if anyone can identify him as the person Dolleen had been meeting over the last three years."

"What makes you think they'll tell you anything?" asked Lucy. "After all, you're not the police."

"Lucy's right." Jazz crossed his arms. "I should go

with you. The Harlequin is in West Hollywood, not too far from my shop. I go there sometimes after work. The bartender is an old friend of mine. He'll talk to me."

"Can you go this afternoon?"

Jazz pulled out his cell phone again and scrolled through the screen. "Yes. But I have to be back in my store by five. Johnny's coming in for a fitting." Johnny Depp, one of Jazz's loyal customers, ordered seasonal clothes from the designer four times a year. No doubt Jazz would be fitting the actor with his new summer line.

"What did you find out from your encounter with Dolly's neighbor yesterday?" he asked. "Is she the one who's been lying to the police about me?"

"Yes, she's the witness, all right. And we can prove she's lying." I went into detail about my meeting with Kiki Hawkins. "I also recognized her voice. She's definitely the mysterious intruder from the night you and I broke in. She admitted to having a key to Dolleen's place for emergencies. But she denied knowing about the padlock key to the storage space."

Jazz seemed to hang on my every word. "That's a lie! She knew about the storage key because we were there when she came looking for it. Did you get any sense of why this witch would lie about me?"

"Actually, no."

"Well, what is she like?"

"Petite, a mousy forty with a much younger husband." I describe the handsome Mr. Hawkins and my mistaking him for the pool guy. "I suspect Kiki is the one with the money, which would explain why they're together. Don't worry, Jazz. If she tries to lie under oath, Deke will destroy her."

"Is that before or after they put me in an orange jumpsuit? What did you find out about Dolly's funeral?"

Poor Jazz. I kept forgetting he wasn't just fighting to prove he didn't kill Dolleen. He was also mourning the passing of a close friend.

I patted his arm. "I didn't forget to ask. She'll be buried in Forest Lawn Glendale tomorrow morning at eleven. I'll meet you there."

"Me too," said Birdie and Lucy together.

He nodded and typed something into his cell phone.

We returned to the living room and began working on our quilts. Birdie's current appliqué project consisted of a wreath of cabbage roses and colorful spring flowers layered petal by petal on a mint-green background with an overall leafy shadow print.

Lucy pieced pink basket blocks for a baby quilt. Her oldest son, Ray, and his wife, Tanya, went through a marital crisis last year but had reconciled. Now they were expecting a fourth child, their first girl.

Jazz worked on a Dresden Plate block, which consisted of a twelve-inch circle composed of fabric arranged in rays, much like a child's drawing of the sun. He'd cut up Russell's old silk neckties to create the wedges for the plate, using the pointed tips to create a serrated edge. The plate was then appliquéd to a fifteen-inch square of shirting with narrow blue and white stripes, yielding a colorful and masculine overall effect.

I hand-stitched the seams of my Prairie Braid

quilt. As always, my breathing slowed down to match the steady rhythm of the needle as I sewed each piece of the pattern. Quilting proved better than Xanax for calming the body and the mind.

After our lunch break, Lucy and Birdie insisted on accompanying me to the Harlequin Hotel. I unpinned both Dolleen's and Jonathan's photos from the murder board and jumped in the back seat of Lucy's vintage Caddy. We followed Jazz's Mercedes over Coldwater Canyon into West Hollywood.


The Harlequin Hotel occupied a converted art deco apartment building just off Sunset Boulevard on Sweetzer. The architecture over the doorway suggested a three-story fan folded into white plaster pleats. Lucy surrendered the car keys to the valet, and we joined Jazz at the entrance, where he waited with Zsa Zsa.

Inside a carpeted lobby no one seemed to notice or care about the animal in his arms. This was Hollywood, after all. He pointed to a dimly lit room to our right and said in a confidential voice, "That's where we'll find Kevin. Just let me do the talking."

The small bar area was about the size of my living room, with dark wood paneling and a giant mirror behind the polished wooden counter. Eight round cocktail tables and chairs crowded the floor and six stools were pushed against the bar. The bartender reminded me of a thousand other aging wannabe actors, with bleached blond hair going thin and a tight black T-shirt showing off biceps gone slightly flabby. He spared us a curious look and then said, "Hey, Jazz. You're early."

Jazz sashayed up to the bar and plunked on a stool, motioning for the three of us to join him. "Hi, Kev. These are my friends: Birdie, Martha, and Lucy. Birdie was Rusty's wife."

Kevin's eyes widened in surprise. "Really? I'm so sorry for your loss. I've known Jazz and Rusty for years." He leaned across the bar and rubbed the top of Zsa Zsa's head. "I was the headliner at Finocchio's in San Francisco for many years. Jazz made all my costumes until Rusty stole him away." He winked. "When the club closed down at the end of 1999, I moved to LA to perform at Rage on Santa Monica Boulevard."

He reached underneath the bar for a chilled bottle of Pinot Grigio with the cork already removed. "I just do this job in between gigs. Can I pour you some wine? On the house."

Lucy waved her hand in the air. "Thanks, hon. Not for me. I'm driving."

Birdie and I also declined.

Jazz said, "Kevin, we're trying to locate someone." He looked at me, and I handed him the photos from the murder board. "This woman used to come here regularly in the afternoons. Do you recognize her?"

The bartender picked up the photo of Dolleen and almost immediately said, "Yeah. I recognize her. She had a thing going with some guy. They never stayed overnight or anything like that. But I saw them going upstairs."

My heart sped up. I knew Jazz asked to do all the talking, but I couldn't help myself. "Would you also recognize the man with her?"

Jazz scowled at me and then handed Kevin the photo of Jonathan.

The bartender slowly shook his head. "There's a definite resemblance, but this isn't the same man. For one thing, the guy with her was *very* buff."

My heart raced a little more. "Are you certain?"

Kevin nodded. "Oh, yeah. I wouldn't forget a cute butt like his. I think she called him Jimmy. Does that help?"

"The name *Jimmy* hasn't come up in our investigation yet, but it's an important piece of information."

So, the J folder didn't belong to Jonathan; it belonged to Jimmy. I must have been really tired yesterday to have overlooked the obvious. Now, however, I knew the name of the person missing from my murder board. And I was fairly certain I knew who Jimmy was.

# CHAPTER 20

As we waited outside the Harlequin Hotel for the valet to bring our cars, I realized my cell phone had been on mute. A little icon told me I had a voice mail, which turned out to be from Emma Fishblatt. "There's something you should know. Please call me back as soon as you can."

I tried her number, but she didn't answer. Was she ill? Did something happen to her? I told my friends about Emma's message. "We need to check on her."

Jazz pulled a tiny bone-shaped biscuit out of his pocket and fed it to Zsa Zsa. "I can't go. I've got to get back to the shop."

Just then the valet appeared with his blue Mercedes S class and held open the driver's door.

Jazz secured the dog carrier on the front passenger seat and rounded the car to his side. "Let me know what happens." He threw us an air kiss and drove off.

Lucy checked her watch. "It's four, and rush hour has already started. Even though Park La Brea is not that far from here, it might take us a while to reach her."

Birdie adjusted her black fanny pack. "I wonder what she wants."

"I don't know, but maybe Emma can tell us about Dolleen's affair. She may even know who it was with."

"I wonder why she didn't say something before." Birdie frowned.

"When we first spoke to her, we didn't know about the Harlequin Hotel." I shrugged. "Maybe Emma didn't volunteer the information because she tried to protect Dolleen's reputation. After all, she was still married to David, even though he sat in prison."

Lucy snorted. "In this day and age? Having an affair, especially under those circumstances, would hardly raise an eyebrow."

"Yes, but Emma's from a different era, one with very strict social rules. Do you remember what she said about her father? He wouldn't let her get married before her older sister. And because the sister never married, Emma was forced into spinsterhood. Someone like her might be very sensitive about social norms."

The valet reappeared with the black Caddy. Lucy walked to the driver's side and handed him a five. "Well, we shall soon find out."

We drove south on Sweetzer until we hit Fountain Avenue, then turned east. Cars crawled along the major Boulevards and Avenues, so we turned south on Detroit Street to Emma's house. With all the stop signs along the way, we probably didn't save much time, but at least we were moving.

"How are the wedding plans coming along?" Lucy smiled at Birdie.

"Everything's a mess!" Birdie waved a hand in the air. "Apparently, there's a huge division among the Watson cousins. A small faction insists our marriage won't be valid unless we say our vows in church. With a 'real' minister officiating. They're threatening to boycott the wedding if Phoebe performs the ceremony in the great outdoors. Honestly!"

"How many people are we talking about, hon?" Lucy glanced at Birdie.

"At least two extended families. That's a lot of cousins, because those people take procreation as a serious mandate from God."

"Good grief. What does Denver say?"

Birdie sighed. "He claims he doesn't care, but I know he'd be hurt if some of the cousins didn't show up. They're even claiming it's incest for a man to marry his brother's wife."

"What?" I could no longer remain silent. "That's baloney! There's a specific commandment in Torah compelling a man to marry his brother's wife if the brother dies without a son—which Russell did."

"Really?" Birdie turned in her seat to look at me. "I think Denny would feel much better if he had something like that to show the cousins. Where in the Bible can we find the passage?"

"Deuteronomy. Just Google *Leverite marriage*."

"What about the rest of the clan?" asked Lucy.

Birdie smiled. "They're a mixed bunch of atheists

and old hippies. They'll show up regardless." She giggled. "They'd probably love to see me in the last wedding costume Jazz designed."

"The green-and-black stripe with the ten-foot train?" Lucy smiled. "I could easily see Kevin the bartender wearing it in his heyday as a female impersonator, can't you? But the thought of you wearing that costume horrifies me. Don't tell Jazz I said so."

When we finally arrived at our destination, I spied a familiar silver Camry sitting on the street in front of Emma's duplex. "Oh, no!" I said. "That's Arlo's car."

"*Uh-oh*. What now?" asked Lucy.

I swallowed. "Emma's message sounded urgent. I say we go inside."

"But won't Arlo be mad?" Birdie grabbed her long, white braid for comfort.

"Mad about what? We're checking up on an elderly friend. Besides, what if Kaplan is also inside? Emma said he threatened her before. She might welcome the presence of three allies right about now."

Lucy unbuckled her seatbelt and opened the car door. "Let's do it."

We hustled to the front porch and knocked loudly.

Emma peeked out at us and quickly opened her door. Her spotted skin stretched tightly over her knobby knuckles as she clutched the top of her pink hand-knitted cardigan. Her face told me everything I needed to know.

"Don't worry," I whispered. "Just let me handle this."

She nodded quietly and stepped aside to let us in.

Kaplan and Beavers stood in the middle of the room. I recognized the tactic. Make the suspect sit down while you stand over them to assert your power and show them who's in charge—a form of psychological intimidation.

Beavers's dark eyes flashed in anger when he saw me. "This is classic."

Kaplan shouted, "What the hell?"

"Language, Detective. Watch it." I gestured with my head toward Emma.

"I told you I'd arrest you for interfering with our investigation," he snarled.

"Interfering? We're only checking up on a friend of my uncle Isaac. Can we help it if she's also a friend of your murder victim?" I turned toward Emma and winked. "Sorry we're a little late. We got hung up in traffic. Are you ready to go shopping at the Farmer's Market?"

A wave of comprehension swept over her face, and she didn't miss a beat. "Yes, I'm ready. It's so nice of Isaac to arrange for you to take me." Emma was almost eighty and still sharp as a tack. As far as I could tell, she didn't have to worry about the Fishblatt curse.

"We're not through!" Kaplan crossed impatient arms over his chest.

"Are you going to arrest this elderly woman?" I smiled sweetly. "Have you Mirandized her?"

Emma sidled next to me and grabbed my left arm for support. She pretended to be muddled and confused. "My goodness. Do I need a lawyer?" She squeezed my arm twice in a secret signal.

*That's my girl. She's playing along perfectly.*

The four of us stood together and waited for a response from the police. Beavers didn't speak at first. But by the look in his eyes, I knew he'd figured out what we just did. Finally, he spoke. "We have no intention of arresting you, Miss Fishblatt. But we do want to ask one more thing. Do you have any idea who would benefit from Ms. Doyle's death?"

Emma squeezed my arm hard. "No, but I presume her lawyer could tell you. Now really, I have to leave for the market. So, if there's nothing else?" I couldn't tell from Emma's answer whether or not she knew anything more.

Beavers's expression broadcast frustration, but he backed off and grunted. "Not at the moment."

Kaplan wasn't so sanguine. He growled at me on his way to the door. "You don't fool me one bit."

Lucy walked with the two detectives and shut the front door behind them. "You haven't heard the last of them, hon."

Emma sighed and let go of my arm. "Thank you for standing up for me. Why are you here?"

"I heard your voice mail and became worried when you didn't pick up your phone."

Emma sighed. "I'm glad you came. Thank goodness they're gone."

"They're not gone, dear." Birdie stood at the bay window looking out to the street. "They're still sitting in Arlo's car. I think they want to see if we were telling the truth about taking Emma shopping."

"Well, let's not give Kaplan a reason to charge me

with interfering in a police investigation, then." I grabbed Emma's hand and smiled. "It's been ages since I've been to the Farmer's Market. If nothing else, we can stop for some pastries at the Russian bakery."

"Can we go to Du-Par's for an early bite?" Emma's eyes filled. "That's where Dolly used to take me."

A quick glance at Lucy and Birdie told me the answer was yes. Almost simultaneously they reached for their cell phones. Ray Mondello and Denver Watson would have to fend for themselves tonight.

"What a great idea," I said.

Emma exchanged her fuzzy pink slippers for sensible black shoes with two-inch chubby heels. She sat in the front seat of Lucy's Caddy, clutching a black vinyl handbag on her lap while Birdie and I sat in the back. At nearly five, the traffic crawled through every street. We slowly headed for the corner of Third and Fairfax and the iconic LA landmark, the Farmer's Market.

The Market began life in 1934 as a place where local growers sold fresh produce first from the backs of their trucks and eventually from permanent stalls. Over time, as the surrounding farmland gave way to urban development, the Market became an oasis in the growing city landscape. Even in the present, it remained a favorite of Angelinos and a must-see destination for tourists beguiled by the sweet and savory smells filling the air.

I turned slightly in my seat to look out the car's back window. The silver Camry stayed right on our tail. Lucy's turn signal ticked steadily as she slowed and entered the parking lot. The detectives didn't follow us but continued north toward the San Fernando Valley. I raised my hand and wiggled my fingers in farewell as they passed by. Kaplan looked pissed.

Shoppers navigated through an obstacle course of outdoor tables and wooden chairs to visit the restaurants, specialty shops, and food stalls. This could be a daunting experience for the elderly, especially when the market was crowded. Du-Par's restaurant, on the other hand, was located on the perimeter and easily accessible from the street. I suspected that was why Emma chose to dine there.

Inside Du-Par's, the hostess showed us to a booth upholstered in red leatherette. Patterned carpeting muffled our footsteps. I sat next to Emma on one side, and Lucy sat with Birdie on the other. The hostess handed us menus consisting of typical diner selections. In addition to using fresh ingredients, Du-Par's was famous for its bakery featuring a large selection of pies.

"What are you having?" I turned to face Emma.

"I always order the same thing." She smiled. "Braised tri-tip and lemon meringue pie for dessert."

The waiter brought us a basket of warm dinner rolls and took our orders.

When he left, I faced Emma again. "We now know Dolleen regularly met a man at the Harlequin Hotel. Did you know?"

The old woman clasped her hands together and pursed her lips. "At a hotel? Are you saying Dolly was having an affair?"

"Yes. We have e-mails and a witness to prove it."

I showed her Jonathan Shapira's picture. "Do you know him?"

Emma nodded. "Of course. That's Jonathan, Dolly's stepson."

"What do you know about their relationship?"

"They were good friends, and he sometimes helped her with legal matters. I'm pretty sure he helped her make out a will. I can't believe Dolly had an affair with her stepson." Emma looked at the table. "That wouldn't be proper."

I sighed. "I don't believe Dolleen met with Jonathan at the hotel. The witness said she called the man *Jimmy*. Did she ever mention the name to you?"

Emma briefly closed her eyes. "*Hmm*. Not so I recall." She cleared her throat. "But I'm glad it wasn't Jonathan. I can't imagine what his mother would do if she found out he carried on an affair with her ex-husband's new wife."

The more I learned about David Shapira's first wife, Shelley, the more I realized how deep her anger and jealousy ran. She hated Dolleen, the woman who broke up her marriage. Not for the first time, I wondered how much more Shelley might hate her if she suspected an affair between her son, Jonathan, and Dolleen.

"What about Abel Shapira, David's father? You used to date him. Did he ever mention how he felt about Dolleen?"

"He never said anything bad to me. I do know David counted on Dolly to take care of his father, so Dolly gave him a generous allowance. Abel knew which side of his bread was buttered, so it was to his advantage to stay on good terms with her."

Emma stopped speaking when the waiter appeared with our food. Chicken-fried steak for Lucy, gourmet meatloaf for Birdie, and a burger with extra onions for me. The plates were hot, and the portions generous.

"What do you know about Dolleen's neighbors, the Hawkinses?" I picked up my sandwich with both hands and took a bite.

Emma cut a dainty piece of braised tri tip and lifted the fork to her mouth with her left hand, European style. "Dolly and the wife were very close and spent a lot of time together. She said Kiki was like an older sister."

Emma's account supported Kiki's story. "What about the husband?"

"The husband's name was James. I think she must've had a good relationship with him as well. She said the three of them often spent evenings watching movies or playing scrabble."

*Just as I suspected!* James Hawkins was the Jimmy missing from my murder board. He must've sent the e-mails we found in Dolleen's J folder; Mr. Igo4you. From my glimpse of him cleaning the pool, he certainly fit the description of her buff lover given to us by Kevin the bartender.

That raised a new question. Did Kiki find out Dolleen carried on an affair with her husband? Did she murder her best friend for that betrayal? Could that be the reason she lied to the police and pointed a finger at Jazz?

"Emma, did Dolleen ever mention having feelings for James?"

"Not that I recall." The old woman stopped suddenly and her eyes widened. "Oh my. Do you think he's Dolly's Jimmy?"

# CHAPTER 21

We left Du-Par's and entered the Farmer's Market, slowly threading our way through the scattered tables and chairs to the Russian bakery located in one of the middle stalls. I treated Emma to a fresh supply of hamantaschen, shortbread cookies filled with fruit paste. I didn't ask her why she bought leaven so close to Passover, because most Jews weren't like Uncle Isaac. They didn't literally rid their houses of all leaven. They just didn't use it during the eight days of the festival.

"Thank you," she said. "I always like to keep a supply in the freezer for company."

Twenty minutes later, we deposited the older woman safely in her home. What was it with the sluggish metabolism of some seniors? The temperature inside felt as hot as Death Valley in August.

She hugged the pink bakery box with one hand and her black vinyl handbag with the other. "What shall I do if the police come around again?"

"It's probably safe to answer their questions. After all, we want the same thing—to find Dolleen's killer.

However, if you feel you need an attorney, I can refer you to the same person who is helping Jazz. By the way, do you have a ride to Dolleen's funeral tomorrow morning?"

"Yes. I'm driving some of the people from the center. You know"—Emma dipped her chin—"some of the others Dolly helped." If the nearly 80-year-old Emma was anything like the 60-something Lucy, she'd take forever to drive to Glendale. I hoped she planned to leave early.

We said our good-byes at seven and headed back toward the freeway.

"Dolleen's neighbor, James Hawkins, has got to be the lover," I said.

Lucy maneuvered the Caddy onto the on-ramp of the 405 Freeway, heading north. "Everything points his way." She looked over her left shoulder for oncoming traffic and sped up as she merged into the nearest lane.

Birdie hung on to the grab bar.

I relaxed into the buttery soft leather of the backseat. "If James's wife, Kiki, discovered the affair, she'd have a motive for murder."

We cruised at a steady 50 miles per hour in the slow lane. Rush hour had passed, and cars zipped by us on the left. Freeways made Lucy nervous, so she always hugged the right shoulder at a reduced speed. If I were driving, we'd be home by now.

Birdie let go of the clutch bar and turned slightly in her seat to look at me. "That would also explain why she lied to the police about witnessing Jazz leaving Dolleen's place on the night of the murder.

So, why do you think she came after the key to the storage facility?"

"Good question. Maybe she wanted to destroy any evidence identifying her husband as Dolleen's lover. Since Arlo and Kaplan have Dolleen's computer, it's only a matter of time before they ask these same questions and come to the same conclusion we did—Kiki Hawkins could've killed her out of jealousy and rage."

"The police can get there another way." Birdie tapped the side of her head like Hercule Poirot. "They can find out who Igo4you is simply by tracing the e-mails. There's plenty of technology to do that now."

I smiled at Birdie and her knowledge of TV forensics. "You're absolutely right. They have the means to get there much faster. The only question is, do they have the will to do it?"

We pulled up to my house just before eight. The front was dark, but a light burned behind the drapes in the windows. The hairs on the back of my neck bristled. Something felt way off. We left the house around two, when there was plenty of daylight. How did a lamp get turned on? Crusher's Harley was nowhere to be found, which meant he couldn't be home yet. Besides, if he'd gotten here before me, he'd have turned on the porch light so I wouldn't stumble in the dark. Plus, the drapes had been open this morning to let in the natural light, so important to quilting. Now they were closed.

"Bye, hon." Lucy twisted around in the driver's seat to smile and wink at me. "What Ray doesn't know won't hurt him."

I pulled out my cell phone. "Uh, Lucy, can you wait until I call Yossi? Something doesn't feel right."

"Isn't that him?" Birdie pointed to the house. We all watched a person's shadow move across the living room toward the window. The edge of the drape flicked open just enough for someone to peek out and see Lucy's car. Then it quickly closed again. My gut tightened when I realized the shadow was much shorter than Crusher's six foot six inches.

"That's not Yossi!" I pressed the icon next to his name, but the call went straight to voice mail. "Yossi, call me. Someone's in the house."

Next I called Detective Arlo Beavers. He picked up on the fourth ring. "When I saw it was you, I almost didn't answer. But I want to know. What the hell were you trying to accomplish earlier today?"

My voice shook. "Arlo, I just got home, and I'm sitting in Lucy's car outside my house. There's someone inside!"

"Probably your boyfriend. If you don't want him there, get a lawyer and change your locks. I haven't got time for this."

"Wait! It's not Yossi. Do you think I'd call you if I weren't really terrified? I need your help."

"Only if you tell me what you know when I get there. Otherwise, I'll notify dispatch and send some uniforms to clean up your latest mess."

"Deal."

"You're lucky I'm only a couple minutes away. Sit tight."

Two minutes later we heard the sirens. Two black and whites showed up, along with Beavers, who drove a car I didn't recognize. He stepped out of a black Ford and, thankfully, Kaplan wasn't with him. I didn't think I could deal with his hostility in the midst of everything else.

As soon as Beavers parked, I jumped out of Lucy's car and rushed over to him. "Thank you so much for coming, Arlo. He's still in there."

"Give me your key." He reached under his jacket and pulled out his gun from his shoulder holster.

I ran back to the car, quickly retrieved my house key, and handed it to Beavers. He pointed to Lucy's Caddy. "Get back in the car and stay there until I tell you otherwise." He gestured to the uniforms. With two fingers, he sent one pair to the rear of the house, guns drawn. The other two followed him to my front door, Glocks in hand.

I slipped into the backseat of Lucy's car. Nobody spoke. We held our breaths and watched Beavers unlock the front door.

Suddenly, they burst through to the inside and shouted, "LAPD! Hands up!"

"Don't shoot! Don't shoot!" a woman's voice screamed.

Lucy's mouth fell open. "Paulina was right! The killer's a woman! She must've known you were closing in so she came here to kill you too."

We heard the woman sobbing inside the house but couldn't make out the conversation. After ten minutes, Beavers appeared in the doorway and motioned for me to come inside. The four uniforms got back in their squad cars and drove away.

"I want to hear this." Lucy unbuckled her seatbelt.

"Me too." Birdie opened her door. "Even though Dolleen's neighbor Kiki is the most obvious suspect, my money's still on the ex-wife, Shelley. It's always the one you least expect."

If Birdie's words could be turned into solid gold, we'd all be rich. The woman sitting in my house was the last person I'd suspect of murder. In fact, there was no way she could've been Dolleen's killer. Apparently, Beavers agreed, because she sat on my sofa. Without handcuffs.

Birdie and Lucy stood with their mouths open in disbelief. I sat down next to the trembling woman and spoke in a soft voice. "Hello, Sonia. What were you doing here? You gave me quite a scare." Sonia Spiegelman, aging flower child, one-time girlfriend of Mick Jagger, and neighborhood *yenta*, lived across the street from me. I'd given her a key to my house in case of an emergency. Her mascara and green eye makeup were smeared over her face from crying. I felt awful.

She glanced at Beavers, who stood with his arms crossed. "I noticed you and your friends drive off this afternoon." Okay. Sonia was nosey; that was the job of a yenta—to know everyone else's business. But to her credit, she did organize a super neighborhood watch, The Eyes of Encino, and took her role as captain very seriously.

"When you hadn't come home for several hours, I realized Bumper must be hungry. So, I let myself in to feed him." She spoke with hooded eyes and a scold in her voice. "It was long past meal time, Martha. His bowl was completely empty. After he ate, we sat for a little snuggle."

I sighed. Sonia bonded with my cat and took great care of him when I went out of town.

"When I heard a car drive up," she continued, "I peeked out the window and saw your friend Lucy's Cadillac. I decided to wait inside for you to say hello." She sniffed. "I was only trying to help out."

"Of course you were, Sonia. Thank you for looking out for Bumper. But maybe next time you can call me first to give me a heads-up?"

Sonia pulled back a little. "I did call you. And when you didn't answer, I left a message."

"Really?" I looked at my cell phone. Sure enough, an icon indicated I had a couple new voice mails. "Sorry. I've just got to learn how to work this thing better."

Lucy yawned. "I'm glad we got this straightened out and everyone's okay. Birdie and I are going home now. Be at my house by ten tomorrow morning, and we'll drive to Dolleen's funeral together." She patted Beavers's shoulder on the way to the door. "Nice to see you again, Arlo."

"Yes," said Birdie. "So nice to see you again, dear."

Sonia stood and looked at Beavers. "If it's all right, I want to go too."

I walked her to the door. "Are you sure you won't stay for a glass of wine? You look like you could use one right about now."

She sighed and lowered her voice. "No, but you're right about my needing something for my nerves. I'm going to spend the rest of the evening with Mister B." Mister B was Sonia's bong. She had a prescription for medical marijuana to treat a mysterious ailment I had yet to figure out.

As soon as I closed the front door, Beavers said, "Now it's time for you to live up to your end of the bargain. You can begin by explaining what that thing is in the other room."

"By 'thing,' I'm assuming you mean my murder board?"

He rolled his eyes. "For the love of God! This time you've gone off the deep end."

"Not really. Let me show you." I headed for my sewing room and he followed. I picked up a fresh note card, wrote a new entry and pinned it up on the white flannel sheet. "This is what we found out today."

JAMES HAWKINS—NEIGHBOR
Kiki's husband
Probable lover
Dolleen's J folder
Mister Igo4you (?)

Then I added one item to the note under his wife's name: *Jealous over husband's affair?*

Beavers studied the information pinned to the flannel sheet in silence. He finally turned to me and said, "Some of your information came directly off the victim's computer. How did you get hold of it?"

*Think fast, Martha.* "Would you believe that in addition to the hate mail she gave to Jazz for safekeeping, Dolleen also entrusted him with a flash drive containing her computer files?" I searched his eyes and held my breath.

Beavers knew me well enough to figure out when I improvised with the facts. I could tell he didn't believe a word I said. He pointed to the flannel sheet. "How do you explain these photocopies of bank statements we found in a file cabinet and *not* in her computer?"

I pressed my lips together, turned my palms out, and hummed an *I don't know* sound.

He narrowed his eyes and pointed to one of Emma's list of names. "What's this?"

I revealed how, with Emma's help, Dolleen singled out the most desperate seniors to reimburse. The next list he examined belonged to the seniors who did not receive any reimbursement. When I finished sharing everything I knew, I said, "Dolleen could've been killed for two very different reasons. Either for money or because of the love affair. If it was the latter, I'd take a very close look at her neighbor, James Hawkins. But if money was the motive, your job will be a lot harder. After all, David Shapira bilked hundreds of people."

Beavers said, "Thanks for the insight."

I ignored the snarkasm. "Have you looked into those horrible letters from Kurt Nixon and C. Evelyn? They threatened Dolleen specifically."

"Surprisingly, we thought of that all on our own."

"And?"

He regarded me for a moment. "I have to admit, you've been resourceful. I've always given you credit for being very smart. You're good at figuring things out. You might've made a hell of a cop." I smiled at the unaccustomed praise until he held up his hand. "The problem is, Martha, you're not a cop." He gestured toward the murder board. "I don't believe you came by any of this information legally. You're impulsive and reckless, and you're breaking the law."

"Someone has to prove Jazz Fletcher didn't kill

Dolleen Doyle. And since neither you nor Kaplan seemed interested in looking elsewhere for the murderer, the job fell to his friends. Me, Lucy, and Birdie."

Just then, the back door squeaked open.

"Listen!" I whispered. "Someone's sneaking into the house."

Arlo reached for his gun again and pointed to the closet. "Hide!" he hissed.

My heart pounded wildly. I ducked inside. "Be careful, Arlo." Before I pulled the closet door closed, I saw him press up against wall, waiting to surprise the home invaders if they entered the sewing room. I said a little prayer. I'd never forgive myself if anything happened to Beavers.

Boots pounded into the sewing room, and a familiar voice shouted, "Federal Agents!"

*Oh crap.* I'd forgotten to call Yossi back. I opened the door a crack and peeked out.

Crusher stood poised to shoot. Beside him stood his friend Malo, an ATF agent I knew very well and a member of the Valley Eagles motorcycle club. Two additional voices shouted from my bedroom and the guest room down the hall. "Clear. Clear."

Crusher, my current boyfriend, and Beavers, my ex, stared at each other, slowly lowered their guns, and holstered their weapons.

"Where's my *fiancée*?" Crusher growled with emphasis on the last word.

Beavers slowly shook his head and jerked his thumb backward toward the closet.

I pushed the door all the way open and stepped out of my hiding place. Five pairs of eyes stared at me.

I wiggled my fingertips. "Hi."

Malo's face relaxed into a grin, stretching the vertical lines tattooed on his cheeks. "*Esa!*" This Latino with a black ponytail just called me *homegirl*. Then he started to laugh.

# CHAPTER 22

Wednesday morning at ten, Lucy, Birdie, and I drove in the Caddy to the LA suburb of Glendale for Dolleen's funeral. Lucy sighed. "It seems like the only time we get to gussy up anymore is to bury somebody." Today my orange-haired friend wore a black linen dress and three-inch heels that boosted her height to well over six feet. Birdie wore lavender polyester, and I wore a gray suit.

Forest Lawn Memorial Park was a tourist destination for pilgrims who came to view the final resting places of many of the Hollywood elite. The huge complex incorporated three churches, mausoleums, and a hodgepodge of buildings with lavish architecture.

"I hope we get to see the Michelangelos," said Birdie.

"I hope we see Michael Jackson," replied Lucy.

Forest Lawn didn't have the actual marble statues, but it had acquired exact replicas of the iconic *David*, *Moses*, and *La Pietà*. These exquisite fakes were strategically placed around the grounds, along with other inspiring works of art. Guests could visit a stained-glass version of Da Vinci's *Last Supper* and two of the world's largest paintings depicting panoramic views of the crucifixion of Christ and his resurrection.

We drove through the gates on a tree-lined main drive. Mature shade trees dotted the manicured green hills as far as the eye could see. A more contemplative visitor could simply sit and enjoy the many gardens and the breathtaking view of the downtown LA skyline. Forest Lawn had something for everyone—living or dead.

We followed the signs to our destination, Wee Kirk o' the Heather, one of the three sister churches at Forest Lawn.

"Oh look." Birdie pointed to a stone tableau poised in the middle of a pond.

A woman with a pained expression stared down at a baby in a basket. I guessed it was supposed to be the moment, forever frozen in white marble, when Pharaoh's daughter discovered the baby Moses.

Wee Kirk, a small building clad in rough lime-stone brick, was tucked under shade trees. Jazz stood in the parking lot next to his Mercedes, talking to someone just out of sight behind him. He wore a black suit and carried a black doggie tote for Zsa Zsa.

"*Yoo-hoo!*" Lucy sang and waved as we walked toward him.

Jazz turned to look at us and waved back with one hand, while holding his little Maltese in the other. She wore a plain black dress and a black hat held on by an elastic band under her chin. A tiny veil of black netting hung over her eyes. When Jazz moved, we saw who'd been standing behind him— a dark-haired woman in a purple velvet cape. Paulina Polinskaya.

One by one, Jazz kissed the air beside our cheeks. "I'm so glad to see you. Paulina says Dolly's going to show up today."

*Of course she's going to show up. Who else would be occupying her casket?*

A naked Chihuahua poked her head out of the purple carrier draped over Paulina's arm. "Hathor insisted on paying her respects this morning." Was it my imagination, or did the dog, like Paulina, have dark lines painted around her eyes?

I knew from previous experience funerals were also where Paulina hustled a lot of new business from grieving people anxious to contact the dead. I guessed that somewhere inside Hathor's dog carrier a pocket bulged with purple brochures extolling her five-star rating on Yelp.

Jazz placed Zsa Zsa back in her carrier, and we joined a stream of visitors heading toward the church. On the way, we passed three squad cars, a couple of LAPD motorcycles, Beavers's silver Camry, and a black SUV with a blue-and-gold U.S. Marshal's logo on the door. Two LAPD officers stood in front of the double oak doors. One examined purses and bags, the other waved a hand-held metal detector over each mourner.

"Why the security?" asked Lucy.

"Maybe Dolleen's husband is here. If so, I'd sure like to talk to him."

When Jazz stepped up to be wanded, the policeman asked him to open the black tote bag. The cop stared at Zsa Zsa. "What's that?"

"*Who's* that?" Jazz corrected him. "She's my little girl, Zsa Zsa Galore. She goes with me everywhere. Zsa Zsa, say hello to the nice officer."

"No dogs allowed."

Jazz gasped. "I won't leave her in the car. Besides, isn't it against the law to leave dogs and children alone in a vehicle?"

I stepped forward. "She's a service dog, officer."

"Where's her jacket, then?" He jerked his thumb at the little Maltese, referring to the yellow vest worn by all service dogs when on duty.

Jazz sniffed. "She's wearing mourning attire. In honor of Dolly." For the first time, I noticed Jazz had painted Zsa Zsa's toenails black for today's occasion.

Paulina also stepped forward and extracted the Chihuahua from a purple carrier. "And this is Hathor. She lived with the departed. She wishes to say farewell."

Arlo Beavers came to the doorway and looked out at the crowd milling behind us. "What's the holdup, Mike?" Then he recognized me. "Of course. I should've known. What is it this time, Martha?"

The officer pointed to the dogs.

I said, "This is Dolleen's Chihuahua, remember? The Maltese is Jazz's service dog. They won't cause any problems. I guarantee it."

Beavers snorted. "A guarantee from you is what I live for. Let 'em in, Mike."

*Thank you,* I mouthed as we filed inside. An odd expression covered his face.

The sanctuary of Wee Kirk consisted of two rows of wooden pews on either side of a center aisle. Dolleen's polished walnut casket, covered with a spray of white and red roses, stood on a bier in front. Behind her, a plain golden cross sat on an altar draped with a white cloth. Bach played softly in the background, and hushed voices murmured in quiet conversation.

In the second pew from the front on the left side of the aisle sat three men. Two wore matching blue blazers and sat on either side of the third man in a black suit. I assumed those were the U.S. Marshals protecting the guy in the middle. They chose seats closest to a side door. Probably so they could quickly bundle the black suit outside in the event of any trouble.

Black suit turned his face to speak to blue blazer on his right. His hair was freshly barbered and the shoulders of his jacket fit perfectly. I couldn't read his expression, but I recognized his profile immediately.

I nudged Lucy with my elbow. "I was right. That's David Shapira. He's the reason for all this security."

"All the way from Leavenworth?" Lucy's jaw dropped. "How'd he manage to pull that off?"

Birdie tilted her head. "Remember, dear, he's a legendary con artist. He must've talked them into giving him some kind of compassionate leave to attend his wife's funeral."

"At taxpayer expense?" I wondered how much an LAPD security detail, two U.S. marshals, and three roundtrip airline tickets from Leavenworth, Kansas, would cost—not to mention lodging and meals. "What a waste. Instead of ending up in jail, he could've used the same skill set to become a member of Congress."

Paulina squinted her eyes. "His aura's dark."

*Duh.* She certainly was queen of the obvious today.

I wanted to position myself as close to David Shapira as possible without actually sitting on his lap. We filed into the pew directly behind him. Before sitting down, Paulina approached Dolleen's casket. She briefly rested her hand on the wood, closed her eyes, and muttered something. Every eye in the room watched this dark-haired woman in a purple cape glide back to our pew.

"What was *that* for?" I asked in a low voice.

Paulina leaned toward me and whispered, "I asked Dolleen if her killer was in this room. She said yes."

*Right.* However, despite my complete and utter skepticism, I checked all the faces in the room to see who it might be. Just in case.

David's son, Jonathan, and his father, Abel, sat in the pew next to the marshals. Three generations of Shapira men. The federal escorts didn't allow any physical contact, not even a handshake.

The neighbors, Kiki and James Hawkins, sat on the right side of the aisle. Kiki leaned into James and wiped her eyes. Were those tears an act? Had she really killed Dolleen out of jealousy?

Emma Fishblatt and four other seniors from the Jewish Center on Pico Boulevard sat in the pew behind them. I'd recognized her light-blue Cutlass in the parking lot. A few dozen other people were scattered in the rest of the pews on both sides of the aisle.

Birdie also scanned the room. "I'm impressed with the turnout."

"I recognize some of Dolly's loyal clients from her manscaping salon," Jazz said. "They're the smooth ones."

LAPD detectives Arlo Beavers and Noah Kaplan stood on either side of the double entry doors. A woman around fifty, with an expensive hairdo, sat in the last pew. She stared at the Shapira men with tight lips. I'd only viewed old photos on the Internet. Nevertheless, there was no mistaking Shelley Shapira. Why would David's ex-wife send his new wife off into the next world? Was Birdie right about her being the killer? Did she come to gloat over her victim? She'd never returned my call. I'd try to wangle an interview today.

The room continued to buzz with quiet chatter while we waited for the service to begin. The Chihuahua poked her head out of the purple carrier, sniffed the air, curled her lips, and began to howl. All conversation stopped and every head turned our way, including Abel, Jonathan, David, and the marshals. A cloud settled over Jonathan's face when he recognized me. Abel briefly locked gazes and turned back around. I couldn't read his expression.

David raised his brows in question marks when he witnessed our exchange. I smiled weakly at him and said over the dog's howls, "I'm so sorry for your loss."

I glanced at the back of the room. Beavers scowled at me and made a cutting gesture across his throat, as the dog continued to wail. I bit the corner of my lip and nodded. I did guarantee the dog's good behavior, after all. If she didn't stop her keening, she'd have to go outside.

Paulina managed to calm the dog into silence then leaned over and whispered, "I told you the killer's in this room. Hathor has picked up the scent."

# CHAPTER 23

"Can Hathor say who the killer is?" Jazz swiveled his head like a security camera panning across the faces.

Paulina stroked the shivering dog. "She's suffering a PTSD flashback right now. Maybe later."

The Maltese wiggled out of Jazz's arms and sat next to the Chihuahua on Paulina's lap. Zsa Zsa's little black hat wobbled up and down as she licked the top of Hathor's head in an attempt to comfort her.

A female minister in a black robe and white clerical collar walked to the front of the chapel and stood behind Dolleen's bier. Gray strands peppered her short hair, and the skin on her neck had lost its battle with gravity. She was joined by a young female rabbi wearing a prayer shawl, a yarmulke on top of her dark hair, and serious, black-rimmed glasses. I gave Jonathan credit. In arranging this funeral, he respected Dolleen's decision not to abandon her Christian faith. She'd entered into an interfaith marriage, and now she'd have an interfaith funeral.

The minister cleared her throat into a microphone

and the room became silent. "Good morning, everyone. My name is Reverend Hazelwood. I've known Dolleen Doyle ever since she came to LA as a wide-eyed girl from a small Midwestern town. She developed a deep sense of compassion growing up in an orphanage. Her faith in the Lord was strong, and she tried to lead a Christian life.

"Dolly learned a trade in the beauty industry and hoped one day to own her own business. Then she met her husband, David, and for a while her life took on an entirely new direction. But, even in the midst of her own life challenges, she never lost her desire to help others. She was generous and giving and never turned down anyone who asked for help."

Jazz held his hand over his mouth, stifling sobs.

The minister continued, "Even though we will miss her, we are comforted to know Dolly has gone home to be with the Lord. Let us pray."

An organist played the moving hymn "Just As I Am" during the silent prayer.

The minister's words confirmed what I'd already discovered about Dolleen's character. I felt a sense of sadness and personal loss for a woman I'd never even met. I could only imagine what her close friend Jazz must be feeling.

After the prayer, the rabbi stepped forward and introduced herself as Rabbi Julie. She looked at the Shapira men sitting in a line. "I had the great pleasure of welcoming Dolly and her husband, David, to congregation Klal Yisrael. Not only were the couple major benefactors, they became valued members of our community. Yet Dolly was modest in her generosity. She found joy in serving whenever asked, volunteering in our day school and sitting on countless committees.

"Her tragic death reminds us of a basic tenet of our faith—to make every day count for a greater purpose, *tikkun olam*, to repair the world. We should seize every opportunity to perform even the smallest good deed. Dolly was a shining example of this to people of all faiths."

Jazz blew his nose into a tissue.

The rabbi pronounced a traditional blessing for the Shapiras. "May you be comforted among the mourners of Zion and Jerusalem."

Jonathan made his way to the front of the room and delivered a similar eulogy, extolling the sweetness and generosity of the deceased. He faltered when he spotted something in the back of the room. I twisted in my seat just in time to observe Shelley quickly leaving the church.

There went my chance for an interview.

Visibly shaken, Jonathan hurried through the rest of the eulogy. His voice broke in sadness. "Even though Dolly wasn't Jewish, she would've wanted me to say this prayer for her." He reached in his pocket and pulled out a black silk yarmulke, which he placed on his head. The rabbi stood next to him. Jonathan's father, David, and Grandfather Abel stood and each placed a yarmulke on their heads. Knowing what came next, I also stood. So did the seniors from the Jewish Center. Taking an uncertain cue, everyone else in the church slowly rose to their feet. Those of us who knew it by heart recited the Kaddish, the Jewish prayer for the dead. David Shapira's shoulders shook as he wept.

At the conclusion of the service, six pallbearers carried Dolleen's casket to a waiting hearse outside. Everyone climbed into their cars and caravanned up a winding road to her grave on one of the manicured green hillsides.

Lucy shifted the Caddy into second gear during our slow procession up the hill. "From what we just heard, Dolleen didn't have an enemy in the world. It makes you wonder who would want to kill such a nice person."

"Well, people always say nice things about the departed during a funeral, dear," Birdie said. "But the reality is, she did have at least one deadly enemy, and it only takes one to get murdered."

We parked on the side of the road behind the hearse. Bird songs filled the trees on that morning in early spring. We walked across a lawn with identical concrete slabs identifying the permanent residents and stopped at a big hole in the ground. The rabbi sang *El Maleh Rachamim*, God of Mercy, while the attendants lowered the casket into the ground. Both clergy women led the crowd in reciting the twenty-third psalm. And then it was over.

With the marshals right behind him, David Shapira stood back from the grave, with Jonathan and Abel beside him in an impromptu reception line. How could I get David Shapira alone long enough to ask him questions? My friends and I approached them and murmured our sympathy. The crowd behind us propelled us forward, making it impossible to linger. Lucy, Birdie, Jazz, and I stood under a nearby tree, watching the parade of mourners. Paulina started working the crowd, handing out business cards.

I bit my lip. "I've got to figure out a way to talk to him."

"And ask him what?" Jazz piped in. "It's not as if he knows you."

"Well," said Birdie, "for one thing, to find out if he ordered a hit from inside the big house. Maybe he promised to give his ex-wife Shelley more money if she offed Dolleen."

"What would be his motive?" I asked the amateur criminologist.

Birdie shrugged. "Maybe he didn't like the way Dolleen paid off all those seniors. He'd gone to great lengths to keep those Cayman Island accounts a secret. Maybe he wanted to make sure his fortune wouldn't be gone by the time he got out of prison."

Lucy turned down the corners of her mouth. "Or . . . maybe David's ex, Shelley, convinced him their son, Jonathan, became Dolleen's lover. And when David found out, maybe he hired someone to get rid of her."

I held up my hand. "Let's not jump to conclusions. We don't know if he and his ex-wife were even on speaking terms. And we certainly don't know if he was aware of Dolleen's affair, or his ex-wife's suspicions about their son being her lover. No, I'm just going to come right out and ask if he knew who might've wanted her dead and why."

"I'm sorry, but I have to leave." Jazz's voice trembled. "My heart is breaking for poor Dolly."

"Of course, dear. We understand." Birdie squeezed his free hand.

He choked back a sob and waved a weak good-bye.

From our vantage point, we watched Emma and the four other seniors make their way to David Shapira. Emma planted herself in front of him and began to loudly scold him for stealing her money. "I'm all on my own, barely scraping together enough money to support my sister. Dear Sarah has the Fishblatt curse. Do you know how much it costs to care for the demented?"

David opened his mouth to respond, but Emma rolled right over him. "After you took my money, you *gonif*, I couldn't pay her bills. We almost lost our house. I was forced to take out a reverse mortgage to get by, and now I'm stuck in a house as old as me! Do you think I'm having fun surrounded by hundreds of condos? Do you think I enjoyed watching our quiet neighborhood turn into Sodom and Gomorrah? How could you do such a terrible thing to an old woman?"

"Not now, Emma." Abel reached his hand toward her.

She pointed to the old man. "I blame you too! The apple doesn't fall far from the tree, Abel Shapira." The other seniors crowded around and everyone began to speak at once. I saw my chance and hurried over to the scene of confusion.

Emma's tight white curls bobbed as she vigorously shook her finger at David Shapira. "Dolly was an angel, may she rest in peace. You didn't deserve her."

Tears filled David's eyes and his lips trembled.

"She was my angel too." Either he genuinely grieved over his wife's death, or he was a darn good actor. My guess was the latter. Con artists were sociopaths, and sociopaths were incapable of empathy. I'd bet my little Honda Civic the man was putting on an act for the crowd.

He surveyed the collection of angry faces in front of him and sighed. "Believe me, I never meant for any of you to get hurt." His voice softened and oozed a smarmy sincerity. "I worked hard on your behalf. I spent sleepless nights worrying about each of you."

*Oh, brother.* I could see how an innocent girl from a small town in Kansas could be swept away by a rich, handsome, and oh-so-charming scoundrel like David Shapira.

His face folded into a sincere smile. "It's Emma, isn't it? I'm not a thief, Emma. I invested your money according to best practices, but the timing was bad. How could I know the economy was about to collapse?" His voice became indignant. "I blame those greedy Wall Street shysters. Don't you see? They hurt all of us. I'm the real victim—yet I'm the one who ended up in jail."

What a crock! Did he really expect anyone to believe he wasn't one of the worst Wall Street shysters of all time?

Emma crossed her arms. "You're right where you belong, you good-for-nothing!"

*That's my girl. Don't be taken in by his con.*

The marshals tugged on David's arms, clearly marking an end to the conversation. Time to return their prisoner to Leavenworth.

"Wait," he pleaded with them. "Please. I have one more thing I need to tell these good people."

They kept their hands on his arms but allowed him to turn around and face the group again.

David's eyes filled once again with crocodile tears. "I knew how Dolly helped some of you. I asked her to do it."

*What?* I seriously doubted that.

"And I'm asking my son, Johnny, to finish what she started."

Did he intend for Jonathan to continue paying back those nine people on Dolleen's list? Could that even be possible, given the Feds now knew where to find the money? I peeked at Jonathan, who couldn't hide the surprise on his face as his father shamelessly took credit for Dolleen's efforts to pay restitution.

By now I'd pushed my way to Emma's side. I blurted, "Why do you think she was killed, Mr. Shapira? Do you know who might have done it?"

Jonathan glowered at me. "Dad, you don't have to speak to this woman."

David raised his cuffed hands together in a gesture of peace. "It's all right, Johnny." He looked at me. "I know who killed her and so do the police. Dolly loaned a lot of money to a friend who took advantage of her generosity. Of course, he never intended to pay it back. And when she called in the loan, he murdered my poor, defenseless wife so he wouldn't have to pay her."

*He's blaming Jazz?* I looked around. Thankfully, Jazz had already gone, which might explain why David Shapira found the nerve to accuse him.

Jazz couldn't defend himself, but I could. "You're a pathological liar, and I can prove it!"

His smug reaction made me see red, so I decided to wipe the smirk off his face. "Dolleen moved on from you. She took a lover. What do you think about *that?*"

His face turned to stone. He looked at Jonathan, who merely gave a curt shake of his head. Without a word, David Shapira turned around and the marshals led him away.

"That crook!" I muttered through my teeth at Lucy. "He knows more than he lets on, and he's using poor Jazz as a scapegoat. I really wouldn't put it past him to have hired someone to kill Dolleen."

# CHAPTER 24

On the way back to the car, the lean, six-foot-tall Beavers intercepted me and gently pulled me aside. He gestured with his head toward Dolleen's grave. "What was all that back there?"

"The nerve of the guy, blaming Jazz for his wife's murder. He knows more than he's saying."

"Maybe. But are you sure you want to go around antagonizing people? Everyone on your so-called murder board was here today. If one of them is the real killer, and if they think you're getting too close, you could become their next target."

"Does this mean you no longer consider Jazz a suspect?" I closed my eyes and pictured the white flannel sheet in my sewing room with all the evidence pinned to it. Suddenly my eyes flew open. "Are you saying *everyone* on my murder board was here today? Including Kurt Nixon and C. Evelyn? The guys who wrote those horrible messages threatening Dolleen?"

I waited for Beavers's lips to move or his head to

nod, telling me I was right. But he merely gazed at me with those dark eyes.

Finally, he said, "Is it true? You and Levy?"

*Huh?* "I have no idea what you're talking about, Arlo. Just please tell me: Were Nixon and Evelyn here today, or were they not?"

"You know I can't tell you. I can only caution you to back away while you still can." He cleared his throat. "So, is it true what Levy said last night? You're engaged?"

*That's what he means.*

Beavers's face became unreadable. Probably from years of practice as an interrogator.

Well, I could also be inscrutable. I'd answer a question with another question. "Why? Would it make a difference to you?"

"I can only caution you to back away while you still can," he repeated.

"What the heck does *that* mean?" My cheeks burned. "Do you know something about Yossi I don't?"

His eyes softened and he took my hand. "I'd hate to see you make a bad mistake, is all."

How dare he make me doubt Crusher! I pulled my hand away. "You don't get to say that without telling me why."

"Listen. Levy operates by his own rules. He's got a reputation for being a . . ."—he hesitated—"rogue agent. Rumor has it he's crossed the line more than once."

Was that why the straight-arrow Beavers always disliked Crusher? "You're talking about rumor and innuendo, Arlo." Angry tears blurred my vision. "What are you accusing him of? Theft? Drugs?

Murder?" Somehow I just couldn't picture Crusher going over to the dark side.

Beavers seemed to choose his words carefully. "They say he's into black ops. One day, a guy like him may be forced to disappear on you again. Maybe forever. Do you really want to live with that uncertainty?"

"You never liked Yossi. Even before he and I started dating. Why should I listen to what you have to say now?"

"Because I . . . I'm still in love with you."

I felt sucker-punched. My mouth flew open and I rocked back on my heels. "What?"

He stepped close and grabbed both my hands. The scent of his woodsy cologne evoked more intimate times together. "Last night, when I thought you were in danger, I got scared. When I asked myself why, I realized how much you still matter to me. Then, when I saw your murder board"—a grin played on his lips—"I also remembered how much fun it was to be with such a smart woman. Even if you are a pain in the ass sometimes."

The usually proper and professional LAPD detective rested his gaze on my breasts and whispered in a quiet voice. "And then there's the incredible sex. Mind and body. You're the complete package."

"I hardly know what to say, Arlo." I pulled away. "It's been months since we, you know. I assumed you'd moved on, like I did."

"Never. I've always loved you. And when Levy said you were his fiancée last night, I could barely keep my cool." Beavers cupped my chin in his hand. "You deserve someone who'll never disappear on you. I'm that guy, Martha. And if you want to get married, I'll be that guy too."

"Oh my God! Are you proposing?"

He blinked rapidly. "I think I am."

"Right in the middle of a cemetery?"

He looked around, as if becoming aware of our surroundings for the first time and grinned. "Not the most romantic place. But, yeah, it looks that way."

"I'm speechless." *For a change.*

He walked me back to the Caddy. "Promise you'll think about what I've said. All of it. And remember, as a bonus, you'll get Artie too." He referred to his German shepherd, Arthur, one of my favorite people in the whole world.

He opened the car door for me and I slid into the backseat. He stuck his head inside the car and greeted Lucy and Birdie. Then he turned his face and gave me a soft, lingering kiss on the lips. "Be careful, honey," he said and closed the door.

Lucy and Birdie both gaped at me and then exploded with questions.

"*Honey?*"

"What just happened?"

"I thought you are engaged to Yossi."

"How long has this been going on?"

I wiggled my head slowly, trying to clear the fog of disbelief. "He just asked me to marry him."

"Get out!" Lucy started the engine. "Are you sure? What did he say, exactly?"

While we left Forest Lawn in the rearview mirror and headed back toward Encino, I repeated our conversation, including the warning about Dolleen's killer and the rumors about Crusher.

"Do you believe him, dear?" Birdie's hand went for her braid. "About Yossi, I mean."

"I wish I knew what he meant by Yossi 'crossing the line.' Undercover agents often have to improvise. But does that necessarily make him a dangerous rogue?"

"Well, hon," Lucy said, "Arlo was right about one thing. Yossi did disappear on you for five months a year ago. And given the job he has, it could happen again."

"Yes, but Arlo disappeared from my life, too, when he cheated on me with Arthur's veterinarian. Who's to say he won't do the same thing again?"

"I'm getting a strong feeling." Lucy rubbed her arm. I braced myself for one of her mystical insights. "I believe Arlo has learned his lesson. He means what he says."

"All due respect, Lucy, how can you know?"

She looked at me in the rearview mirror. "Admit it, girlfriend. I've never been wrong."

"Do you still have feelings for Arlo, dear?" Birdie's voice was gentle, but her question landed in my gut.

I thought about the last time we'd been together, eight months ago. Crusher had disappeared, and I let Beavers back into my bed. It happened so easily. He was hard to resist, and we'd both been overwhelmed by desire. I scrubbed my face with my hands. "I don't know what I feel right now."

"Listen, hon," said Lucy, "Birdie and Denver waited forty years to be together, and only now are they getting married. If you have doubts about who you ought to be with, my best advice is not to commit to anyone right now. Take your time to decide."

Once back home, I felt relieved not to see Crusher's Harley parked in the driveway. I opened the door, hurried to the murder board in my sewing room, and added more notes to David Shapira's card. I stared at the note cards and other evidence pinned to the flannel sheet, hoping for a brilliant flash of insight.

But I could only think about my astonishing conversation with Arlo Beavers in the cemetery. So, I did what always helped when I needed to sort things out. I opened a package of M&Ms. Then I unfolded Birdie and Denver's Barn Raising quilt, grabbed my sewing kit, settled on my cream-colored sofa, and let the steady rhythm of the needle order my thoughts.

Could Crusher have "crossed the line"? Could it have been as bad as Beavers hinted? By definition, black ops were secret actions taken on behalf of the government that were illegal—like torture and assassinations—using the rationalization the ends justified the means. Could I be with someone who executed the Machiavellian schemes of those maniacs in Washington running our government?

I didn't doubt Crusher loved me. And I was pretty sure I loved him back. But I also knew Beavers wasn't exaggerating. Crusher could disappear again. During his last time away, he never contacted me or returned my calls. I suffered with anxiety, doubt, anger, and depression. Could I live through more long, silent absences? I cursed Beavers for planting those seeds of doubt.

And what about Arlo Beavers? Why did I have such strong feelings every time I was around him? I knew of no reason to doubt his shocking declaration of love today because, with the exception of his dalliance with Arthur's vet, Arlo Beavers was as straight as a laser beam. He'd never say he wanted to marry me unless he meant it. The downside of being so absolute and straightforward, however, was his need to always be in control. How could I live with the inevitable power struggles?

Last night, after the awkward confrontation between Beavers and Crusher in my sewing room, I'd insisted on spending the night alone. I wanted to avoid dealing with Crusher's probing questions or possible hurt feelings. Now, thanks to Beavers, our relationship had just become more complicated and troubling.

Up to now, I'd managed just fine as a single woman. Did I really want to give up my independence to either one of them? Lucy had nailed it. If Birdie could wait forty years for her one true love, I could wait a little longer.

Around two in the afternoon, my stomach growled loudly. I'd been so rattled, something almost unthinkable happened. I'd forgotten to eat lunch. Thank goodness I found some chopped liver and deli rye left over from yesterday. As soon as I laid the quilt aside on the sofa, Bumper jumped on it, turned around to make a nest, and settled in the folds. Cats were like that. They thought they owned everything. Like all my other quilts, I'd have to wash

Bumper's orange hair out of this one before giving it to Birdie and Denver.

I brought my sandwich back to the sofa and stared out the front window. I ate with one hand and fed a little chicken liver to a purring cat on the finger-tip of the other. Bumper became especially devoted whenever protein was involved.

I heard the roar of the Harley before I saw it. Crusher came around the corner and pulled into the driveway. He removed his helmet to reveal a black nylon do-rag as today's head covering. Anyone would be intimidated by the sight of this six-foot-six, 300-pound bearded biker.

I couldn't get Beavers's warning out of my head. My heart pounded in anticipation of the unavoidable confrontation looming because of it. Nevertheless, I wanted nothing but the truth.

His key turned in the front door and he grinned as soon as he saw me. "Babe!" He reached me in a few steps, sat on the sofa, and gathered me in his arms, kissing me hard. "I got to thinking about last night. I didn't like the way Beavers looked at you."

"Really? How, exactly, did he look?" My pulse hammered in my throat.

"You didn't see it? The dude still wants you. So, I've decided we need to make this official."

Crusher slid to the floor on his knees, reached into his pocket, and pulled out a fuzzy black box. He opened it and showed me a ring with a huge solitaire diamond, at least three carats. "I want everyone to know you are my *beshert*." He called me his destiny, his soul mate. "Please accept this token of my love and marry me already."

The diamond absorbed the light and sent it back out in fractured rays of rainbow colors. I gasped at the stunning perfection of the stone. The clarity seemed pure to the naked eye. How would it look under magnification? Would Crusher stand up to the same close scrutiny?

More important, how did a federal agent afford such a ring? Beavers's words erupted in my brain. *Back away while you still can.* "This must've cost a fortune, Yossi."

Crusher grinned. "I told you, babe. I know a guy." When I didn't move, he took the ring out of the box, grabbed my left hand, and slipped the diamond on my finger. A perfect fit. "Do you like it?"

The sparkling gem sat like a giant warning to the world: Unavailable. Keep Away.

"Yossi, we have to talk."

His face collapsed into folds of confusion. "Not the reaction I hoped for. Look, babe, you've been hurt in the past. I get it. But you should know by now I'm crazy about you. I thought you felt the same." The frustration oozed between his next words. "What is the problem?"

"I guess I haven't made peace yet with the uncertainty of your job. You get an assignment, you disappear, you don't communicate, and then you show up again. We've never really talked about what you do when you're working. I don't know how deeply you're involved with the Israelis. I mean, does the ATF even know you're working with the *Shin Bet* too?"

His face became a mask. "We've been over this before. Even if I wanted to, I couldn't answer those questions. My work is classified." He studied my face for a moment. "Why is this coming up now? Has something happened?"

"I've heard rumors. Someone suggested you were a rogue agent. They accused you of having crossed the line. I need to know if you're involved in black ops and all the terrible things those people do. Is there any truth to the rumors?" I searched his eyes for a reaction. I didn't have to wait long.

"That *mamser* Beavers!" He spat out the Yiddish word for *bastard*. "He tried to poison you against me. Am I right?" He stood and began to pace without waiting for an answer. "I saw it in his face last night."

"Does it matter who warned me? Just tell me the truth, Yossi. I need to know what you really do."

"I told you, my work is classified. You'll just have to trust me."

Trust was my biggest issue. The only persons I really trusted were my friends Lucy, her husband, Ray, Birdie, my daughter, Quincy, and my uncle Isaac. Until today I also thought I trusted Crusher.

He stroked the sides of my face with the backs of his fingers. "Forget Beavers. Don't let his crap come between us."

I offered him a smile. "I have to admit, I've been warming to the idea of becoming Mrs. Levy."

"Then what's the sudden doubt?"

"I want to trust you, Yossi, but trust goes both ways. You need to tell me everything. Until you do, I can't accept your ring." I slipped the diamond off my finger and handed it back to him.

Crusher frowned, put it back in the box, and pressed it into my hands. "Keep this. We're not through with this conversation." Then he took my hand and led me into the bedroom.

That afternoon, he managed to convince me he loved me. Twice. But he offered no further explanation of his work as the *other* kind of undercover agent.

# CHAPTER 25

Thursday morning, I sat alone in my sewing room with my third cup of coffee staring at the murder board when Jazz called. "I've got some time today, so I can come over and help you stitch the Barn Raising quilt. Also, I've designed another wedding dress for Birdie. I'd like you to take a look before I show it to her."

"Sure. What time? I'd really welcome the distraction."

"Half hour. I'm also bringing a drawing of your wedding dress." I could hear the smile in his voice. "It's fabulous."

The last thing I wanted to think about was a wedding dress and Jazz's idea of fabulous. Besides, even if I did want to get married, whose proposal should I accept? A generous, laid-back undercover ATF agent with a secret life and Israeli connections he refused to discuss or an upright, uptight LAPD detective with Native American roots, whose life was an open book? A future filled with anxiety and uncertainty or one that was reliable and predictable but not as exciting? A three-carat flawless diamond sitting in a black fuzzy box or my favorite German shepherd?

Jazz and Zsa Zsa showed up thirty minutes later, wearing matching blue chambray shirts. As soon as he sat down, he pulled a sketchpad out of Zsa Zsa's carrier. "This is my newest design for Birdie."

I examined the drawing. Jazz imagined Birdie with a halo of hair and a bun on top of her head. He designed a gathered maxi skirt with a wide waistband and on-seam pockets in a yellow and blue floral print. The bib of a gauzy white blouse featured several rows of small pin-tucks down either side of a placket with pearl buttons. The full, long sleeves, also delicately pleated, ended in gathers at three-inch wrist bands. Tiny strips of lace edged the high-banded collar and cuffs. Samples of the delicate floral print and white cotton lawn were taped to the page.

"You nailed it this time, Jazz. I absolutely love this. It's elegant, yet simple." I fingered the fabric swatches. "This floral print keeps it from being too formal for Birdie's taste. I think she'll be quite comfortable wearing this."

He heaved a huge sigh. "Thank God! Now, what do you think of this?" He turned the page to the next drawing labeled *Martha*. He'd drawn the same outfit, only everything was white, and the busty model held a parasol—more *Downton Abbey* than *Little House on the Prairie*. A swatch of ivory silk clung to the page. He watched for my reaction.

*Oy vey!* I chose my words carefully. "I love the old-fashioned simplicity of this silhouette."

"Great! Because I thought it would be sensational if you and Birdie had a double wedding and wore matching dresses."

I did an internal eye roll. "Unfortunately, I'm not in the market for a wedding dress, Jazz. Why don't you just concentrate on Birdie for now?"

He tapped his fingers together. "Why? Has something happened between you and Yossi? Come on, dish." He reached over and squeezed my hand. "We've been through so much, I feel like you're my little sister."

I sighed heavily. "It's complicated." I told him about Arlo's proposal in the cemetery, his accusations about Crusher's work in black ops, and Crusher's silence on the subject. I even mentioned the three-carat diamond sitting in the box on my nightstand. "So, you see why I can't even think about marriage now?"

He closed the sketchpad and put it back in the tote. "Okay. I won't mention your dress again." He made a zipping motion across his lips. "But don't you think you're being a little hard on Yossi for being secretive? I'm pretty sure when he took the job with the ATF he swore some kind of oath not to spill the beans."

"There are ways of saying stuff while still leaving some of the beans in the can."

Jazz's cell phone chirped. He read a text, quickly responded, and shoved his phone back in his pocket, trying to hide a smile.

"Okay, Jazz. I don't mean to be nosy, but I've noticed you doing a lot of texting lately. Does this have anything to do with a certain state trooper in Oregon?"

The shock on his face told me I'd scored. "You're scary! How'd you know?"

Lucy, Birdie, Jazz, and I drove to Oregon last year to bury Russell Watson in the family plot in McMinnville. On the way, we encountered local law enforcement when someone ran us off the road. Then we spent several hours at the state police headquarters. When they finally allowed us to leave, I glimpsed the head trooper slip a small piece of paper to Jazz.

I smiled. "Just a lucky guess. It's Trooper Franklin, right?"

Color rose in Jazz's cheeks. "His name's Grover. We're going to meet up in McMinnville at Birdie's wedding."

"Speaking of which, we'd better finish this." I handed him Birdie's Barn Raising quilt. I didn't have a large frame where multiple hands could gather around and sew at the same time, so Jazz stretched the quilt in his fourteen-inch hoop and stitched on it alone. I resumed working on my charm quilt, the project I'd temporarily abandoned when we started on Birdie's wedding quilt.

It wasn't uncommon for serious quilters to keep several WIPs—works in progress—going at the same time. Switching back and forth between different projects in various stages of construction provided variety and a break from boredom. I settled back and stitched the seams of the fabric rectangles in my Prairie Braid quilt, also known as French Braid or Friendship Braid. It wasn't unusual for a pattern to acquire more than one name, depending on where it had traveled and how many decades it had been around.

"Dolleen's funeral must've been very painful for you," I said. "You seemed so upset when you left the cemetery yesterday."

Jazz put down his needle and sighed. "I just needed to get out of there and be by myself for a while."

"Well, you missed the Emma Fishblatt show."

"The what?"

"Emma confronted David Shapira and gave him and his father, Abel, an old-fashioned tongue lashing."

He chuckled. "She seemed like such a meek little thing. Good for her. I'm sure she spoke for all of his victims. How did he react?"

"He tried to justify his actions. He had the gall to claim he was the victim. He also tried to take credit for the restitution payments. But Emma didn't buy a word of it."

"Did you get the chance to speak to him?"

I cut a fresh length of thread from the spool and chose my words carefully. "Yes. I asked him if he knew who killed his wife and, well, he blamed you. He said you did it because of the loan."

"Oh my God!" Jazz covered his mouth.

"Don't worry. I stood up for you. I called him a liar and asked if he knew his wife had taken a lover. That shut him up. But I got the distinct impression he knew and didn't like it. Before I could ask him anything else, the marshals took him away."

"My life could be over," he moaned. "And all

because of those stupid texts I sent." He pressed his fist into his lips.

"If it's any consolation, Arlo seemed impressed with the evidence we've gathered. I got the impression he also suspected everyone on my murder board."

Just then my phone rang. An unfamiliar voice spoke. "Is this Mrs. Rose? My name is Lillian Gould. I attended Dolly's funeral yesterday." Lillian's deep voice sounded like a stevedore with a cold.

I put her on speaker so Jazz could hear the conversation too. "Yes, this is Martha Rose. You said you were at the cemetery? How did you know her?"

"The same way Emma did. Dolly gave me money every month."

"I'm so sorry for your loss, Mrs. Gould. Dolleen seemed like such a nice person. She helped so many people."

"You told David Shapira your friend didn't kill Dolly and you were going to prove it. Well, I'm calling because I think I can help you."

Jazz raised his eyebrows and leaned toward the phone. I put my finger to my lips and cautioned him not to speak. "Please go ahead. I'm listening."

"Not over the phone. Come over to my house and I'll be glad to tell you what I know."

At two in the afternoon, Jazz and I headed south on the 405 Freeway toward West LA. He parked the Mercedes in front of a modest, two-story apartment building south of Pico Boulevard, not too far from the small house where I grew up and where my uncle Isaac still lived.

We pushed through a wrought iron gate at the entryway into an open courtyard. I quickly located Apartment C and rang the bell. A zaftig woman I recognized from yesterday answered the door. Heavy women seemed to fall into two categories: those who still cared about their grooming and those who'd given up. Lillian fell into the former group. Her voluminous green caftan fell in soft, clean folds. Bright red fingernails glistened against the bulging knuckles and puffy skin of her hands. Rhinestone earrings tugged her lobes downward, and a neat auburn wig covered her head. I guessed her age to be somewhere between 60 and 100.

I introduced Jazz and Zsa Zsa as we took seats on a green velvet sofa that had seen better days.

Lillian glanced at the Maltese. "Cute dog. Don't let it pee on my floor."

I found her blunt manner refreshing.

Lillian studied Jazz's face. "You were at the funeral yesterday too. You must be the one accused of killing Dolly." She delivered her statement in a gravelly voice, without an ounce of fear.

"I didn't do it." Jazz raised his chin and met her gaze.

She nodded once and plopped her bulk in an overstuffed easy chair with white, crocheted antimacassars on the arms and behind the head. "I believe you." She reached over to the coffee table separating us and opened a white box of See's candy. She extracted an almond cluster covered in milk chocolate and thrust the half empty container in our direction, another reason to like Lillian Gould. "Help yourself."

"No thanks." Jazz gave a little wave of his hand.

I, on the other hand, seized a butterscotch square. "What is it you wanted to tell me?"

She bit off half the almond cluster and spoke through her teeth. "Dolly was into something illegal." The big woman sat back and crunched, waiting for our reaction.

# CHAPTER 26

Lillian licked the chocolate from her fingertips. "Emma told us yesterday all about Dolly's so-called affair at the Harlequin Hotel."

I wondered how Dolleen would feel if she knew the chatty Emma Fishblatt so freely gossiped about something so private.

Lillian must've read my mind. "Emma can't help herself. Haven't you noticed? She has a tendency to run off at the mouth. Anyways, I thought you should know I saw Dolly there last month."

I sat forward in my seat. "At the Harlequin?"

"Yeah. Tuesday afternoons there's a four o'clock happy hour. They serve all the free buffalo wings you can eat. Me and my friend were there last month with an overpriced bottle of chardonnay and a plate full of wings. I looked up and saw Dolly stop at the entrance of the bar, looking for someone."

"Did you talk to her?"

"Nah. I'm pretty sure she didn't see me. The place was crowded, and me and my friend sat in a dark corner. Anyway, Dolly spotted a man standing at the bar and quietly waved at him. He followed her upstairs, carrying a satchel. A half hour later, she came downstairs carrying the same satchel and left the hotel. Five minutes later he came down minus the satchel and also left."

"Can you describe this man?"

"Yeah. Young. Handsome. Great tush."

Jazz and I looked at each other. James Hawkins!

"We think they were having an affair," I said.

"That's the thing. I don't think hanky-panky's what she was up to. I did the math. Dolly shelled out nearly ninety grand every month to our little group, and she hinted we weren't the only ones receiving checks."

Lillian wasn't wrong. Those numbers matched the evidence we'd found.

"Go on," I urged.

"All that money couldn't have come from her business. I was a bookkeeper for fifty years, honey." She tapped her chest with a scarlet fingernail. "I worked for some real shysters. I know numbers. On the books and off the books. Look. The Feds never recovered half the money Shapira stole. My guess is the cash is stashed somewhere the government can't get at it. Like the Caymans. Dolly musta known where her husband buried the money and used it to pay us back."

"So, why didn't she just give you one lump sum? Why did she bother with all those monthly payments?"

"Two reasons. First, any check over ten grand would alert the IRS and trigger an audit. Second, she probably laundered the money through her

business. Because of that, she couldn't run too much
cash through her books because that would also
alert the IRS. I think Dolly processed small amounts
every month to make the money look like legitimate profit."

Jazz squared his shoulders. "Well, that doesn't
prove Dolly was shady. She just wanted to pay you
back as best she could. Make everything right."

"Gawd, are you that naïve?" Lillian snorted.
"Dolly obviously had access to the money. If she was
such a good person, why didn't she just hand everything over to the government and be done with it.
Let them reimburse *all* of the victims?" Lillian reached
for a chocolate-covered caramel and popped it in
her mouth.

My eyes drifted to the pieces of See's candy in the
white box, calling to me from their frilly brown
paper cups. I snatched a milk chocolate patty. When
I bit into it, a brace of mint from the sweet, white
filling erupted in my mouth.

Jazz frowned. "If Dolly had turned the money
over to the government, it would've taken years for
you to see a penny. Maybe she knew you needed the
help right now and didn't want to make you wait."

"The satchel exchange," I said, bringing the conversation back to Lillian's revelation. "You think
that's how Dolleen got the cash?"

She swallowed. "I figure the guy with the satchel
was a courier Dolly paid to bring over money every
month from the islands. She distributed some of it
to a chosen few, just enough to ease her conscience.
But she chose to hang on to the rest of those millions

rather than give them up to the Feds. In my book, that makes her as much of a thief as her husband."

"You're wrong!" Jazz said. "I knew Dolly better than you. She'd never steal from people."

The assertion Dolleen was complicit in David's elaborate fraud completely contradicted my impression of her. Still, Lillian made sense. Why didn't Dolleen turn all the money over to the Feds? Until I knew more, I had to consider that maybe I'd misjudged the victim. Maybe she was more deeply involved in her husband's schemes than Jazz realized. "Do you know of anyone who might've wanted to kill her?"

"How about everyone who ever invested with David Shapira—including me? Every time I looked at Zillow, I wanted to kill someone. I inherited a couple small apartment buildings in Santa Monica from my parents. Even though they were rent controlled, they brought in a tidy income because the properties were mortgage free. In 2007, when the real estate market tanked, David Shapira convinced me I'd be better off to sell the buildings and invest my money with him." She growled. "Like an idiot, I listened. Four million dollars. Gone. And now those buildings have tripled in value." She pointed to the walls around her. "Thank God I hung on to this place, or I'd be out on the street."

Lillian blew out a puff of angry air. "Yeah, we were all infuriated, but none of our group is responsible for her murder. We may not've liked having our money doled out in dribs and drabs, but face it: no more Dolly means no more money. Between all of us, we had maybe ten million reasons to want her alive. Now we're screwed. Once again."

"Do you believe what David Shapira said yesterday when he promised Jonathan would continue to make reimbursement payments?"

"Hah!" Lillian snorted. "I was stupid enough to believe that schmuck once, and look where it got me."

I stood to leave. "Thanks for the information, Lillian. Call me if you think of anything else."

"Yes, thanks," said Jazz. "I appreciate your help, even if you are wrong about Dolly."

"No problem." She rocked forward and pushed her bulk up from the chair with a grunt. "Emma told me you're Isaac's niece. He's very quiet. I guess you could say kinda brainy. I see him playing chess at the center."

I nodded. "He likes spending time there."

"He never married, did he?"

*Where is this going?* "No, he was too busy taking care of all of us."

"Is he gay?" She glanced at Jazz.

I searched her face for any sign of contempt, but I only saw curiosity. Lillian didn't seem the type to be on the prowl, like Emma, and probably every other widow at the center.

"No," I said as I moved toward the door.

She shrugged. "Just curious. I hear he has a regular poker game going with Morty and a couple others."

"That's right." I reached for the doorknob.

The big woman smiled. "I got as far as the finals in the lady's division in Vegas. Tell him if a spot in the game ever opens up, I want in. Meanwhile, I'll do some digging and see what else I can find out about Dolly."

Jazz drove without speaking on the way back to the Valley. As we crested the top of the Sepulveda pass, I broke the silence. "I think Lillian is right about the courier."

He shifted in his seat and frowned. "But she was wrong about Dolly being a thief."

"Still, Lillian brought up a good point. Why didn't Dolleen give all the money back to the Feds?"

"She must've had her reasons." He clamped his jaw shut.

"There's another thing. From Lillian's description, the courier was James Hawkins. His e-mail name, Igo4you, didn't mean he was attracted to her; it meant he traveled for her."

"I know, right?"

"So, maybe we have to reconsider their relationship. Lillian said Dolleen and James met up at the hotel and stayed only a half hour. Does that sound like the behavior of a couple of lovers having a tryst? I think they exchanged the cash in a room where they wouldn't be seen. Then each left the hotel alone so as not to draw attention."

Jazz looked over his shoulder to change lanes and transition from the 405 to the westbound 101 Freeway. "So, what about the last message we found in the J folder? The one where he wrote *she's suspicious*?"

"Kiki's not off the hook as a suspect. She'd still have a motive for murder if she found out about their meetings at the Harlequin and assumed they were having an affair."

Jazz parked in front of my house and got out to give Zsa Zsa a bathroom break on the lawn. When she finished, he put her back in the carrier. "I'm heading back to West Hollywood. The traffic's going to be heinous." He kissed the air on both sides of my face, European style, and drove off.

I put my purse on the hall table and bent down to pet my cat, Bumper, when my phone rang. I looked at caller ID but didn't recognize the number. Fully expecting to hear a telemarketer lie to me about home repairs or everlasting lightbulbs, I was totally unprepared for what came next.

"This is Shelley Shapira returning your call."

# CHAPTER 27

Oh my God. David Shapira's ex-wife and the woman with a huge motive to kill Dolleen Doyle was on the phone. "Thank you for calling me back, Mrs. Shapira."

"Jonathan told me not to."

"But you did anyway . . ."

"How dare you go to my son, claiming you've got evidence against me in Dolleen Doyle's murder!"

"I'm more than willing to discuss this with you. Is there some place we can meet?"

"I don't have time for this. Just tell me how much it'll take to make you go away."

Underneath the arrogance, I detected a bit of panic in her voice. If I could tap into her fear, maybe I could push her into talking to me face to face. I needed more than a voice on the phone to gauge her reactions. "I'm sorry, Mrs. Shapira, but that won't work for me. I'm not after money. However, I am willing to meet you anywhere, any time, for a conversation." I held my breath, waiting for her response.

The silence stretched as she considered my offer. At last she said, "Tonight at nine. The Black Market in Studio City. Don't tell Jonathan." She ended the call.

I wished I didn't have to leave the house again, especially so late, but at least I didn't have to drive far. At 9 p.m., the Black Market would be a quick trip east on the 101 Freeway. And the effort of going out would be worth the chance to quiz one of the major players in Dolleen's drama.

The Black Market turned out to be a trendy, new night spot. A dark wooden bar with hundreds of bottles of liquor ran the length of the long, narrow interior. Dark leather booths lined the opposite wall, and a long line of bistro tables marched down the middle. A brick ceiling, rounded like a vault, created a cave-like atmosphere. A large crowd pushed the noise level high. Shelley was smart. Our conversation couldn't be easily overheard in this place.

Dozens of customers pushed against the bar, and most of the tables and booths were taken. Even at this hour, people munched on plates of savory appetizers and snacks with their cocktails. I scanned the faces and spotted Shelley sitting alone in a booth toward the back.

"Thank you for meeting me." I slid into the seat facing her.

Her manicured hands rested on the table on either side of a tall glass of something blue and bubbly. Even in her fifties, the perfectly coiffed Shelly Shapira looked like a catalogue model for Saks Fifth Avenue. And the diamonds in her cocktail ring could've choked a horse. She studied my face before she spoke. "I watched you confront David yesterday."

"Really? You left the church when Jonathan got up to speak. I thought you'd gone home. Frankly, I don't get it. Why were you there in the first place?"

The waitress appeared at our table with a menu. I ordered a Coke Zero, no ice, and passed on the food.

Shelley's lips compressed into tiny folds as she sipped her drink through a red plastic straw. When the waitress left, she said, "I wanted the satisfaction of seeing Dolleen put in the ground." A smile played at the corner of her mouth. "Do I shock you?"

"Not really. I think it's pretty common knowledge you blamed her for breaking up your marriage. Who wouldn't be furious?"

Shelley's green eyes darkened. "You're right. It's no secret I disliked the little slut, but I hated David more. Let me tell you just what kind of man he was."

"Okay." I was glad she wanted to vent. The more I knew, the better.

She seemed to gather herself together and gazed into the empty place over my shoulder. "We met in grad school. I studied art history and he majored in finance. He was smart and funny and ambitious. I was so much in love, I didn't recognize what a player he was, even back then. When I got pregnant, we married. It didn't bother me I had to drop out of school. David was three months away from an MBA, so I figured he'd get a job and support our family and we'd live happily ever after."

She closed her eyes. "He got a job at Bear Stearns

right after graduation. Stupidly, I thought his late
hours were a sign he was determined to get ahead
by working overtime. On the evening my water
broke, I called his office, but nobody answered the
phone. David's father, Abel, ended up taking me
to the hospital." She opened her eyes and looked
straight at me. "David showed up after midnight
and apologized. He said he'd gone drinking with
'the boys' to celebrate a killing they'd made on the
market that day. But when he kissed me, I smelled
someone else's perfume."

"I can sympathize," I said. "My ex-husband also
cheated."

She sighed. "Then you know what I'm talking
about. I was devastated, of course, but I fooled myself
into thinking that being a father would change
him." Shelley's eyes still bore the pain she must've
endured with David's betrayals.

"Did it change him?" I asked, knowing full well
what the answer would be.

She made a dismissive gesture. "The more successful he became, the worse his cheating got. Even when
one of his mistresses gave birth to a child by him,
another boy, I continued the pretense of a happy
marriage. For my son's sake, I put up with years of
David's philandering because I wanted to spare
Johnny the embarrassment of growing up in a fractured home. Our arrangement worked until David
decided to trade me in for a shiksa half his age."

"After all you put up with, you must've been beside
yourself. Maybe even angry enough to kill . . ."

Shelley shifted forward in her seat. "Furious and
humiliated, yes. But not enough to kill her. The

truth is, Dolleen Doyle did me a favor. Although I didn't get as much as I deserved, I got a huge settlement in the divorce. Little Miss Kansas was just the latest in a parade of women over the years and happened to be in the right place when David hit his midlife crisis."

"Your divorce happened years ago, yet you never remarried. Are you still in love with him?"

"You're joking," she scoffed. "I never remarried because I learned my lesson. I'm too smart to ever trust anyone in the same way I trusted him. She pointed her finger at me. "You said you've been through the same thing. Would you ever get married again?"

Shelley's question hit me between the eyes. Could I ever get over my mistrust and make a commitment? If so, who would it be? Crusher or Beavers?

"What about Jonathan and Dolleen?" I asked, shifting the focus away from me. "I heard a rumor they were having an affair."

"Preposterous!"

I watched carefully as her hands tightened into fists and then relaxed.

"Johnny would never touch her."

"Are you sure? Didn't they travel to Leavenworth together to visit your ex-husband? Dolleen was very pretty and close to your son's age. A long trip like that—they must've spent the night in a hotel and returned the next day. Anything could've happened. Someone said you 'went ballistic' when you found out."

"Is this the so-called evidence you claim to have against me?"

"It's a line of questioning the police would be interested in."

"What makes you think they haven't already asked? Look. I objected to their traveling together only because I knew what the gossip would be, and I was right. The minute they returned to LAX, the paparazzi were all over them. Johnny made a huge mistake leaving town with her. It looked very bad for him."

Shelley's statement rang true. She was a woman who was all about appearances—enduring an unfaithful spouse to maintain the façade of a marriage. I could easily believe she'd also try to protect her son's image. The question was, how far would she go to do just that?

I wasn't ready to drop the subject. "Yet they did have some kind of relationship."

"Johnny was her lawyer." She grabbed the straw and took a fortifying drink.

I sensed she wouldn't be goaded into saying more, so I tried another line of questioning. "Okay. Let's leave their relationship aside for the moment. During all those years you were married, didn't you have at least an inkling about David's crimes?"

Shelley narrowed her eyes. "You've got your nerve accusing me like that. David went to his office every day, and I took care of our family and entertained his clients. In case you haven't been listening, David and I didn't exactly have a close relationship. We hardly spoke. As far as I knew, he ran a legitimate business. And for your information, the FBI's satisfied I'm innocent."

Shelley could be lying. It was possible she knew all about David's activities, even participated in his scams. It was also possible she could've made a deal with the FBI, trading her inside knowledge for immunity in the prosecution of her ex-husband.

She tensed up and began scooting toward the end of the booth.

I raised a placating hand. "Please don't leave, Shelley. I'm not blaming you. You were put in the position of trying to defend your home and your marriage. Anyone would've done the same thing."

She stopped moving but remained on high alert.

"The reason I ask is I'm trying to figure out how much Dolleen knew about David's activities and if that's somehow behind her murder. You say you didn't know what your ex-husband was up to until it was too late. That happens to a lot of wives. But he could've recruited his new wife to participate in his schemes. We do know that right up to the time she died, she had access to his offshore accounts."

"How do you know that?"

"Because she made regular reimbursement payments to a few of his victims. Elderly people from the senior center on Pico Boulevard. And she hinted there were others she paid every month."

"Really?" She laughed. "That's delicious. David must've been *fried* to discover she gave his precious dollars away while he sat rotting in prison. I wouldn't put it past him to hire someone to stop her from spending his money." She sat back and sipped her drink.

I touched the side of my head. "Actually, the same

thought crossed my mind. And yet yesterday, at the funeral, he insisted the reimbursement payments were his idea. He even claimed your son will continue to make those payments."

She paused and slowly bobbed her head in understanding. "So, that's what David meant. But you can't seriously believe him. Nothing but lies ever came out of his mouth. From the looks of it, not even the old woman he talked to believed what he said."

"Still, I have to ask. Since Dolleen is dead, does Jonathan now have access to his father's money?"

"That would be illegal." She crossed her arms. "Johnny was right. You lied about having evidence implicating me. I don't know what you're up to, but we're done here." She grabbed her turquoise leather clutch and stood. "I assume drinks are on you." The elegant Shelley Shapira walked out of the Black Market without looking back, turning several heads in her wake.

As I walked to my car parked on Ventura Boulevard, my cell phone rang. "Babe, it's late. Are you okay?" Crusher must've come home and discovered the empty house.

"Yeah, I'm in Studio City. I'll be home soon and tell you all about it."

Twenty minutes later we stood in my sewing room in front of the murder board. "I need to update some of these cards. I've learned a lot of really important stuff today."

He went to the kitchen and brought back two

bottles of Heineken. He watched in silence, pulling on the bottle, until I finished writing. I pinned up the last card, took a big gulp of beer, and began rolling my shoulders, trying to undo the stiffness in my neck.

"You've had a long day." He put his empty bottle down, moved behind me, and began kneading my shoulders with his strong hands, forcing them to drop down from where they hunched around my ears.

I relaxed into the massage and closed my eyes. "Yeah. I found the answers to some questions, but new ones popped up." I told him about my conversation with Lillian Gould, taking sips of beer as I spoke. "The thing she said about James Hawkins being a courier and not a lover made a lot of sense. She also suggested Dolleen wasn't as innocent as everyone assumed."

"Did she get specific?"

"Yeah. She made a good point. Why did Dolleen continue to smuggle cash into the country and launder it through her business? Why didn't she just turn over the hidden accounts to the Feds so all of David's victims could be reimbursed?"

I finished the beer while describing my meeting with Shelley Shapira. "I think she knows a lot more than she admits to, but she wasn't about to confide in me."

I moaned as he dug into the muscles at the top of my shoulders, the location of two painful trigger points of fibromyalgia. The spasm in my neck began to relax.

"That feels so good, Yossi." A wave of fatigue enveloped me. "But I'm cooked. I need to go to bed."

He kissed the crook of my neck, tickling me with his beard and sending electricity down my spine. "Trust me. I'm going to make you feel even better."

# CHAPTER 28

Friday morning I woke up refreshed, relaxed, and ready to cook Shabbat dinner for Crusher, Uncle Isaac, Morty, and his girlfriend, Marilyn. Uncle Isaac strictly avoided combining meat and milk dishes in the same meal, according to the laws of *kashrut*. But mixing dairy with fish was permitted, so I built my menu around grilled salmon, sautéed spinach, potatoes au gratin, and a homemade rhubarb pie with a buttery crust.

I'd just taken the pie out of the oven at ten when Jazz called. "I'm so disappointed! I'm at Birdie's and she doesn't like the newest wedding dress design. *Quelle* disaster."

"I'm sorry, Jazz. I thought for sure she'd love it. What are you going to do now?"

"I don't know. I could still make the outfit for you. Are you sure you don't want a double wedding?"

Shelley Shapira's question flashed through my mind. *Will you ever get married again?*

"I'm not ready." *Maybe I'd never be.*

"Well, then, how about the rest of your wardrobe?

I could take you shopping. Show you how to take it up a notch." He paused. "Several notches."

I could be so insulted. But Jazz was right. Except for Shabbat and funerals, I lived in size sixteen stretch denim jeans and T-shirts, not to mention my comfortable navy-blue rubber Crocs. "I might be open to a couple of suggestions. Maybe after Passover."

"When's that?"

"The first night is on Friday, a week from today."

"Okay. We can go the day after, on Saturday. We could have brunch at Le Bistro." He wasn't about to let me off the hook.

"*Um*, it doesn't quite work that way, Jazz." Rather than a long tutorial on the intricacies of the holiday, I'd give him the simple explanation. "Passover lasts for eight days. The first two nights we have a special celebration dinner called a Seder. We eat matzah instead of bread at every meal, so it's kind of difficult to go out to eat. Too many food restrictions."

"Okay, I get it. But don't think I'm going to forget. I've been dying to give you a makeover for months."

"Do I have to give up my Crocs?"

"*Oy vey*!" said my non-Jewish friend. "You might as well walk around in a set of Buick tires."

After the call ended, I covered my dining room table with a white cloth and began setting my *bubbie*'s gleaming silver next to the Bavarian china plates with the blue rim. I was humming the *na-na* part of "Hey Jude" when something Shelley Shapira said began tugging at my brain. It had seemed insignificant at the time, but when I put it together with a remark Kevin the bartender had made, the sudden truth took my breath away. I stopped humming and headed for the car. Time to confront both Hawkinses.

The Corvette and the Toyota pickup were parked in their driveway, which meant both Kiki and James were home. James answered the door, wearing a pair of tight jeans and flip-flops. He clutched a shirt. Every muscle in his arms and bare torso stood out in high definition. Now that I saw his face up close, I knew I was right. He tilted his head. "Yes?"

"I want to know why you lied to the police and tried to implicate my friend in Dolleen's murder."

He hung on to the door, speechless for a moment. "Do I know you?"

"Martha Rose. I've already spoken to your wife. Are you going to let me in, or do I have to go to the police?"

James Hawkins stepped aside and allowed me to enter the sunny living room with a view of their sparkling blue swimming pool.

Kiki hurried in from the kitchen, wearing a pair of white shorts and a tank top. "What are you doing here?" She looked at her husband. "Jimmy? What's going on?"

"I think we all better sit down" I said as I settled in an easy chair upholstered in yellow.

James buttoned on his shirt and began to pace. Kiki sat on the edge of the sofa, looking rapidly back and forth between the two of us.

He stopped walking, assumed a wide stance, crossed

his arms, and glared at me. "You've got two minutes." He was attempting to assert control, but I wasn't about to let that happen.

"I've figured out your secret. I know you were meeting Dolleen at a hotel in Hollywood."

The news didn't seem to shock Kiki. She stretched her hand toward her husband. "Jimmy?"

James sat beside her and placed an arm around her shoulders. He drew her body into his, surprising me with the tenderness of the gesture. "Stay calm," he murmured. They waited for me to continue.

"When I first learned about your meetings at the Harlequin Hotel, I thought you and Dolleen were having an affair." I pointed toward Kiki. "That would give you a solid motive for murdering her, and it would also explain why you lied to the police about seeing Jazz come out of Dolleen's house the night she was killed."

Kiki rapidly shook her head. "I didn't. I would never . . ."

I looked once more at James. "But then I found a witness who observed you walking into the Harlequin carrying the same satchel Dolleen carried out a half hour later. Hardly long enough for a romantic tryst, but plenty of time to hide in a room, count the money you carried, and collect your cut. You weren't having an affair. You were Dolleen's courier, smuggling in cash from the Caymans. I'm sure if the police look at your passport, they'll find your trips coincide with the cash withdrawals from David Shapira's offshore accounts."

By now James had worked his jaw muscles into a tight knot. "What do you want? Money?"

I knew I was on to something. That was the third time someone connected to this case offered to pay me off. "The truth. One of the things puzzling me is why Dolleen chose *you*. But then something Shelley Shapira mentioned last night changed my mind. You have a much bigger stake in the game than I first imagined."

Kiki began to shiver and James pulled her even closer.

"Shelley told me about David's endless affairs and how he had a son with one of his girlfriends. At first that didn't mean much. But then I remembered something Kevin, the bartender at the Harlequin, said when I showed him a picture of Jonathan Shapira. He said Jonathan looked a lot like the man Dolleen was meeting. And now we're in the same room, I can see the resemblance. You and Jonathan are half-brothers, aren't you? You are David Shapira's other son."

James leaned forward and put his head in his hands. "Christ."

Suddenly Kiki came to life. "You leave him alone! He didn't kill Dolly. Neither of us did."

"Then why were you so anxious to get into Dolleen's storage unit?"

"I don't know what you mean," she said.

"No more lies! Jazz and I were hiding in Dolleen's bedroom the night you came for the key to the unit. You threw the box on the floor when you found it empty. Remember?"

Kiki blinked. "Oh my God. You were there? I only wanted to protect my husband. Dolly told me she kept all the records in her storage place. I just wanted to destroy anything connecting the money transfers to Jimmy before the police discovered them. Unfortunately, the police must've gotten to the key first."

I didn't bother to tell her that Jazz and I were the ones who found the key. "So, you knew all along what your husband and Dolleen were up to?"

"Of course. I knew they weren't having an affair." She smiled at James.

I looked at him. "Then what did you mean in your last message to Dolleen when you wrote *she's suspicious?*"

He sat up and said to Kiki, "Please, precious, can you bring us each a drink of water?"

She stood, kissed his forehead, and walked toward the kitchen. I marveled at the tenderness between such an unlikely couple. James appeared to be in his early twenties, strikingly handsome and fit. In contrast, the plain little Kiki was around forty and badly in need of some blond highlights and lip gloss. Yet they seemed devoted. How did something like that happen?

He lowered his voice to a whisper. "Dolly was helping me plan a surprise trip for my anniversary. Kiki found one of the brochures and asked me why I was looking at European cruises. I thought for sure she'd guessed what I was up to."

Kiki came back into the room with three glasses and a pitcher of ice water on a tray. She poured each of us a drink and sat next to her husband, putting a protective hand on his knee.

"Thanks." James took a long drink.

"How long have you been working for Dolleen?" I asked.

James placed the glass on the coffee table. "I didn't work for Dolly. I worked for David."

"You call your father by his first name?"

"He prefers it that way. So do I. To save his 'real' family from embarrassment, he insisted I be raised with my mother's last name. If he refused to claim me, why should I claim him?"

Kiki reached behind him and stroked his back.

Encouraged by her gesture, James continued, "Underneath all his charm, David was a cold SOB. But he always took care of me and my mother. Not out of kindness or even guilt. He paid both of us hush money until the whole world found out what a fraud he was. After he confessed, he no longer had a reason to keep her quiet. Before he went to prison, he arranged for automatic withdrawals from the offshore accounts. He said he would no longer support both me and my mother. So, if I wanted my allowance to continue, I'd have to smuggle the cash into the country every month."

I raised my glass and sipped. The cold water felt good on my throat. "So, you're saying Dolleen never managed those accounts?"

"Exactly."

That would explain why Dolleen hadn't helped more people or didn't surrender the cash to the government. She couldn't have because she never controlled those accounts.

James ran his fingers through his hair. "I brought the cash to her, but David determined how much and when. Around $200K every month got divided four ways. Jonathan, Abel, and I each got $20K. Dolly got $40K."

How wrong could I have been? The income and lavish lifestyle belonged to James, not Kiki—which made their attraction to each other all the more unusual. "And the rest of the money?"

"David instructed Dolly to invest the other $100 K in a legitimate retirement account for when he got out of prison. He figured with good behavior he'd be free in five years."

"But," I said, "it turns out Dolleen had other plans for the money. Did David know she didn't invest the funds according to his wishes?"

"I never told him. Why would I? But I did notice she'd gotten nervous lately."

"Jimmy's right." Kiki spoke up. "She didn't seem herself, but she never said what was bothering her."

Was Shelley right? Did David find out what Dolly really did with his money? How angry would he be?

"Do you think David had her killed?"

Kiki gasped.

James held up his hand. "Honest. We don't know who killed her. Look, I'm sorry about your friend. Don't blame Kiki. I happened to look out the living room window that night and see his distinctive license plate. Then when we found out Dolly had been murdered, I got the idea to point the police in his direction."

"What about Dolleen's will? Who benefits from her death?"

James and Kiki looked at each other.

Kiki said, "We don't know for sure. But I guarantee you, it's not us. She once mentioned something about an orphanage in Kansas. Jonathan handled her legal affairs. You'll have to ask him."

"Since Dolleen's death, who controls the money from the offshore accounts now?"

James shrugged. "I suppose Jonathan does."

"One last question. How did you and Dolleen come to live next door to each other?"

James said, "Both these houses belong to David."

"How is it the Feds never confiscated these properties?"

"The deeds are in Jonathan's name," Kiki piped up.

James kneaded his eyes with his fingers. "I wish to God Dolly was still alive."

I believed him. Dolleen had been worth far more to them alive than dead. Now that the police were examining every aspect of her life, they'd eventually discover the truth about James smuggling cash into the country. Sadly, it appeared both Hawkinses were headed toward prison.

He took a deep breath. "Are you going to turn us in?"

We were interrupted by someone pounding on the front door. "LAPD. Open up."

Kiki covered her face and moaned. I moved over to her while James got up slowly and opened the door. Detectives Beavers and Kaplan strode into the room, flashing their IDs. Kaplan did a double take when he saw me sitting on the sofa next to a frightened Kiki.

"What the—?" the young detective sputtered.

I was less interested in the hapless Kaplan and more interested in reading the whole three-volume story passing over Beavers's face.

I smiled and stood. "I was just leaving."

"Not fair!" Kaplan shouted at me. "You don't always get to talk to the witnesses before we do. I'm sick of this." He turned to Beavers. "Tell her."

Beavers's eyes crinkled at the corners as he watched me walk toward the door. He slowly shook his head and his mustache twitched. "Just get on with it, Noah."

# CHAPTER 29

I drove straight from the Hawkins house in Tarzana to Lucy's house in Encino. Ten minutes later I sat in her kitchen, watching her chop veggies, and told her about my visits with Lillian Gould, Shelley Shapira, and the Hawkinses. "Kiki knew all about the smuggling. She knew James wasn't having an affair. I don't think either one of them wanted Dolleen dead. Her murder has brought the police to their door. They're in deep trouble."

Lucy stopped chopping and handed me a glass of water. "What about Shelley, the ex-wife? From what you've told me, she's a tiger when it comes to her son. She could've killed Dolleen to put Jonathan in control of all David's money."

"Wow. That sounds like a plot ripped straight out of the case files of Detective William Shakespeare."

"Well, don't forget what Paulina said." Lucy referred to the communiqué the psychic Paulina Polinskaya allegedly received from Dolleen's ghost and verified by her Chihuahua, Hathor. "The killer was a woman. And if it turns out to be Shelley Shapira, then Birdie nailed it. She's insisted all along the ex did it."

"If you recall, Paulina also claimed the killer wore white sneakers. I just can't see the elegant Shelley Shapira wearing shoes like that."

"She would if she played tennis," said Lucy.

I wasn't convinced. "I'll give you this. Shelley's shrewd and smart and even admitted to hating Dolleen. But I'm more inclined to believe Jonathan might've done it."

Lucy bit into a slice of carrot. "Really? I got the impression from you he tried to live down his father's crimes."

"I thought the same thing until I discovered he's been aiding and abetting his father all along. Jonathan transferred some of David's real estate assets, those two houses in Tarzana, to his own name. God knows what else he's hiding. And he's been receiving payments of $20K a month from those offshore accounts. He handled Dolleen's legal affairs. He could've discovered she wasn't investing the $100K for David and tipped off his father."

"And you think the father told Jonathan to get rid of her?" Lucy asked.

"That's one possibility. Let's face it. Dozens, maybe hundreds, of people hated David. However, I have to go with what I feel in my gut. I think Dolly's killer is closer to home."

"Paulina said the same thing." Lucy rubbed seasoning into a roast, placed it in the nest of vegetables, and covered the pan. Then she sat across from me at the table. "Your gut is often right,

Martha, but it's also been dangerously wrong. Just promise me you'll be careful."

Ten minutes later I was back in my own kitchen. The digital clock on the stove blinked steadily, an indication there had been a power outage in my absence. Unfortunately, power surges in Encino were not uncommon. I reset all the clocks in the house and sliced red rose potatoes for the au gratin.

In a few hours, five of us would gather in my dining room to usher in the Sabbath. I thought about Emma Fishblatt and Lillian Gould, two seniors who'd likely be spending the evening alone. On a whim, I called and invited each of them to join us. To my surprise, they both accepted. I wasn't worried about having enough food; I always cooked extra.

At six in the evening, the smell of baked, cheesy potatoes and rosemary filled the house. Mountains of spinach wilted in hot olive oil and garlic, and the salmon sat in a pan on the counter ready to bake in the oven. When Crusher came home, I told him about James Hawkins's confession.

"Clever of you to figure out James was David's secret son. Nice work. If neither one of the Hawkinses murdered the vic, you can narrow your search."

"Yeah, but I'm still left with the question of motive."

"Work the money angle, babe. If it's not love, it boils down to money. Now if you'll excuse me, I've got to shower and change."

I heard the loud engine of Morty's car pull into

the driveway ten minutes later. The ninety-year-old
Morty still carried a valid driver's license and drove
a gold Buick. I'd tried several times to convince my
uncle not to risk riding with the older man. But
Uncle Isaac always pointed out the last time Morty
had an accident was in 1996, and it was the other
guy's fault.

My uncle entered the house first, wearing his
good slacks, a dress shirt, and his embroidered
Bukharian skull cap. "Good Shabbos, *faigela*." He
kissed my cheek. "I brought company."

Morty wore a brown suit. A diamond stick pin
glittered in the blue tie he always wore because it
matched his eyes. He handed me a bouquet of
white roses and grinned, false teeth clacking.
"*Shabbos blumen* for the *shaina maidel*." Sabbath
flowers for the pretty girl. I was flabbergasted not to
see his girlfriend, Marilyn, standing behind him.
Instead, I looked once more into the hooded eyes
of Abel Shapira.

Morty must've read the surprise on my face.
"Marilyn went to her granddaughter's recital tonight,
so Isaac suggested we bring our friend Abel."

Abel wore a blue-striped dress shirt, with a black
ribbon of mourning pinned to his collar, and the
same gold Rolex watch. My uncle patted the man's
back. "I thought he shouldn't be alone, especially
after burying his daughter-in-law this week, may she
rest in peace."

Why in the world would Abel accept an invitation
to my house after the way I confronted his son at
Dolleen's funeral?

Abel silently scrutinized my reaction. He seemed

to enjoy my shock because his hangdog expression shifted slightly on the spectrum from completely miserable to mildly satisfied. "Good Shabbos. I've been looking forward to this."

*What does that mean?* Was he preparing to rake me over the coals for what happened at Forest Lawn? Neither my uncle nor Morty attended the funeral, so they didn't know I'd confronted David. I'm sure, if they knew, they wouldn't have brought his father, Abel. Now it was too late. I'd just have to make the best of an awkward situation.

Uncle Isaac noticed the extra plates at the table. "Who else is coming, *faigela*?"

My heart sank as I realized how truly awful this evening would be. "A couple of ladies from the Jewish Center. I believe you know them both." If I'd known Abel was coming, I never would have invited Emma Fishblatt. She started the whole ugly confrontation at Dolleen's graveside. She'd also blamed Abel. Now they were going to be sitting at the same table together. My table.

Crusher emerged from the bedroom, smelling like lemon verbena soap. He wore black trousers, a crisp white shirt, and a white crocheted head covering. His face broke into a broad grin when he saw the three old men. "Shabbat Shalom!" He shook their hands and gave them each a man-hug. Then he handed black silk yarmulkes to Morty and Abel.

A half hour later, the doorbell rang. Emma and Lillian arrived right on JST, Jewish Standard Time. Late.

"Shabbat Shalom." I put on my best smile. "I'm so

glad you could both make it on such short notice. Come in, come in."

Emma wore a blue polyester shirtwaist dress, a single strand of pearls, and a blue hand-knit cardigan. She smiled and stepped into the house. "I made these for you." She handed me a Ziploc bag with a few frozen hamantaschen, the shortbread cookies I'd bought for her at the Russian bakery earlier in the week.

Lillian followed Emma into the house, wearing a beige caftan with metallic gold embroidery around the neck and down the front, over her ample bosom. False eyelashes raked the air every time she blinked, and bright red lipstick migrated up the thousand creases around her lips. She smiled broadly and thrust a box in my direction. "I know you like these."

I brightened at the sight of one box of See's assorted nuts and chews wrapped in white paper and sealed with gold foil stickers. I guided the two women into the dining room, where the men were standing around schmoozing. Emma eyes lit up when she noticed Uncle Isaac, and her hand flew to her tight white curls. Then she saw Abel and stiffened. She whirled around and faced me, eyes blazing. "What is *he* doing here?"

I glanced at Lillian, to see if she would react the same way to Abel, the man who persuaded her to invest with his son. She snorted like a bull preparing to thunder across the room and gore someone.

Abel clenched his fists and looked at Uncle Isaac. "What is this? Some kind of ambush?"

Uncle Isaac scratched his head and looked at me. "*Nu?* What is he talking about?"

Emma gritted her teeth and pointed at Abel. "I will not sit at the same table as that man!"

Lillian growled like she was grinding coffee beans in her throat. "He talked me into investing with his son. I'll break the little putz in two!"

*Oh crap!*

# CHAPTER 30

I spread my hands and smiled nervously at the tense gathering. "Well, everyone, it's kind of a funny story." Nobody smiled. "*Um*, my uncle Isaac surprised me tonight by bringing Abel so he wouldn't be alone during this time of mourning. Meanwhile, I invited Emma and Lillian for the same reason. Neither my uncle nor I knew what the other was doing, so obviously bringing you all together was an honest mistake. I know you have . . . issues. But it's Shabbat. Can we pretend this is Switzerland and try to set aside our differences, just for tonight?"

I took Emma's hand. "I would be honored if you said the blessing over the candles."

She shrugged and glanced at Uncle Isaac.

Then I turned to Lillian. "Didn't you say you wanted to speak to my uncle and Morty about something?" I mouthed the word *poker*.

Lillian said, "Yeah, okay."

Emma simpered in my uncle's direction. "I *bench lecht* every Friday night." She used the Yiddish expression for blessing the candles.

He smiled politely. I handed her my blue scarf, which she draped over her helmet of curls. She walked over to the sideboard, where two short, white candles stood in my *bubbie*'s silver candleholders. She made three dramatic swoops of her hands over the twin flames, covered her entire face, and enunciated every word of the blessing with slow gravitas. A regular Sarah Bernhardt.

Lillian rolled her eyes at me. Crusher fought to keep a straight face.

After the *omein*, I sat Emma and Lillian at one end of the table, on either side of Uncle Isaac, who presided over the meal. Morty sat next to Emma and I sat next to Lillian, directly across the table. I placed Abel on the other side of me and Crusher at the end. We sang the traditional blessings over the wine and raisin challah. The room vibrated with tension, but so far, the guests kept silent. *Thank God.*

As I walked the hot dishes of food to the table, the lights in the house flickered.

"What happened?" Uncle Isaac asked.

"Unfortunately, our part of the grid gets the occasional electrical surge and brownout. It's annoying, but nothing to worry about."

Lillian helped herself to a mountain of crusty au gratin, tapping the serving spoon on her plate to dislodge every last morsel. She squinted at Uncle Isaac and declared, in her raspy baritone, "So, I understand you play poker on a regular basis. How about dealing me in sometime?"

*So much for the subtle approach.*

Too polite to be rude, Uncle Isaac said, "Well,

maybe sometime, when we have an opening. Do you know how to play?"

"Do I know how to play? Honey, I can give you a run for your money. Texas Hold'em. Draw. Stud—five and seven card. H-O-R-S-E. Omaha High-Low. Whatever you want. Except Strip." She laughed and winked. "I only play that game one-on-one."

A rosy flush crept up my uncle's cheeks. Crusher glanced at me and tried to hide another smile.

"We're not so fancy-shmancy." Morty flapped his hand in the air. "And we play for quarters, not boobs. Maybe you'd be happier riding the charter bus with the ladies for the nickel slots at the Indian casino."

"*Puhleez*," she scoffed, "gimme a break. Are you going to turn me down because I'm not a guy? Listen, big shot. I placed third in the Poker Olympics in Vegas. Ladies' division."

"Ladies' division? Could've fooled me," Abel muttered into a forkful of spinach.

If Lillian's looks could kill, Abel would be on his way to the undertaker.

She continued, "I walked away with ten grand."

Morty glanced at Uncle Isaac. "I guess we could try it out once. See how everyone gets along."

Lillian beamed. "Where do I sign up?"

Emma glared at her friend, apparently angry at being outdistanced in the race to snag my uncle. She angled her body slightly away from Lillian and batted her eyes at my uncle. "My father never would have approved of women engaging in such a crass endeavor. Papa taught us to respect certain rules of behavior. He was a stickler for tradition." She batted her eyes and smiled. "You remind me of him, Isaac."

Abel sneered. "Rules? So, what do you call taking money every month from Dolly?"

"You shut up!" Emma's veneer slipped. "It was my money to begin with. If it wasn't for you and your lousy son, I wouldn't have been forced to take out a reverse mortgage and accept Dolly's handouts!"

Lillian put down her fork and snarled. "David stole millions from me and you have the chutzpah to sit there and criticize us for wanting our money back? You funneled victims to your son for his Ponzi scheme. You think you're such a *k'nocker*, but you're nothing but chump change."

Crusher telegraphed a *What were you thinking?* look to me and said, "Maybe we all better take a deep breath."

Lillian pointed to Abel. "Breath, *schmeth*. I'll breathe deeper when you're in jail!"

Abel waved his hand. "Ah, stop *hocking my tchainek* already." He dismissed both women by likening their words to the rattling of a teakettle on the stove.

The lights flickered again, distracting everyone for a moment. In the silence following, I jumped up. "I see we're out of wine. I'll just go and open another bottle."

Crusher stood. "I'll help you."

I could tell he wanted to say something, but because my house was designed with an open plan, we were still within earshot in the kitchen. So, he grabbed my hand and led me down the hall into the sewing room. As soon as he closed the door, his huge shoulders began to shake with silent laughter.

"Oh my God." A snort escaped and he wheezed with quiet hilarity until his face turned red and tears rolled down his cheeks. I couldn't help myself and gave in to the contagion of his mirth. He finally took a breath. "Where did you dig them up?"

"These are two of the seniors Dolleen reimbursed. Her death devastated poor Emma because they were as close as mother and daughter. I wanted to do a *mitzvah* and invite them to dinner. Unfortunately, Uncle Isaac had the same idea for Abel. To tell you the truth, I'm puzzled. I mean, after the way I confronted David at Dolleen's funeral, why would Abel agree to come to my house? I don't trust him."

Crusher pulled me to him and gave me a sweet kiss. "Don't worry, babe. I've got your back."

We hurried back to the kitchen, opened another bottle of Baron Herzog kosher Chardonnay, and returned to the table, where Crusher topped off everyone's glass.

Toward the end of the meal I asked, "Who would like a scoop of butter pecan ice cream on their pie?"

Every hand rose except Emma's. "I'm allergic to nuts."

"Takes one to know one," said Abel.

Emma threw him a withering look. "Just because I wouldn't let you go all the way with me, doesn't make me a nut. It makes me a decent woman, and you a dirty old man."

*Please God, take that picture from my mind.*

"You got me all hot and bothered then tried to trick me into getting married. But I saw right through your scheme." Abel sneered. "You're nothing but a tease." He left the table and headed for the restroom.

I stood and began gathering the dinner dishes. "Okay, I'll just get the dessert now. I'm pretty sure I have some vanilla ice cream in the freezer. Would you like some, Emma?"

She glanced at my uncle then stared at the table, playing with her dessert fork. "That would be lovely."

Crusher helped clear the dinner dishes and poured a boiling kettle of water into a teapot, releasing the aroma of peppermint and black tea. I put the hamantaschen cookies on a plate, opened the box of See's candy, and scooped six portions of butter pecan. I used a separate spoon to scoop the vanilla ice cream. If I'd done my job right tonight, everyone would leave with a very full stomach.

I carried all the desserts to the table on a tray, being careful to serve Emma the pie a la vanilla ice cream. When I returned to the kitchen for the teapot, the lights flickered again. Then the house went dark. Only the Sabbath candles cast a very faint glow from the sideboard in the corner. A minute later, the lights came on again. Abel had returned from the restroom and sat in his place next to me.

I poured everyone's tea and took my seat. "I hope the DWP fixes this problem soon."

Emma screamed and dropped her fork. "Someone's trying to poison me!" In front of her on the table sat a piece of rhubarb pie with a scoop of Butter Pecan ice cream. She glared at Abel. "First you kill Dolly, and now you want me dead."

Uncle Isaac looked at his plate. "No, no, I'm sure you're wrong. Here's the vanilla ice cream, right here. We'll switch. I'm sure Martha made an honest mistake when she served the pie. Right, *faigela*?" His eyes pleaded with me to make this go away.

I'd been very careful to serve Emma the vanilla ice cream. Someone exchanged the plates when the lights went out. Did Abel make the switch? The only other person with easy access to the plate was Lillian, who sat directly opposite Emma. But what would her motive be? Getting rid of the competition in the race for my uncle didn't seem like a good enough reason.

I took a deep breath. "I'm so sorry, Emma. Uncle Isaac is right. I must've made a mistake."

Uncle Isaac placed the pie a la vanilla in front of Emma, but she made a face and pushed it away.

"At least have some tea," he said.

"No, thank you." She dabbed her eyes with her napkin. "I'm quite full."

Abel put his fork down. His forehead folded into deep creases and his pupils became pinpoints as he glared at me.

*Uh-oh, here it comes.*

He leaned toward me and said in a low voice, "I came here tonight to tell you to back off. You weren't satisfied to harass Johnny. Oh no. You also had to go and bother Shelley."

I straightened in surprise. "You're still in contact with your ex-daughter-in-law? Why would she tell you about meeting me, yet keep it a secret from her son? What exactly is your relationship with her?"

"We both want what's best for Johnny." He

leaned closer. "You're playing a dangerous game. Back off or the same thing that happened to Dolly could happen to you."

The hairs on the back of my neck rose along with my voice. "Are you threatening me?"

All conversation stopped and every face turned our way.

"No. I'm warning you." He lifted his cup of tea and saluted me. "Friendly, like."

Now I was mad. "Even if you did scare me—which you don't—it's too late to back off. I know all your family secrets, including the fact James Hawkins is also David's son, your grandson."

Abel put the cup down, and it jiggled in the saucer. "Who told you that?"

"James was only too happy to reveal Dolly gave both you and Jonathan dirty cash every month— cash that James smuggled into the country. Your *Johnny* was up to his eyeballs in conspiracy. Here's something else I know. Since Jonathan managed Dolleen's legal affairs, he must've been the one who discovered she gave away David's money rather than investing it. I'm guessing Jonathan told David, and David got so mad he had Dolleen killed. Maybe Jonathan did it himself. Maybe even you."

"I told you so." Emma crossed her arms and sat back in her chair.

Abel stood abruptly. "Don't say I didn't warn you!" He walked out of the house.

"Good riddance to bad rubbish," Emma snapped at his back.

Through my front window, I saw Abel standing

on the curb next to the street, talking on his cell phone.

I looked at Lillian and screwed my face into an apology. She immediately got the message and heaved her body out of the chair. "This was a lovely dinner, Martha. Thanks for inviting us." She retrieved her purse, where she'd dropped it on the sofa, wrote on a piece of paper, and handed it to Uncle Isaac. "Here's my number. Call me when you set up your next game." She elbowed him in the side and winked. "Or just call me."

Emma stared daggers at Lillian, who was now her chief rival in the quest for my uncle's attention.

Lillian cracked a lopsided smile, like she knew exactly what she had done. "Come on, Emma, time for us to hit the road too." She walked toward the door and stopped to whisper in my ear. "I owe you one. Call me later. Emma told me something interesting about Dolly on the way over here tonight."

I stood at the door and watched them leave. Abel refused to look at the two women as they got in the blue Cutlass and drove away. I watched him standing on the curb for another ten minutes until a car stopped to pick him up. I'd assumed he'd called Uber until I glimpsed the driver.

Shelley Shapira.

# CHAPTER 31

Uncle Isaac, Morty, and Crusher took their tea to the living room while I cleaned up. Every nerve in my body crackled from the stress of the evening. What had Emma told Lillian?

Certain enough time had passed for Lillian to have reached her apartment, after an hour I retreated to the privacy of my sewing room and punched in her number. "I'm sorry about this evening. I had no idea Abel was going to be here. Are you free to talk?"

"Emma dropped me off five minutes ago. I'm alone."

"You wanted to tell me something Emma said?"

"Yeah. I think it could help your friend. Dolly's death may've meant the end of our monthly checks, but they were going to stop anyway. Turns out, the Feds knew all about the smuggling and money laundering. They approached Dolly and offered her a deal if she would hand over the info on the offshore accounts and any other assets David had hidden."

"No wonder someone said she'd been nervous lately. Did she accept the deal?"

"Yeah. But before accepting, Dolly insisted on immunity for all of the seniors and that we be allowed to keep the money she'd already paid us. She even got them to agree not to hit us up for back taxes. Emma said Dolly told her all about the arrangement just before she died."

"That must've been a huge relief to all of you."

"Yes and no." Lillian coughed a deep, smoker's cough. "The other part of the deal was once the government recovered the offshore money, we wouldn't be eligible for any further compensation. So, even if Dolly hadn't been killed, we were never going to see another penny."

And neither would David, Abel, or Jonathan. Dolly's testimony would put them all in prison—a compelling motive for murder.

"Why did Emma wait so long to say anything?"

A candy paper rattled in the background. Lillian spoke around something in her mouth. "Emma can't keep a secret. I think she just needed to tell somebody. Let it out. Like you saw tonight, she's not good at nuance."

*That's the pot calling the kettle black.* "Speaking of tonight, I definitely did not put the wrong dessert in front of Emma."

"I didn't think you were so dumb," she said.

"You were sitting closer to her than me. Did you see anything? Do you think Abel could've switched plates?"

"The lights going out disoriented me for a minute.

I didn't see him, but I wouldn't put anything past the little putz."

After listening to his threat tonight, I agreed. "I appreciate the info, Lillian."

She smacked her lips. "Like I said, I owed you one. Thanks for setting me up with Isaac and Morty. G'night."

The pieces of the puzzle were coming together. Jazz said he saw FBI agent Kay B. Lancet at the West Valley police station. In addition to handing over her file on David Shapira, she must've briefed Beavers on the FBI's deal with Dolleen. I felt elated. In the face of all the new evidence, Beavers would have to rule out Jazz as Dolleen's killer and rule *in* the entire Shapira family. Ex-wife included.

When I returned to the living room, Morty said, "This was some evening. I haven't seen such a dinner since my wife, may she rest in peace, died. Her brother Sol used to fight with her that way. He was a real no-goodnik. He rooked their parents with one sour deal after another. He's dead now—may he *schvitz* in the devil's Turkish bath without a drink of water."

Uncle Isaac cleared his throat. "I'm not blaming you, *faigela*, but we barely avoided a disaster tonight. God forbid Emma should eat the ice cream with nuts."

*Like the whole evening wasn't already a catastrophe?* "But Uncle Isaac, I didn't make a mistake. I was very careful to serve her the vanilla ice cream. The dessert plates were switched while the lights were out. Emma was right. Someone did try to poison her."

"*Has v'halila*!" God forbid. "Who would do such a thing?"

I sighed. "I know none of us did it. That leaves Lillian and Abel, and I don't think it was Lillian. That leaves only one other person. Abel. He could've made the switch in the dark when he came back to the table."

Uncle Isaac shook his head slowly. "I never would have guessed it. Come on, Morty." He stood. "I need to get some rest."

The old men wished us a peaceful Sabbath and made their way outside to Morty's Buick.

Crusher poured two more cups of tea while I told him about my conversation with Lillian. All the while, he seemed distracted and made no comment.

"Yossi? Is something wrong?"

He put down his cup. "I have something to tell you, babe."

My stomach lurched. I knew what was coming next. "You're leaving again, aren't you?"

He reached for my hand. "The call came while you were in the other room talking on the phone. I've got to head out tonight."

I hated this part of his job. Crusher's assignments often took him out of LA, and even out of the country. Sometimes he returned within a day or two, but other times he was gone for weeks or months. And he could never risk contacting me while he worked undercover. I never knew how long he'd be gone, and I worried every minute for his safety.

Beavers challenged me to consider whether I could live with a husband who disappeared on me all the time. Now those words haunted me.

\* \* \*

At 5 a.m. Saturday morning, I woke with a pounding migraine. The tension from the disastrous dinner and Crusher's departure had caught up with me. The muscles in my shoulders and neck clenched like angry fists. I shuffled into the kitchen and took a Soma and a headache pill. Then I prepared a pot of strong French roast. The extra caffeine would help. I rubbed some White Flower oil into all the places that hurt and draped a moist heat pack around my neck.

Sipping a cup of hot coffee, I reclined on the sofa and covered myself in my blue and white quilt. My cat, Bumper, always knew when I was in pain. He curled into a circle in my lap and purred softly, offering me his furry comfort. He was still there when I woke up three hours later, all traces of the headache gone. As soon as I stirred, his altruism evaporated, and he ran into the kitchen demanding breakfast.

At eight thirty I called Beavers. "Arlo, we have to talk."

"Have you thought more about our conversation on Wednesday?"

Was he kidding? I could think of nothing else last night after Crusher left, but I wasn't going to confess that to Beavers. "No," I lied. "I'm calling about Dolleen's murder. I've just learned some important information I want to run by you."

"I can be at your place in twenty minutes." His voice turned sarcastic. "That is, if Levy isn't there."

My heart squeezed at the reminder my boyfriend

disappeared on another clandestine assignment. "No, I'm alone. I'll see you in twenty."

Beavers showed up with his German shepherd.

I bent down and hugged my canine buddy. "Hey, Arthur, how's my favorite guy?"

He wagged his tail in response and gave me a huge lick on the side of my face. When I stood up again, the dog turned his attention to Bumper's rear end.

Beavers wore a western shirt, tight jeans, and cowboy boots. "Artie misses you. Like me." He took a step closer, seducing me with his woodsy cologne. "But I told him we needed to play it cool."

I took a step backward. "Arlo, you're making my life too complicated right now. Can we please talk about Dolleen's murder?"

I steered him to the kitchen table, a cup of fresh hot coffee, and a plate of hamantaschen left over from the night before. He bit into one of the cookies. "What's so urgent?"

I told him I knew about Dolleen's deal with the FBI. "Don't you see? The entire Shapira family had millions of reasons to keep Dolleen from telling the Feds what she knew. Any one of them had motive to keep her from talking. It's possible they all could've been in on it. Even the ex-wife, Shelley."

"The ex?"

I told him about my confrontation with Abel the night before. "He admitted to being in contact with his former daughter-in-law. He knew I talked to Shelley. And when he left here last night, she came to pick him up. She's very protective of her son. I wouldn't be surprised if she were in on the whole plot."

Beavers's expression settled somewhere between sympathetic and impatient. "I'm sorry to disappoint you, Martha, but everyone in the Shapira family has a solid alibi. I can't place any of them near Dolleen Doyle's house when she was murdered. We even checked out the ex-wife. She also came up clean."

"What?" I felt momentarily disoriented. I thought I'd finally figured out the real motive for Dolleen's murder and even narrowed down the suspects. "Are you certain? I mean, if your dim-witted partner Kaplan verified any of those alibis, you should double check."

He shrugged an apology. "I'm sorry, but those are the facts."

I immediately thought of Birdie Watson's husband's death last year and how his murder by a hired assassin had been disguised to look like a bank robbery gone wrong. "Well, couldn't the family have hired a hit man?"

"Hit men don't use dumbbells as a weapon. They dispatch their victims more quickly and cleanly, usually with a bullet, knife, or garrote. Whacking someone on the head is more a crime of anger and opportunity—not the result of a business transaction. Until we can find more evidence to the contrary, your friend remains a person of interest."

Panic rose in my throat. "Well, what about those two people who wrote messages threatening Dolleen?"

"So far, we haven't been able to link either one of them to her murder."

"But there must be dozens of David's victims who

wanted revenge." I was already depressed about Crusher's leaving on assignment, so it didn't take much for the bad news about Jazz to produce a lump in my throat. "Arlo, please believe me. Jazz couldn't have killed Dolleen. You can't arrest him. You know what could happen to a gay man in jail."

I got up from the table and staggered toward the coffeepot. A sense of futility washed over me. I clutched the edge of the sink and began to softly cry. Beavers came over and gathered me in his arms.

When I didn't resist, he kissed the top of my head and murmured. "I'm so sorry, honey. I really am. I know how hard you've tried." I leaned into his embrace and accepted the comfort of his strong arms and soft caress. He took a deep breath and then blew it out. "I shouldn't tell you this, but even though your friend is still the only one we can place at the murder scene, I don't think he did it."

I raised my head to look in his face. "Do you really mean that?"

He nodded and stroked my cheek. Then he kissed me gently on the lips. I kissed him back.

A deep voice said, "Martha?"

I hadn't heard the door open. I pulled away, stunned, and stared at Crusher. He looked as if he'd been punched in the stomach.

*Oh my God.*

His nostrils flared. "It didn't take you long, did it? And here I thought you were afraid to commit because you thought I'd cheat on you. But it's really the other way around, isn't it?"

I desperately wanted to reassure him, but I also

felt annoyed by his accusation. "Really? That's the first thing that comes to your mind? Not that Arlo comforted me because Jazz could still go to jail or that you disappeared on me again? I know how this must look to you, Yossi, but it's not what you think."

He stared angrily at Beavers. "This isn't you cheating on me only hours after I leave?"

Exasperation quickly replaced my shock. "Well, you're the one who chose to go, not Arlo." The minute the words left my mouth, I knew I'd said the wrong thing. I glanced from one to the other.

Beavers's dark eyes twinkled. Crusher's blue eyes smoldered.

In an attempt to salvage the situation, I spoke softly. "Why did you come back?"

Crusher took my house key off his key ring and threw it into the brass dish on my hall table. "Doesn't matter now." He turned and abruptly walked out the door.

My jaw dropped and my face went numb as I realized he'd just broken up with me. I don't know how long I'd stood staring at the door when Beavers gently laid his hand on my shoulder. He turned me around to face him. "Do you want to talk about this?"

I rapidly blinked away tears. "No."

"He doesn't deserve you."

"Somehow I don't find those words comforting. Please, I just need to be alone."

"You know I love you, right?"

"So did Yossi. And look how that just ended."

"His leaving you isn't a bad thing," he said.

"I'll call you later." He kissed my forehead and left with Arthur.

My whole body ached from the stress, and I felt my headache returning, so I took another dose of medicine. Then I grabbed the phone and called the only person who could help me now. "Lucy, can I bring Birdie's Barn Raising quilt over? I know you wanted a chance to put your own stitches in it, and I've been too busy. Besides, I really need to talk."

"I know that tone of voice, girlfriend. You're having man problems, aren't you?"

"You don't know the half of it." My voice broke. "I think Yossi's gone for good. He just stormed out of here without his key."

"Why would he do that? Did you have a fight?"

"Worse," I groaned.

"Well, come right over and fill me in on the other half, hon. I'm all yours."

# CHAPTER 32

Lucy's kitchen still smelled like bacon and eggs from breakfast. She sat next to me at the pine table, put her arm around my shoulders, and squeezed while I poured my heart out.

"The thing is," I moaned. "I wasn't exactly cheating on Yossi."

"Well, what do you call kissing another man?"

I cringed slightly. "Arlo attempted to comfort me, and I guess I just got swept up in the moment."

"*Uh-huh.* I'm comforting you right now, yet I don't see you locking lips with me."

I laughed for the first time since the fiasco at dinner the night before.

"I know how Arlo is," she continued. "You must've encouraged him somehow. Otherwise he would've backed off."

I plunked my elbows on the table and sank my face into my hands. "Okay, maybe I do have some feelings left for Arlo. But I wasn't cheating. At least not like Yossi thought. I feel like crap."

She pushed a plate of brownies in front of me. "Here. This should help."

I bit into a soft brownie with a crispy crust. My best friend had her priorities straight. Chocolate always made things better.

"Tell me what to do," I said with my mouth full.

She shifted positions so she could face me. "I'm right about one thing. You've got a long ways to go before you're ready to get married. Despite what Paulina said." Lucy referred to the psychic's prediction I'd be married by the end of summer. "Now tell me why Arlo *comforted* you." She made air quotes with her fingers.

"I thought I'd figured the whole thing out." I told Lucy about Dolleen's deal with the Feds and how the whole Shapira family could've conspired to kill her to keep from losing control of the money. "But Arlo told me they all have alibis, including the ex-wife."

"They still could've been responsible," she said. "They could've hired a killer."

"Asked and answered. Dolleen's murder was a crime of passion."

"What about Dolleen's neighbors? They also had a lot to lose."

"As far as James and Kiki Hawkins were concerned, Dolleen was worth much more to them alive. Her death exposed their criminal activities. No, my gut tells me both of them are innocent of her murder."

"But if the Shapira family didn't kill her, and

neither did the neighbors," said Lucy, "then who? And why?"

Suddenly I had an idea. "I know someone who just might help us answer those questions." I stood and moved toward the front door.

"Wait a minute, Martha. Where are you going?"

I told her where I was headed.

The southbound traffic on the Sepulveda Pass ran fairly light at noon. My knuckles turned white from gripping the steering wheel too tightly. What if I hit another dead end? What would happen to Jazz? Arlo confided he didn't think Jazz killed Dolleen. Nevertheless, he still remained their best suspect.

I took Wilshire Boulevard east to Detroit Street, turned north, and parked in the driveway behind Emma Fishblatt's Cutlass.

The old woman and Dolleen were very close. I always suspected Emma knew more than she'd been willing to tell, and Lillian had confirmed as much the night before when she revealed Emma knew about Dolleen's arrangement with the FBI. What other evidence could she be withholding?

I took a deep breath and rang the bell.

The peephole window opened and a pair of blue eyes widened in surprise. "Just a moment." She closed the opening and unlocked the door, stepping aside to let me in. "Please excuse my appearance. I didn't anticipate any company today."

A scarf knotted on top of her head made her

look like an aged Rosie the Riveter. She wore a short-sleeved white blouse, revealing wrinkled and saggy arms, and loose navy-blue trousers with an elastic waist band. Emma smiled sweetly. "I hope you didn't drive all this way just to apologize about last night."

"Actually, I came to talk some more about Dolleen."

She gestured for me to take a seat in the living room. "My poor Dolly. I miss her every day. I don't know what more I could possibly tell you." She clasped her hands tightly in her lap.

"I just have a few more questions." I spoke gently, hoping not to upset her by asking again about the money she lost. "I spoke to Lillian last night, and she told me something disturbing. She said Dolleen advised you about the arrangement she made with the Feds. Why did you keep it to yourself all this time? We could use that kind of information to prove Jazz is innocent."

Emma pressed her lips together. "That's the last time I tell Lillian anything."

"She only wanted to help," I said.

She studied my face for a moment and sighed. "Oh dear. I have a feeling this is going to be a difficult conversation. Shall I make us some tea first? We'll probably need it." As she moved across the room, I noticed, for the first time, she wore white sneakers.

Like the sun slowly breaching the horizon at dawn, a new wariness lit up my brain. Even though I doubted the psychic's claim about the killer's shoes, I decided not to accept anything to eat or drink from Emma. I tried to be careful not to telegraph my new suspicions.

I smiled. "Maybe later, thanks."

"Are you sure? I have all kinds." Before I could answer, she scurried to the kitchen. After a minute, she returned with an assortment of teabags in a black lacquered presentation box. "Dolly gave this to me last Mother's Day. Just pick what you like and I'll boil some water."

What the heck—didn't everyone in LA wear white sneakers? Although someone might be able to adulterate a pot of tea, a random tea bag sealed in foil was probably safe. I chose a strong Irish Breakfast, with a picture of a green shamrock, and kept the packet in my hands. I followed her back to the kitchen and watched her every move. Emma hummed to herself as she filled the kettle with tap water and placed it on the burner. She placed two teacups and saucers on the table, along with a holder filled with paper packets of sweeteners. I opened a tiny, sealed envelope of stevia and emptied it into my cup. I casually stuck the end of my finger into the powder and licked my fingertip. So far, so safe.

We chatted about cooking for the upcoming holiday until the water boiled. I opened the foil packet and brought the teabag to my nose. It didn't smell like anything more sinister than strong black tea. Emma poured the scalding water into both our cups. If she suspected I didn't trust her, she didn't show it.

"Milk or lemon?" she asked.

Even though I liked my tea with milk, I refused to take a chance she could've somehow contaminated it. I shook my head and smiled. "No thanks, I'm good."

We returned to the living room. Emma raised her cup to her lips. "You're right, of course. I have been holding back. My father taught me never to reveal too much about my personal business. He said other people would take advantage of me if I did." She tilted her head. "If you don't mind my saying so, Martha, you look exhausted."

The strong hot tea felt good going down. "This hasn't been easy for any of us." I wouldn't tell her about my terrible morning. "So, how did you feel about Dolleen's deal with the FBI?"

"How should I feel?" Her eyes narrowed almost imperceptibly.

"Well, on the one hand, she managed to shield you from prosecution and the tentacles of the IRS. On the other hand, though, she agreed to a deal cutting you out of any future reimbursement. You were never going to see another penny of your money."

A shadow slid across her face, and her hand tightened around the cup. "She should never have agreed to let the government cut me off."

"Those payments were going to stop no matter what Dolleen did. To her credit, she managed to give half your money back before the Feds caught up with her. She didn't have to do that, you know. Doesn't that prove she tried to look after you?"

"A lot you know. She always said I was like her mother. If she loved me like she said she did, why couldn't she continue to pay me out of her own pocket?"

"Sounds like you were really angry with her." I drained my cup.

Her eyes flashed. "I begged Dolly to continue those monthly checks because without them, I couldn't keep my sister in assisted living for the memory impaired. It wasn't poor Sarah's fault she inherited the Fishblatt curse. But you know what Dolly said? She told me I'd have to take Sarah out of private care and put her in a *county* facility. Imagine! A Fishblatt stuck in a place like that." She raised her chin. "Papa would never have allowed it."

At last. The real motive for Dolleen's murder.

"You know what I think, Emma? I think you went to Dolleen's house the day she died. That's when she told you about her deal with the government, including the fact you would be ineligible for any future reimbursement. You tried to talk her out of it, but she told you it was too late. There would be no more money."

The old woman's body went rigid. She didn't move a muscle.

"As if that weren't bad enough," I continued, "she didn't offer to keep on giving you monthly checks from her own personal account. You must've felt deeply disappointed. And abandoned."

Emma angrily swiped at a tear in the corner of her eye.

"I don't think you meant to kill her. But when Dolleen suggested you put Sarah in a county facility, I think you lost it. You spotted the hand weight, picked it up, and hit her over the head."

Emma watched me carefully but remained silent.

I pressed on. "Afterward, you knew enough about the Shapira family to steer the investigation in their direction. You tried everything you could to convince me and the police that one of them was guilty. You even went so far as to switch your own dessert last night while the lights were out, so you could blame Abel."

Suddenly I began to feel strangely lightheaded. Something horrible was happening. Emma's face became blurry and the room began to spin.

"You look unwell, Martha. Is anything wrong?"

I felt my arms going weak. Emma put something in my tea! But that was impossible, wasn't it? I'd been so careful. "What did you do, Emma? How?"

Panic rose in my throat and cut off my words. *Call Arlo, Martha.* I fumbled my cell phone out of my purse but couldn't focus on the screen.

The old woman came over and snatched the phone out of my hands. She stood next to me as I slid toward the floor. The last thing I saw before sinking into oblivion were the white sneakers on her feet.

# CHAPTER 33

I floated up out of the blackness and, with my eyes still closed, sniffed the unmistakable odor of eau du hospital. The swish of people bustled around me and a machine beeped nearby. My throat felt raw and raspy and my insides hurt. I stirred slightly and felt the sting of an IV needle taped to my right hand. Why did they always put the needle in the hand you needed to use for other things?

"She's moving." My best friend Lucy's voice, heavy with relief.

"Martha dear, are you awake?" Birdie's voice fluttering, full of anticipation.

I groaned in response, my lids still too heavy to open.

"Look, Zsa Zsa. Auntie Martha's awake." Jazz.

"*Baruch HaShem*!" Uncle Isaac praising God with a catch in his throat. "I'm right here, *faigela*."

"You're in the Ronald Reagan Medical Center at UCLA, hon." Lucy again.

I managed to open my eyes and blinked against

the light. I scanned all the concerned faces in the room, looking for the one voice I didn't hear. As I feared, Yossi Levy, aka Crusher, was missing.

Birdie wrapped her arm around Lucy's waist, leaning against the tall woman for support. "We were so worried, dear."

Jazz carried Zsa Zsa close to his chest. She wore a tiny white nurse's cap and little blue cape. "Thank God. I couldn't stand to lose my best friend." He sniffed and then smiled. "And besides, I was afraid I'd never get the chance to redo your wardrobe."

"What happened? How did I get here?"

Lucy cleared her throat. "After you left my house, I got a very bad feeling. One of the strongest ever. So, I called Arlo and told him what you were up to."

"And it's a good thing Lucy has ESP," said Jazz. "By the time Arlo got there, you were unconscious and unresponsive from an overdose. The paramedics rushed you here to the ED."

Fog still curled around my brain. "An overdose?"

Birdie's eyebrows pushed together. "They did a gastric lavage and put something in your IV to counteract the side effects and wake you up again."

"They said you might feel sore for a while." Lucy smiled. "But you'll live."

I still couldn't figure out what they were talking about. "What kind of overdose?"

Jazz spoke up. "They found your regular meds in your system, along with a lethal cocktail of Xanax and Ambien. That sweet little old lady, Emma Fishblatt, tried to kill you."

The more they talked, the more the haze began

to dissipate, and the events of the morning slowly came into focus. I managed to catch Lucy's eye and motioned for her to come nearer. She moved to the head of the bed and leaned in close.

I whispered so nobody else in the room could hear me. "Did you call Yossi?"

My friend patted my arm in a sympathetic gesture. "I tried, hon, but he's not answering. I did leave a couple messages, though."

Tears sprang to my eyes.

"Listen. You know as well as I do, if he's on assignment, he can't respond and take the chance of blowing his cover."

I picked up the hem of the white sheet covering me and dabbed the tears from my cheek. "Or he doesn't care."

"Don't jump to conclusions," she said. "Of course he cares. He's just hurt right now, but I'm sure he still loves you."

Beavers's deep voice interrupted our conversation. "Welcome back." He'd just entered my room with his young partner and approached the foot of my bed, wearing jeans and a crooked smile.

Detective Noah Kaplan remained by the door, trying not to look at me.

I caught his eye, pointed at him, and mouthed the word *zero*—reminding him that by not listening to me he missed yet another opportunity to solve a case.

His dark eyes flashed and he looked away again.

Beavers pulled out a pen and small pad of paper,

preparing to take notes the low-tech way. "What's the last thing you remember?"

I closed my eyes again and tried to claw back through time to recapture the moments before I fell into darkness. "Sitting in Emma's living room. I'd just confronted her about Dolleen when I realized she'd put something in my tea. But I couldn't figure out how. I'd been very careful to watch her every move. Then everything got fuzzy." I opened my eyes again. "I tried to call you, but I blacked out. Lucy said you found me."

Beavers scratched the side of his neck. "It took us a while to get over the hill to Miss Fishblatt's house. When we got there, she refused to answer the door." He pointed to Kaplan standing in the doorway of my room. "Noah and I went 'round back and found her trying to drag you into the yard. For an old lady, she was strong. She'd gotten you as far as the kitchen door."

I propped myself on my elbows. "Emma killed Dolleen."

Beavers nodded. "We know. She broke down and confessed when we found you unconscious on her floor. You were right about her, but once again you underestimated the danger of confronting a killer. Even if she was nearly eighty."

"How did she manage to poison me?"

"Once we got her to the station, she couldn't wait to brag about how clever she'd been. She kept saying something about escaping the Fishblatt curse. Anyway, she knew you suspected her. So, when she went to the kitchen to get the box of teabags, she quickly poured all her pills in the dry kettle. After you selected your teabag and followed her back into the kitchen, she let you watch her fill the kettle with tap water. She knew you'd never suspect the poison was already inside it. The boiling water dissolved the pills, and you were never the wiser."

"But Emma poured her own tea from the same kettle. How come she didn't pass out too?"

"She told us she only pretended to drink. When we examined the scene, we confirmed her cup was still full, while yours was empty."

"Where is she now?"

"In custody."

"What's going to happen to her?" I asked.

"She confessed, so there won't be a trial. The DA ordered a psych eval. Because of her age, she'll probably end up in a locked ward of some overcrowded county facility. Hardly a pleasant place to spend your last years."

"Maybe they'll allow her to bunk with her sister, Sarah." I sank back into the pillows. "Thanks for rescuing me today."

"You mean yesterday. Today is Sunday."

"You've been in a coma, hon," said Lucy.

"It's not uncommon with an overdose like yours," said Beavers. "I've seen it hundreds of times."

Jazz glared at Kaplan. "Now that you know I didn't kill Dolly, you owe me an apology!"

The well-built Detective Kaplan slouched against the door frame, looking like a model in an ad for Levis. He briefly lifted his shoulder in a dismissive shrug. "I'm not going to apologize for doing my job. You were a person of interest in a crime. And we had some pretty strong evidence against you. I was perfectly within my rights to treat you like a suspect."

Jazz looked down his nose at the young detective. "Martha was right. You're a snotty little weasel."

Just then a woman with a head of copper-colored curls rushed into the room and over to my bed. "Mom! Oh, Mom." My daughter, Quincy, threw her arms around me. We held tightly to each other while she cried softly in my neck. "I was so scared when Aunt Lucy called and told me you wouldn't wake up. I took the first red-eye to LAX."

I covered the top of her head with a thousand kisses. "I'm so glad to see you, sweetie." I looked around the room but didn't spot her fiancé. "Did Naveen come with you?"

She sat up on the edge of the bed. "No, and he's not coming to Passover, either. We broke up over a month ago. I just didn't want to talk about it yet. I'm still not ready."

Uncle Isaac laid a hand on her back. "*Nu*, Quincy, girl? Where's my hug?"

She stood and towered four inches above him. She bent down for an embrace. "How are you, *zaydie*?" Quincy grew up calling him *grandpa*, even though he was technically her great uncle.

Detective Noah Kaplan never took his eyes off my beautiful daughter dressed in tight jeans and high-heeled boots. His smile revealed a dimple as he took a step toward her and extended his hand. "You probably don't remember me, but we met a couple of years ago."

A friendly grin transformed her face from beautiful to dazzling. "Sure, I remember you. It's Noah, right?"

*She's flirting?* I wanted to scream at her to stay away from the arrogant young detective.

His whole face brightened. "Yeah. Noah Kaplan. And you're Quincy Rose. An unforgettable name and face to go along with it."

*Crap! He's flirting right back.*

Kaplan ran his fingers through his dark curls and lowered his voice. I heard him say, "Maybe we could grab a coffee some time? Or dinner? I'd really like to take you to dinner." He handed her his business card and gestured toward me with his head. "Call and let me know when you're free."

Beavers fought to keep from smiling as he watched my face tense in undisguised horror at the exchange.

Uncle Isaac spoke up. "Kaplan, did you say?"

"Yes, sir."

"Jewish?"

"Yes, sir."

Oh, no! I knew exactly what my very traditional uncle was doing. Although he respected Quincy's fiancé, Naveen Sharma, he'd never liked the prospect of his great niece marrying outside of the faith. And now she'd announced she was single again, my not-so-subtle uncle would attempt to fan the flames of attraction between my daughter and the young Jewish detective.

"Sooo Kaplan," he said, "do you have somewhere to go for Pesach?"

I groaned, but nobody paid attention.

Lucy and Jazz exchanged a meaningful look but then Lucy shrugged and returned to the main topic. "Admit it, girlfriend. Paulina nailed it. Dolleen's killer *was* a woman, and she was close to Dolleen."

Totally," said Jazz. "*C'est vrai.* But I can't figure out why Dolly's Chihuahua would lie about the white sneakers."

I decided to keep quiet about Emma's Saturday attire. Why encourage the two of them? Besides, as if my own love life weren't in ruins, I now had my daughter's to worry about.

Passover? With *Kaplan?*

# EPILOGUE

Upstairs in the master bedroom of the Watson ranch, Birdie sat in front of the mirror of an old-fashioned walnut vanity. Jazz stood behind her, wearing jeans with a crease ironed down the legs, a blue gingham shirt, and a red bandana tied around his neck. He carefully pinned up her long hair in a halo of white.

Birdie smiled at his reflection and caressed the delicate long sleeves of her white lawn blouse. "You did a lovely job on my wedding outfit, dear."

Jazz raised his eyebrows and adjusted the vintage rhinestone button on the shoulder strap of her white brocade overalls. "Well, it's not what I had in mind, but I'm glad you like it."

Lucy handed her a pair of diamond earrings. "I brought these for you, hon. I thought you'd want to wear 'something borrowed' today." Lucy owned an impressive collection of jewelry given to her over the years by her husband, Ray.

"They're lovely." Birdie smiled and fastened the studs to her earlobes. "I hardly look like myself."

"That's the point," Jazz muttered.

The brand-new Barn Raising wedding quilt we made for the couple lay folded across the foot of their four-poster bed. Zsa Zsa napped on top of it, wearing her little, blue gingham bridesmaid dress and a collar covered with silk flowers.

Jazz sprayed Birdie's hairdo in place. "If Rusty was here, he'd not only approve of this marriage, he'd be happy for you." Jazz referred to Russell Watson, Birdie's dead husband and Jazz's secret lover.

She smiled sweetly. "Thank you, dear. I feel it too. I only wish the two of you could've realized your dream of getting married."

From the way the color crept up Jazz's neck, I suspected he hadn't told Birdie yet about his new friend, Oregon State Trooper Grover Franklin.

I looked out an open bedroom window of the three-story Queen Anne. The faint smell of roses and lilacs wafted up on the balmy spring air. Behind the house stood a red barn and a horse paddock surrounded by a newly painted white rail fence. Beyond that, cattle and horses grazed in the rolling green terrain of the Willamette Valley.

The wedding preparations were completed in the yard below. Blue-checkered tablecloths covered dozens of tables, and neat rows of hay bales faced a temporary stage erected for the ceremony and dancing afterward. Musicians tested the sound system with an electronic tap-tap on the microphone.

Birdie's long-time friend Sandra Prescott, aka Rainbow, presided over the event. Birdie and Rainbow were in charge of food production and preparation when they lived on the Aquarius commune in Ashland, Oregon. The young Birdie married Russell Watson and left Aquarius. The even-younger Rainbow also left and parlayed her talents into a global food empire.

Now, under Rainbow's expert choreography, a dozen servers dressed in white shirts and black slacks bustled in a synchronized dance. They'd been instructed to intercept guests and take the potluck dishes over to a string of long, folding tables. Near the paddock, Watson cousins tended the tri-tip, chicken, and ribs slowly cooking in metal barrels over smoking mesquite.

"Martha?" Lucy's voice pulled me out of my reverie. "The guests are starting to trickle in. Ray just texted me. He said it's almost time, and we need to get dressed. Jazz will stay and help Birdie with her outfit in case he needs to make any last-minute adjustments."

I walked down the hallway into my room and closed the door behind me. Jazz had designed long dresses in blue gingham for the attendants. However, I just couldn't bring myself to put on the white pinafore intended to go over it. You had to draw the line somewhere. With my long curls loosely arranged on top of my head, I looked like a character from Laura Ingalls Wilder. I sprayed a mist of Olene, an extravagant French perfume, and joined the others in the living room.

Lucy wore a gown identical to mine. She'd also declined to wear the pinafore. The conservative Ray wore a blue gingham shirt and knotted red bandana around his neck. Originally from Wyoming, he looked completely at ease in his outfit.

Rainbow—blond, elegant, and dripping with diamonds—chose to wear the white pinafore. She took one look at us and said, "Really? You're afraid of an apron?"

Lucy just rolled her eyes. "It was just too *Wizard of Oz.*"

"May I present the bride?" We all turned our heads to see Jazz descending the stairs with Zsa Zsa on her leash and a glowing Birdie on his arm. Her brocade overalls were cut with wide legs to give the illusion of a skirt. Brand-new white sneakers covered her feet. Woven in her halo of white hair were tiny yellow rosebuds and baby's breath.

Denver rushed over to his bride. He wore jeans, cowboy boots, and a white buckskin jacket with a yellow rose pinned to the lapel. "I always knew you were beautiful, Twink, but today you outshine the stars. I'm a lucky man."

We watched the guests stream onto the property and surrender dishes of food to Rainbow's army of servers. Then they assembled on the hay bales facing the stage, the din of happy chatter filling the air.

Rainbow's cell phone buzzed. She answered it and nodded. "Okay. We're on our way." She turned to the couple and smiled. "Phoebe's ready to perform the ceremony." She reached in a box and handed Birdie a bouquet of blue Dutch iris and yellow roses with sprigs of white baby's breath. Then she handed Lucy and me bouquets of yellow tulips, taking one for herself. "Any time you're ready."

Rainbow led our procession on the arm of one of the Watson cousins. Lucy took Ray's arm, I grabbed Jazz's arm. The bride and groom came last. As we moved across the yard, Rainbow signaled the musicians, who began to play "Unchained Melody," Birdie and Denver's special song. The crowd became quiet, stood, and craned their necks to watch us approach.

Phoebe Marple, the minister who would officiate today, took her place in the middle of the stage behind a standing microphone. Phoebe was another old friend from their days on the commune. She wore a white caftan and a wreath of flowers atop her long, flowing, gray hair. A chorus of five women in purple robes, wielding flat drums and rawhide hammers, stood off to the side next to the musicians.

Ray gave Lucy a look and she nudged a warning with her elbow. If this wedding was anything like Russell Watson's funeral last year, the devoutly Catholic Ray Mondello would be in for a cultural experience.

Birdie and Denver stepped in front of Phoebe, while our small group formed a semicircle behind the couple, also facing Phoebe. The white-robed old woman leaned toward the microphone. "Welcome to this joyous event," she intoned.

The purple-robed ladies pounded a rapid staccato on the drums.

Phoebe raised her hands above her head, looked toward the sky, and pronounced in a stentorian voice, "We call upon the deities to sanctify the sacred circle and the union of these two souls."

Ray looked at Lucy, eyebrows raised in question marks. She casually shrugged one shoulder.

Phoebe instructed Birdie and Denver to face each other and hold hands. She pulled a mixture of rose petals and oak leaves from a cloth bag hanging around her wrist and sprinkled them on the floor as she circled the couple. "This is the sacred ring formed by the element of mother earth and everything that grows upon her. May you always be blessed with abundance."

Drumming.

Then she lit a candle and waved it over the bridal couple's heads. "We bless you with the element of fire. May your hearth always be warmed by the flames of love."

I sighed. At the moment, my own hearth was stone cold because the man I loved had broken up with me.

One of the purple-robed women handed her a smoldering sage bundle. Phoebe walked around the sacred ring flailing the smoke and blessing them with the element of air. Finally, she pulled a salt shaker full of water out of the bag on her wrist and baptized droplets over Birdie and Denver's heads while she blessed them with the element of water.

The purple drummers marched three times around

the sacred ring, pounding a slow rhythm. *Tap, ta-tap, ta-tap.* Then they took their places once again by the musicians.

Phoebe cleared her throat and addressed the couple. "Birdie and Denver, for almost fifty years the two of you have been star-crossed lovers, each married to someone else. Torn apart by your separate life journeys. But one journey has ended and another begins. The time has come at long last for the joining of your souls. You may now exchange symbols of unification."

A guitarist began to sing Paul Stookey's wedding song, "There is Love." The beauty of the song always brought tears to my eyes, and apparently I wasn't the only one. I could hear sniffles from the crowd sitting behind us.

The elderly couple slipped golden rings on each other's fingers. When the song ended, they spoke softly to each other, declaring their love. Denver kissed Birdie, and Phoebe threw her arms in the air and announced, "And so it is sealed." Everyone stood and clapped.

Ray made the sign of the cross.

The newly married couple left the stage and mingled with the guests, accepting congratulations and hugs. I stood, rooted in place next to Jazz, watching the swarm of well-wishers. Slowly, a wave of self-pity engulfed me. Birdie had Denver, Lucy had Ray, and Jazz had Trooper Franklin. I had no one. Tears I'd been fighting since Crusher left stung my eyes, and I blinked rapidly in an effort to dispel them.

Crusher was done with me. He'd made that clear when he returned the key to my house. Despite my happiness for Birdie and Denver on their special day, I couldn't quell the strong urge to submit to the sobs squeezing my heart.

Jazz must've sensed my distress because he stepped closer and put his arms around me. I struggled not to make a sound as silent tears rushed down my cheeks. He reached into his pocket and passed me a folded white handkerchief. "I know what's going on in your head, Martha. Don't give up on Yossi. He'll come to his senses. Remember, *ma chéri*, it's not over 'til the fat lady sings.'"

"I'm the fat lady," I sniffed. "And I'm not singing."

He grabbed my shoulders and pushed me slightly backward so he could inspect me. "Well, you look fabulous in this dress, if I do say so myself. Who knows? Maybe you'll meet some cowboy today and ride off into the sunset."

"That's hardly likely, given my track record."

"I know it'll be a stretch for you," he said, "but go back in the house, put on the pinafore I made to go with the dress, and pretend you're a dumb, helpless female. Believe it or not, some men like that."

We both began to giggle.

During the party, three cowboys did approach me. One used a walker, one smelled like a barn, and one was a dead ringer for the actor Sam Elliot.

When I told him so, he said "I get that a lot. Do you want to dance?"

I shrugged. "Why not?"

We hopped across the dance floor in some kind

of awkward two-step, and he said, "Tell me about yourself, little lady."

*Oh brother!* Was that the best he could do?

I decided not to take Jazz's advice and act like the helpless "little lady." After all, if I was going to be a colossal loser at love, why not be honest about it? "I seem to have a knack for finding dead bodies and solving crimes. In my spare time, I make quilts and screw up relationships. How about you?"

His eyes got that trapped-animal look. When the music stopped, he touched the brim of his hat. "Thanks for the dance." He escaped in the direction of one of the drummers in a purple robe.

I found Lucy and Ray eating ribs at the same table as Jazz and Trooper Franklin. Jazz put down his glass of wine and pointed to the tall fifty-year-old in a dark suit and bolo tie. "Martha, you remember Grover Franklin?"

"Of course," I smiled and offered my hand to the state trooper we'd met the year before.

Jazz glowed when he smiled at the man. Clearly he was smitten. I hoped their friendship would grow into something wonderful for both of them. I sighed. At least one of us was happy.

The musicians played "The Tennessee Waltz," and Lucy and Ray moved toward the dance floor. All of a sudden, Jazz whispered something to Trooper Franklin, and they abruptly left the table without a word of explanation.

*Well, that was a little rude.*

I sensed someone approaching my chair from

behind but didn't bother to look. I was in no mood for any more cowboys.

A large pair of hands rested on my shoulders. Every muscle in my body tensed as I prepared to turn around and confront whoever it was for touching me without my permission.

Then my heart jumped when a familiar voice said, "Babe. May I have this dance?"

**Please turn the page
for a quilting tip from
Mary Marks!**

# MAKE YOUR QUILT YOUR DIARY

American history is not just about the men who fought wars or the titans of industry who built our railroads. It's about the everyday people who made those things happen, immigrants who came to this country from diverse backgrounds and worked hard to raise families. A few achieved great success, and these are the men who dominate our history books.

But what about the women who also built this country? History books may feature a few notable female heroines, from Pocahontas and Harriet Tubman, to Eleanor Roosevelt and Ruth Bader Ginsberg. But the struggles and lives of most ordinary women have gone largely unrecorded and unrecognized.

Fortunately for modern historians and researchers, many of our foremothers detailed their own histories in personal journals and diaries. These women weren't necessarily essayists writing long elegant passages. Some only recorded the barest facts. Some were barely literate. But they all left behind a fascinating glimpse into their lives and times.

Another way women memorialized their experiences was through—you guessed it—their quilts. They sewed their everyday experiences into an almost infinite number of designs. If you look through an encyclopedia of traditional quilt blocks, you'll find thousands of patterns composed of triangles, squares, rectangles, and other geometric shapes. Each block has a name, such as Friendship Star, Grandmother's Flower Garden, Jacob's Ladder, and Log Cabin to name some of the most common ones. These names reflect the things that were important to the quilt makers and tell us a lot about their beliefs and activities.

Some of our foremothers went so far as to record certain specifics in their diaries: when she made it, who it was made for, and other details she thought were important. Some diaries even included tiny swatches of the fabrics used.

Another way we learn about the past is through information sewn directly into the quilt, such as the quilt maker's name and the date the quilt was finished. Many antique quilts have yielded valuable research benchmarks because of that.

Nowadays we have an important tool that is ideal for this task: the computer! Products are available which will stabilize ordinary cotton fabric and allow it to pass through the printer. With just a few key strokes we can create labels with loads of information and sew them onto our quilts, establishing a permanent record that will last as long as the quilt itself.

If you decide to keep a diary or print a label, what you choose to say is up to you. The important thing is to think about future generations and what you want them to know about you, about your life and about the beautiful piece of art you worked so hard to create.

Happy quilting!

# Connect with Us

Visit us online at
**KensingtonBooks.com**
to read more from your favorite authors, see books
by series, view reading group guides, and more.

for sneak peeks, chances to win books and prize packs,
and to share your thoughts with other readers.

facebook.com/kensingtonpublishing
twitter.com/kensingtonbooks

## Tell us what you think!

To share your thoughts, submit a review,
or sign up for our eNewsletters, please visit:
**KensingtonBooks.com/TellUs.**